Fubars

Paddy Bostock

A Wings ePress, Inc
Political Fantasy Novel

Wings ePress, Inc.

Edited by: Jeanne Smith
Copy Edited by: Christie Kraemer
Executive Editor: Jeanne Smith
Cover Artist: Trisha FitzGerald-Jung

All rights reserved

Wings ePress Books
www.wingsepress.com

Copyright © 2019 by: Paddy Bostock
ISBN-13: 978-1-61309-592-8
ISBN-10: 1-61309-592-9

Published In the United States Of America

Wings ePress Inc.
3000 N. Rock Road
Newton, KS 67114

What They Are Saying About
Fubars

An interesting read yet again from Paddy Bostock, this is just what I needed during the long journey I had to take recently.

It starts with how the acronym for FUBAR came about as a slang word and how those associated with the lead character and others find their way around what life throws at them.

I loved Tosh and his Mutt and would have loved it if Tosh did not just take in his mum when she had a "change" of heart once he became famous. That's just my personal opinion, but everyone's POV is different.

Dwayne, Tosh's friend, Tosh's best four-legged friend Mutt and their journey, along with that of their friends is a treat to read. As always, I love Paddy's writing style that's so different from other authors. However, it doesn't take away your reading fun; it's not a slight read. Be prepared for drama, fun, romance and more in this tale, and enjoy the ride!

—Sherin Lloyd
GoodReads Reviews

A mesmerizing and laugh out loud satirical political fantasy tale. Highly recommended!

—Atlantic Way Review

This is a story that will keep you engaged until the last word of the last page. It is unforgettable and unique in that it will leave you thinking and reflecting on the state of the world and your personal life. I just love stories like this.

Is there something in a name? There is, in that names allude to a person and his or her background as well as culture. The characters in *Fubars* have an amazing depth. They are all interesting in their own right because they come from so many different backgrounds and cultural settings. Some of them have shady backgrounds. Others are inspiring, who make one feel inspired.

Fergus Ulysses Barr is a timid person of British descent who is multifaceted. He is selfish and rich. Dwayne Junior Zobinsky is the son of a New York businessman as well as an artist. Tosh is a rebel and wandering musician of sorts. Then there are all the other characters who represent all of us in one way or the other.

One of the themes that emerges as the story unfolds is that reconciliation and harmony are much more possible in private lives than public ones. The only things that are constant are strife and conflict. And we don't have to go far to witness that in our political and cultural arenas.

This is another one of Paddy Bostock's great stories. I have read most of his latest books, and I can honestly say that he is a GREAT storyteller. The characters are real and they have soul. The questions posed are deep and sometimes they even took my breath away.

Rating: 5 stars
—Irene S. Roth
WordPress.com

This novel starts out funny and ends up even funnier.

We regularly face incidences that make us understand how ridiculous or evil some people's behavior or ideas might be. Satire shows—basically ridicules— these times by utilizing humor or hyperbole.

Paddy Bostock weaves a mesmerizing political fantasy tale with intriguing twists and turns that will easily captivate the reader's attention from the beginning. The characters are drawn with great credibility and conviction. It's a fast-paced novel that will keep you engaged from the first page to the last.

I've read this author before and it's safe to say his storylines leave the reader spellbound. Bostock does it again with *Fubars*. The storyline and plot are amazing.

Bostock is so prolific, so inventive, so exactly what I want to read. This book starts good but ends great and this is one book I didn't want to end.

Bostock pays as much attention to his sentences as he does to his plots, shifting or consolidating meaning with the use of a single word. His writing is impeccably honed, full of juxtapositions and qualifications that create a satirical atmosphere that will leave you laughing out loud.

However, it must be said that this story is not for the faint-hearted or easily offended. A word of caution, therefore, for those who are linguistically sensitive. Nevertheless, the themes and outcome are just as affecting in the arresting contemporary political landscape.

Highly recommended and a well-deserved five stars from me.

—Píaras Ó Cíonnaoíth, Irish author and poet

In a field crowded with disappointing tomes, what a pleasure it was to read *Fubars* by Paddy Bostock and be introduced to something exceptionally well written. Fans of satire and comedy will love having a nibble on this one! An absolutely unputdownable book.

—Emerald Book Reviews

Dedication

To Amy, with love

* * *

One

No baby gets the chance to choose its own name, does it? How could it when it can't speak, read, write, or tell a toilet from a toothbrush? No way, that's how. It isn't until much later, and sometimes not even then, that it dares to re-name itself Elvis, or Madonna, or something. Otherwise, it's stuck forever with whatever fashion-of-the moment moniker its parents have lumbered it with. Such was the case with Fergus Ulysses Barr whose parents, Lord Xavier and Lady Hermione Barr, had argued long, hard, loudly, and almost to the point of divorce, over the various ancestral handles best suited to what turned out to be their only offspring. Just as well they lived in a massive manor house called Piddlington Hall in the middle of a massive estate on the outskirts of Little Piddlington In The Marsh, or else they would have disturbed the neighbours. Mind you, they *did* disturb "The Help," Max and Milly Pratchett, who dwelt in a couple of tiny rooms in the east wing overlooking the garages and outdoor lavatories.

"They don't half bloody go *on*, don't they Milly?" said Max night after night as Lady Hermione's pregnancy reached expulsion time. "Can't hardly hear the telly, can we?"

"Toffs for you," Milly would say. "Other hand, they pay the wages, innit?"

"Don't even know if it's a lad or a lass, do they? Him banging on about bleedin' 'Fergus Ulysses,' her 'Phoebe Fiona.' Might as well call it Fido and be done with it. Just wish the little bleeder'd get *born*, that's all. Or not. Image all that howlin' and yowlin' we're going to have to put up with nights."

"Now, now, Maxie, don't...be...naughty. God wouldn't like that, would He? Send you right to hell, He would."

"On a special God bus with Jesus driving," Max would be on the cusp of saying, but always bit his lip just in time. Milly could be a proper bitch when it came to religion even though, in Max's view, she never practised what she preached.

And so, on and on the Pratchetts debated and cavilled up until the very night the doctor and midwife were summoned to usher Fergus Ulysses into the world. And no easy job it was when he got stuck somewhere halfway down the birth canal and sent Lady Hermione into paroxysms of agonized screaming.

Downstairs in the Victorian sitting room, where he'd remained with the dogs because he reckoned birthing to be women's business, Lord Xavier jammed his fingers in his ears and went in search of the Fortnum & Mason Royal Whisky bottle he couldn't find.

"For the love of all that's sacred, woman, shut your damn mouth, will you?" he bellowed three storeys upstairs in the direction of the bedroom as he opened and slammed shut cupboards in search of fiery liquid relief. Which he eventually located in the piano stool of the hundred-year-old inherited Steinway grand nobody played because nobody could. Why the bally bottle was there Lord Xavier neither knew nor cared. Just pulled it out and took several long hard swigs. By the time Fergus Ulysses was dragged out all bloody and bawling, his father-to-be was comatose on a red leather Chesterfield, oblivious to his son's arrival, and Lady Hermione was being hooked up to an IV machine.

So much for Fergus Ulysses' inauspicious birth.

~ * ~

Mind you, until he was sent away to School aged eleven, life for Fergus Ulysses in Piddlington Manor was more or less tolerable mainly because he rarely, if ever, saw either Lord Xavier or Lady

Hermione who were always *busy in Town*. Where Town was the young Fergus Ulysses had no idea. Seemed a somewhat odd name for a place by comparison with Little Piddlington In The Marsh, which he knew was the name of the village where the mansion was located, but nonetheless it was in Town that Mumster and Dadster spent most of their days and nights.

In Dadster's case, this meant frequenting the bars in parliament's Upper House, turning up for the odd debate to earn the stipend he neither needed nor deserved, and spending large amounts of *quality* time with high-class whores in Soho, while Hermione pursued her not very secret affair with Sir George "Ginger" Wigglesworth in Hampstead. Both knew of each other's peccadilloes but had fallen out of love with each other far too long ago to give a monkey's. Obviously, Fergus Ulysses didn't know anything about any of that either. All he knew was neither of them was there with him except for the odd birthday, and at Christmas when neither parent bought him presents, but Dadster would get squiffy and shout at Mumster a lot. One Christmas, he threw her down some stairs, but Mumster seemed all right afterwards, and Max and Milly told him it had all been in fun anyway. Just a bit of a jolly prank so…

Long story short, Fergus Ulysses spent the years from zero to eleven pretty much exclusively with the Pratchetts, and a series of wet nurses, French governesses, horn-rimmed bespectacled home tutors in tweed suits, and the two Labradors, Woofer and Barkie, whom he liked a lot more than the governesses and home tutors who woofed and barked a lot more than the dogs ever did. Woofer and Barkie, one brown the other black, were nice chaps. A lot nicer than any human he'd ever met. Secretly, and for his use only, Fergus Ulysses re-named them William and Lucy, which they appreciated. Followed him around the massive estate like little lambs, they did, when called by those names and, henceforth refused to answer to either Woofer or Barkie, however much Lord Xavier would berate them on one of his infrequent visits. Fergus Ulysses thought that was funny until the latest governess, Justine, with whom Lord Xavier was conducting a clandestine affair, told him he was a "very bad and naughty boy" for calling the dogs different names and upsetting Dadster. But secretly, Fergus Ulysses was pleased as, approaching his eleventh birthday, he'd begun to think of Dadster as a bit of a *wallump*, a word he'd made up himself seeing as, not having mixed with any of the village children, nobody had taught him words like "twat," "fuckwit," or "dickbrain," which might have come in handy in the circs.

As far as education went, he'd learnt to speak more or less grammatically, to read, to write in an awkward sinistral cursive script, and to do simple sums, but that was about the size of his academic development. Far more importantly, from his point of view, were the ideas he thought up when wandering with Lucy and William, and not being forced to sit on chairs and learn things he found largely pointless. Sometimes he would try explaining these ideas to his latest home tutor, but they would normally be dismissed as "absurdly fantastical pre-adolescent whimsy," or just plain "worthless," so he learned to keep them to himself as he flâneured around the estate speaking to trees, flowers, birds, and the squirrels Lucy and William would occasionally lumber after.

And then, bingo, out of the blue, came the day he was bundled into the family Rolls and driven off to one of the nation's most prestigious boarding schools. You'd have thought such a school might have required some evidence of educational prowess, wouldn't you? Intelligence quotient scores, the capacity for multiplication and long division, a gift for spelling or the recitation of canonical poems, that sort of thing. But no. Lord Xavier being an alumnus of the institution, his sprog was welcomed with open arms. Mind you the cheque for half a million pounds, and the promise of further funding for two squash courts, a refurbished swimming pool, and a lacrosse pitch had gone a long way to lubricating ease of entry.

"Doesn't matter if the child's a total duffer, old fellow," Headmaster Quentin Fortesque BA, MA told Lord Xavier. "We'll soon break him in. Transform him into a backbone of the nation just like your good self."

"Jolly Dee, Forters. Whole bloody point of School, eh? Pass the port, would you? Then I'll be awf. Busy, busy, busy in Town, dontcha know. Oh, and by the by, if the little bleeder shits his pants when I'm gone, beat him. Spare the rod and spoil the child, eh?"

"Quite, Lord Barr. Old practices always the best."

"Indeed. Must be awf," said Lord Xavier, quaffing the port in one gulp and leaving Fortesque to close the door behind him.

~ * ~

Until the arrival of NYC banker's son Dwayne Zobinski in his final year, life at School for Fergus improved exponentially after a shaky start. By then, he'd taken to calling himself Fergie for the sake of street cred and to counteract the early years when he had been generally regarded as a "girly dunce" by staff and fellow students alike. Girly because of his small size, chubby pink face and soft, mousey, curly hair; and dunce because he had never played a computer game, couldn't operate a smartphone, thought times tables were pieces of furniture for resting the newspaper on, and "alphabet" described a big win on the horses. This latter misapprehension resulted from having heard Lord Xavier proclaim "Alpha bloody bet, eh?" during a brief visit to Piddlington Manor when he scooped the jackpot in a local fillies race.

Furthermore, the younger Fergus Ulysses was bad at games, never having played any or been allowed to watch them on TV. To him "footer" and "rugger" were enigmas, therefore, the former apparently played with eleven people and a round ball which one kicked and wasn't allowed to handle unless one was a goalkeeper, and the latter with fifteen players and an oval ball for both handling *and* kicking. The only thing both games had in common so far as Fergus Ulysses could tell was the requirement to hurt one's opponents—"tackling" it was called. In the case of rugger, this appeared to be the *sole* purpose of the game which was a hooligans' game played by gentlemen by comparison with soccer which was a gentleman's game played by hooligans, a piece of wisdom imparted ad nauseam every Wednesday and Saturday afternoon by gym master "Horrid" Horace McIlroy, who was reputed to have played "hooker" for Scotland and only ever wore a tracksuit.

In the summer term, it was athletics. And cricket, on the face of it, a gentler pastime, only Fergus quickly recognised it wasn't after witnessing a boy called Cuthbert Cuthbertson being hit on the head by a "bodyliner" and whisked off to hospital in an ambulance being given the kiss of life. So much for the gentler pastime, he concluded. Thereafter, he never batted, never bowled, and only ever fielded on the boundary—at which he was also crap because he couldn't throw the ball far enough or in the right direction to reach the "wicket-keeper" so opponents could be "stumped out."

And as for athletics, forget it. He simply didn't see the point of throwing things, jumping over things, or running flat out over short and long distances despite School's motto *Mens Sana In Corpore Sano*, which Fergus had no means of understanding, seeing as it was in a language other than English—"Laffin" as one of the brainier boys told him.

Anyway, whether it was in footer, rugger, cricket or athletics classes, never mind PT, it was "Horrid" Horace's words, "C'mon Barr, stop faffing about like a faggot and put your back into it, or it's a*nother* week of detentions for you and, maybe, a *beating*," that were branded on Fergus Ulysses's hippocampus in those early days.

Across the coming years, however, through his own reflections and endeavours rather than any useful input from School, the re-branded Fergie managed, radically, to change his image and reinvent himself such that he became a pupil to be respected. It wasn't popularity exactly, because he remained something of a loner, but it marked him out as different or even special. And how did he achieve this miracle? For starters, by growing, working out in the gym, and insisting School's barber give him a number one haircut. Then by developing a broken voice before many of the other boys, by learning to play guitar and, out of the earshot of his teacher, by playing some blues and rock 'n' roll deemed as "groovy" by other boys. Also by climbing through the grades in all academic subjects, bar maths.

But, most importantly of all, by giving as good as he got at footer, at which he became a more than decent right wing back, and even better than he got at rugger, becoming the youngest scrum half ever in the first XV. At cricket, however, he remained only ever mediocre, batting half-way down the order, and still only ever fielding on the boundary, but at least he made the school team. And at athletics, he became a decent sprinter over one and two hundred metres, also making the relay team.

Horrid Horace was astonished, although to give him his due—albeit, he took most of the credit himself—he lavished praise on the finest all-round sportsman he'd produced in years. What Horace didn't know, and just as well neither he nor anybody else did, was that Fergie also wrote poetry, some short pieces which were more like songs for the guitar, but also lengthy, practically Byron-esque epics all of which he kept under his dormitory bed in a locked suitcase. Not that anybody would dare meddle with Fergie's belongings for fear of a bloody nose or worse.

But then in his final year, just before A-levels, Dwayne Zobinski had to arrive, didn't he? Dwayne fucking Zobinski who spoke a whole different brand of English, acted like he owned the universe, and—no good denying it—was a sports superstar. Lousy at cricket, but *victor ludorum* in both track and field on sports' day, straight into School's first XV as a second-row forward at rugger, although all he'd ever played before was American football, and pretty shit hot as a soccer goalkeeper. Okay, he flunked every exam he took, but Quentin Fortesque BA, MA didn't care about that, reckoning as long as the NYC banker father stayed in Town his progeny would be Oxbridge-bound, no question. Oxbridge would let anybody in if he could play rugger, never mind if they were as thick as bricks. And that would be a big feather in School's cap.

"So?" I hear you ask. "What does all this have to do with Fergus Ulysses? Was he jealous of this Yank, or what?"

Answer, no he wasn't, he actually quite liked the guy. What he *didn't* like, however, as Zobinski perused the rugger team sheet one awful day—School team sheets were pinned on a Main Hall noticeboard giving players for the different teams with their initials then surname—was the way, when coming to the scrum half position of a misspelt F.U. Bar, he took a step back, and said, "Holy shit, I ain't playing for no team alongside no guy who got himself called Fubar.

Man, that is toooo...damn...spooky. Gonna lose every damn game we play. Got loser written all over it."

Which was when other members of the team, being British, and not knowing such Americanisms, came to googling "Fubar" to see what it meant. And when they did, all hell broke loose for Fergie, hence the Dwayne *fucking* Zobinski, as news of his acronym spread through School from top to bottom, and the sniggering started wherever he went. Worst of all were nights in the dormitory when the ghostly whispers of foo-baa, fooo-baaa-ha-ha, foooooo-baaaaaaaa-haaa-haaaa-haaaaa began to echo around the beds and down the corridor and wrecked his sleep, however many pillows he jammed over his ears. Pretty much ostracized, Fergus Ulysses never again played for a school sports team, began to lose weight, and failed all his A-levels until Quentin Fortesque BA, MA had enough and, the withdrawal of funds notwithstanding, demanded of Lord Xavier his son be removed from School *sine mora* (pronto).

"What the fuck did you have to call me Fergus fucking Ulysses for, you fucking twats?" eighteen-year-old Fergus raged at Lord Xavier and Lady Hermione as the Rolls rolled towards School's gates. "You never wanted me anyway, and then you had to go and call me stupid names."

It was this unforeseen and unexplained outburst that caused Lady Hermione in the back seat with her only offspring to spill her gin fizz and faint, and chauffeur Ronald (no second name) to lose control of the Rolls and swerve into an old oak tree. As a result of the impact and air-bag failure, Lord Xavier, who was sitting in the front and never bothered with seat belts, was flung forward into the windscreen and suffered concussion followed by brain complications including memory loss—sometimes he thought he was a rabbit—impaired speech, uncontrollable flatulence and penile dysfunction, none of which prevented him from attending the House of Lords, of course, but did put paid to his dalliances with Soho whores and French governesses which, in brief moments of relative consciousness, he regretted to the depths of what remained of his mind.

"Poetic justice," I hear you schadenfreude types saying, and with some reason. But be sure to learn the lesson from this, i.e. to be *very* careful what you call any boy child you may be about to have. If your family name is Witt, for example, be chary of Frank Unwin Charles Kenneth for first names...and so on.

*Any*way, such was the history of Fergus Ulysses Barr from birth to the age of eighteen. What, you will be wondering, happened to him next?

Two

What happened next was the newly self-christened Ringo Barr leapt from the Rolls while the adults were otherwise occupied, paying attention to Lord Xavier's damaged head, and legged it to the cricket pavilion under which he hid till the ambulance had come and gone with Dadster and Mumster in it. Surprising it was that nobody, not even chauffeur Ronald (no second name), noticed his absence, but this was no time for Ringo to worry about such trivia. Maybe when they came to think about it, they'd just assume he'd gone back to School. Which, eventually he did at the very dead of night when he climbed back into the building through a broken window in the chemistry lab, crept up to his dorm and collected the few precious belongings he knew he'd need, before creeping away again, scaling the boundary fence and hot-footing it into the surrounding countryside where he spent a sleepless night in a deserted barn along with four rats, six pigeons, and a stray cat he named Annabelle. At first light, he poked his head through the hole where a door had once been, assured himself the surrounding fields were empty, and hit the road that would take him to the village of Pudstock, from whose station he knew there were trains to take him to London—"Town" as he'd once thought of it.

Unlike the nineteenth-century provincial Dickens waifs who'd headed for the big city before him, however, Ringo came equipped with a change of clothes, the phone he now knew how to operate, his guitar, and the credit card in the name of F. U. Barr Lord Xavier had given him "in case of emergency." Well, this was an emergency, all right and, he hoped, a life-changing one at that. No longer would he tolerate the abuses of first being ignored at home then being mocked at School for being different, then admired for trying to "play up and play the game," then mocked *again*, just because of a misspelt name aberration. No siree. From now on, this would be *his* life to do with as *he* chose.

~ * ~

On the train to Victoria, he thought carefully about his first steps on arrival in the metropolis and concluded there were obvious precautions he needed to take in the probable case of School, or even his parents, having set the police on his tail. Using his credit card, for example, because that could be traced. Okay, he'd had to use it for the train journey, but all that would tell any snooper was he'd gone to London. And London was a big place. But without the card, old-fashioned money, or a place to stay, how was he to survive? On the streets? Possibly. But he would need to avoid the places homeless people would be most likely to frequent because that was where the cops would look first. So no good hiding in plain sight under a blanket on pavements by ATM machines. Or trying to weasel his way into a hostel where, even if he gave a false name there was always the chance of recognition from the mug shots that would have been circulated. This pretty much ruled out the whole of Central London, including outlying tourist traps like Camden Lock. What Ringo reckoned he needed was one of the big parks he'd heard about, somewhere offering shelter at night, and a decent nearby high street where, in disguise, he could play his guitar and make a penny or two. On his phone, he narrowed the parks/green spaces down to what looked like the biggest and wildest, Hampstead Heath and Wimbledon Common, then, trusting to his new friend serendipity, tossed the only coin he possessed to determine which of these would be his new temporary home. It came down heads: Hampstead Heath.

"Oo*kay*, so it's Hampers here I come," said Ringo on arrival at Victoria.

Having left the station, he wandered haphazardly towards Parliament Square then Trafalgar Square, the recent scenes of a million-strong anti-Brexit march. There he stopped to check on his phone the best walking route from his current location and quite a trek it looked, but he was young and he was determined, so with a hey-ho and a nonny, off he set in those dark Brexit-looming days.

"Talk about *fu*bars," he reflected as he trudged. Only recently, a young Englishman would have been able to tread the lands of Europe without let or hindrance, but now who knew? Soon there would be barriers here, barriers there, barriers everywhere. And to what purpose, he wondered. To put the "great" back into Britain and make it once again the "proud and independent" nation it had been until the EU "foreigners" took it over, as he'd read in School's library's determinedly alt-right newspaper section? Ringo didn't like the sound of that at all, but who was he, some eighteen-year-old kid, to change the course of history? Nobody, that was who, meaning his only option was laissez faire. Given his current homeless status, he wouldn't even be able to vote in a second referendum—*if* there were one.

So taking the route suggested by Google maps, onwards he tramped northwards towards Camden Town from where it would be only a couple of miles to Hampstead Heath which, from the maps he'd seen on his phone, looked big enough to hide an army *and* had the advantage of a decent enough high street where he could play his guitar and make a living.

"Bit of a hike," Ringo muttered. "But never mind. Fortune favours the brave, right?"

~ * ~

It was as night was drawing in and darkness beginning to descend that, exhausted, Ringo reached his destination, stumbled onto the Heath, and followed any path he could find that might take him well away from human settlements. It was on the one leading to Kenwood

House he found a cosy little copse to bed down for the night. A shame he hadn't brought a sleeping bag with him but he'd never *owned* a sleeping bag, so that was the end of that little aspiration. He would just have to be a good boy scout about this and improvise as best he could. After all, the army haversack he'd brought from School would suffice as a pillow, and the tatty overcoat he'd found in a bin along the way as a blanket. Plus the calories garnered from an abandoned *croque monsieur* he'd found on a table at Starbucks Belsize Park should keep him warm enough.

It was with this youthful sense of invulnerable optimism bubbling through his veins that Ringo found a patch of soft, relatively dry grass nicely enclosed by trees—elms or oaks he thought, but he'd never been much good at Nature—covered himself in his smelly coat, rolled himself into a foetal ball, rested his head on his haversack, shut his eyes, said "nightie night" to the gibbous moon and, more tired than ever before in his short life, was off in dreamland within seconds.

This state of bliss wasn't to last very long, though. At around two a.m. he felt a wetness on his face and a weight on his outflung arm, which caused him to sit bolt upright and scream, mainly because in the most recent of his dreams he'd been wrestling a tiger called Shere Khan who kept whispering *foooo-baaa* in his ear. Despite his daytime confidence, Ringo could still be dragged back to the bad old days of poor old Fergus Ulysses.

"Aaaaaaggh," he said, which confused Mutt, the Heinz 57 mongrel who reckoned he'd been doing perfectly acceptable things when meeting a human he wished to befriend. Okay, lying on the guy's arm might have been a tad out of order, but the face licking? Mutt didn't think so. In Mutt's book, face licking was an A-Okay move, which deserved reciprocation with a pat on the head at the very least. It was a chagrined Mutt therefore who climbed off Ringo with his tail between his hairy legs when commanded to do so by his master, Tosh.

"Gerroff 'im, boy. He's kippin' innit?" said Tosh. "Sorry bruv, he's only tryin' to be frennly. New around these parts, are you?" he added.

"Yuh-yeah."

"Well, welcome to your new neighbours."

"Suh-sorry. I haven't taken your space, have I?"

"Nah, me 'n' Mutt're just over there," said Tosh, pointing across the darkness to another grassy patch, this one sporting a tiny one-man tent.

"Muh-Mutt?"

"My pal. Man's best friend?"

Ringo smiled, remembering William and Lucy. "You're right about *that*. Sorry about before, Mutt," he said, sitting up and reaching out to muss the dog's ratty ruff, which pleased Mutt so much his tail returned to its normal wag mode, this the first indication of apology acceptance. The second was to pounce on Ringo and knock him flat on his back again, causing merriment all around.

"And your name is...? he asked his new human neighbour when the laughing was over.

"Tosh."

"Just that?"

"Yeah...Tosh."

"Any second name?"

"Nope. An' yours?"

"Ringo. Also no second name."

Tosh swept his russet shoulder-length dreads to one side and arched his eyebrows. "Bleedin' Beatle, is it? How's Paul getting' on these days?"

Ringo shrugged. "I wasn't always called this."

"Only you're not tellin' me what you were called before, right?"

"Right. And neither are you...Tosh."

"Fair enough. Runaway like me, are yer?"

Such was the start of a conversation that would run through the rest of the night. It turned out that Tosh was three years older than Ringo and, from a radically different end of the social spectrum, but the current circumstances rendered that an irrelevance. What united them was both having found themselves at odds with their backgrounds, and for not dissimilar reasons: absent parents. Tosh had never known his father, had only a drunken part-time whore for a mother, and had been bullied at school just like the ex-Fergus Ulysses.

He wasn't stupid but had been made to look that way. Plus there was the mixed race problem that had left him an unwanted member of both the black and the white in-groups. Ringo sympathized.

"Thanks, pal. But you're a posh lad, ain't yer? Tell it from the accent, can't I?" said Tosh. "So what're *you* doin' here?"

Ringo told him. Not *all* of it but enough for Tosh to get the point.

"All that money and still..."

Ringo nodded. "Funny old world, eh?"

"You can say that again, bruv. The rich lad and the poor lad both camped out together with no place to go. Gimme your hand."

So Ringo did and Tosh pulled him into a shoulder-bumping embrace.

"Raaf, raaf," said Mutt, evidently approving of the fraternity. Dawn was creeping into the copse, and that meant wakey wakey time for animals.

"And is that a guitar case I can see behind your baggage?" said Tosh when the shoulder bumping was over and Mutt had taken to sniffing where his master pointed. "Play a bit, do yer...Ringo? Thought you was a drummer? Wanna give us a tune?"

"Wouldn't that be dangerous? Don't want to draw attention, do we?"

"No probs. I know the park geezer who comes round sometimes to check on stuff an' he's all right. Never given me no bother. Not gonna do nothing, isn't Willy. Go on, give us a tune.

So Ringo pulled out the guitar, checked the tuning, and strummed one of his own compositions called "Outsider Blues."

"Nice one, son. *Real* nice," said Tosh at the final E-seventh with the twiddly bit at the end. "Eric Clapton, eat your heart out."

Ringo smiled.

"'Ang on a minute," said Tosh, climbing to his feet and wandering off to his tent, Mutt watching his every step.

He returned with a couple of bongo drums. "Fancy a bit of accompaniment?"

Which marked the first session of the duo, later to become known as, Tosh 'n' The Ring whose brief collaboration was to result in internet fame.

Meanwhile, before full light hit, what Ringo was coming to think of as the "magical copse," Tosh loaned him a spare sleeping bag, and they both slept until noon. In his next dream, Ringo featured as a roving troubadour like Bob Dylan. It was a fun dream this time around.

Three

The following few months were the best of Ringo's short life so far. Never had he enjoyed such freedom, although he quickly learned with liberty comes responsibility. Not that he baulked at that. After all, the responsibility—or lack of it—taken by others for him hadn't exactly been a blessing. And if he fucked up now, well *he* fucked up, and that would be his fault and nobody else's. On the upside, if he didn't it would be to his credit and his alone. Each springtime day passed like a week but was never boring as he and Tosh roamed the Heath with Mutt chasing sticks and dunking himself in ponds. And the evenings were even more fun as he and Tosh put together a little repertoire of rock, blues, reggae, and country numbers in their private copse.

"Ain't been any good music since the sixties and seventies. Or even earlier than that," was Tosh's opinion right up front on their first serious jam, and Ringo reckoned he was right. All that had come since was mindless computerized crap with no social content.

"Where've all the protest singers gone?" he asked.

"Some of them still alive and giggin', Dylan for one. Times they are a-changin' and all that. It's what I like about your songs, kiddo.

Got a bit of meanin' in 'em, innit? We could put some of 'em in our set too, you want."

"Set?"

"Yeah. Only if you're up for it, like. I got this gig couple times a week sittin' in on drums wiv a band at The King and Parrot down Camden way. Nice lads but pretty bollocks at playin' they are, still it's money, right? Reckon they'd let the two of us have a go if I asked nicely."

"And we'd get paid?"

"Like I said."

The need for money was a major part of his new independence Ringo had yet to satisfy. It wasn't as if the few coins he made from busking on Hampstead High Street in his tatty overcoat and the wig Tosh lent him were earning him a living exactly. He'd thought of a McJob somewhere, but concluded that would be too exposed. This manna from Tosh would be a far better alternative.

"One thing though, mate," he said. Ringo really liked saying "mate."

"What? Too shy? You'll get over it."

"No. It's just my old man..."

"Will have told the filth and given 'em pictures of you, right?"

"Right."

"Well, no worries, pal. They've got pics of me too, only for different reasons," said Tosh, sweeping the dreads from his head to reveal an almost entirely shaven head.

Ringo gawped. He never did find out what Tosh's "reasons" were and didn't care to pursue the matter.

"No way anybody's gonna find me. The wigs, innit? Plus taches, beards, specs, the whole bag of works. You wanna see me as a blondie. I...am...something...*else*," he added with a wiggle of his bum.

Ringo laughed. "And you could do the same for...?"

"You? Easy freakin' peasy. Yer own mother wouldn't know yer."

"She didn't anyway."

"Mine neither. Pass the weed, would yer?"

Weed was the other reason Ringo's days had begun to seem driftily longer. Until then, he had never even smoked a cigarette. Not that he toked all that much now, only when sharing.

"Ta," said Tosh through a long exhalation. "So you in the game or ain't yer?"

And Ringo *was*. These days he was up for most anything.

"Only we can't 'ave you calling yerself Ringo, can we?"

"Too Beatley?"

"Too fuckin' Beatley. From now on you're The Ring. Shake on it?"

The pair shook hands long and hard, *so* long and hard Mutt got jealous and reckoned he should join in, his paws still sodden from the most recent pond dip. But did Mutt care? The hell he did. Nor did Tosh and The Ring as, disentangling themselves, the trio danced a little leg-licking dance around the twilit copse. They named it "The Muttadango," which Mutt liked. Mind you, he tired of it quickly once Tosh mentioned Bonios as a reward.

"Raaf, *raaf,*" he said, tail twirling as he made a beeline for Tosh's tiny tent.

~ * ~

The same few months were the worst of Lord Xavier's medium length life so far, and he was much disgruntled about it, the dearth of gruntle evincing itself in sudden explosive outbursts of rage accompanied by excessive breakage of anything in his near vicinity, mainly booze glasses. You know how it is when you've headbutted the windscreen of a crashing Rolls Royce and suffered brain complications. Life is just never the same again, and such was the case with Lord Xavier, whose speech dysfunctions had accelerated to include aphasia, pleonasm, circumlocution, periphrasis, and a rare form of vowel confusion amongst other degenerative conditions, such that he was barely able to make sense in any context, thereby losing yet more gruntle. Especially, whenever he stood to speak in his section of the Mother of Parliaments, faced a wall instead of the Lord Speaker and took to chuntering incomprehensibly on his favourite (only) topic of fox hunting—"fux hinting" as he pronounced it—and yet again faced hoots of derision and amusement from his fellow peers as he forgot the beginning of his sentence, paused, started again from a different place, forgot that...and...so...on.

Bad though this was, things were no easier on the home front where Lady Hermione, now his full time carer, and thus no longer able to dally with Sir George "Ginger" Wigglesworth in Hampstead, took the brunt of his ill-expressed furies. Mind you, at least she managed a smile when he called her a "sally butch." What she found less amusing was the aphasia. At the dinner table, for example, when Lord Xavier wanted a fresh fork and would ask for "one of those prongie thingimmjugs," get furious with "the help" for not knowing what he meant, and start throwing wine glasses around.

You get the picture. Both professionally and domestically, Lord Xavier was a linguistic wreck, unable even to masturbate in the bath because of the penile dysfunction. For anybody else, you might have felt pity.

And whom did he blame for all this in the increasingly rare moments his memory functioned? Fergus Ulysses, of course "The mizrubble angreetfol lattle shatkocker" who'd caused the accident in the first place by disrespecting the parents who "laved and adured" him. Lord Xavier—"Crossbar" (X Barr) as Lady Hermione had dubbed him—swore on the Hooly Babble he would see *that* "little bosturd" in Hull. It was as the result of this resolution, just as Ringo had feared, that he swore to pull hierarchy ("pill horurchy") in Westminster and Scotland Yard to ensure the "twut" was hunted down the length and breadth of the land, then faced a Parliament Square "faring squid" composed of top marksmen from the Royal Fusiliers whose motto, as best he could remember it—which wasn't very well at all—was *honay swat ki molly pence* (*honi soit qui mal y pense*).

Not that he was in any fit condition to organise all this himself, of course. The arrangements he would leave to the sally butch living in his mansion and claiming to be his wife and the lottle twut's mother. It was Lady Hermione, therefore, who was left with the task of raising the matter of her son's disappearance with the Metropolitan Police Commissioner Cynthia Broadbent, who, at least, was a woman.

"That's absolutely *right*, Miss Broadbent. Dis...app...*eared.*" she said when she finally found the MPC's number amidst the detritus on Lord Crossbar's desk.

"Where to?" asked Cynthia, who wasn't the brightest candle in the chandelier.

"If I *knew* where he'd disappeared to, I wouldn't be calling *you*, would I?" replied Lady Hermione reasonably enough.

"Ah-hah," said Cynthia, making a note. "So I s'pose you'll be wanting us to find him for you?"

"That was indeed the purpose of my call, woman."

"Only we're a bit busy at the moment, what with the Brexit riots, and the planet extinction marches and everything."

"I don't care how bally busy you are. You must have some plod on the books to look for my boy."

"Plus we lost a lot of coppers with the government cuts," Cynthia carried on undaunted. "Can't spare the ones we've got left looking for runaways. There're hundreds of 'em around town."

"Madam, I'll have you know we are speaking here of the only son and heir of a leading parliamentary peer of the realm."

"One of the snooty buggers who cut our budget most likely," Cynthia only just stopped herself from saying. Instead, she coughed meaningfully and said, "Is that so?"

"It...is...*so.*"

"And this peer's name?"

"Is Lord Crossb...pardon me, Lord *Xavier* Barr. A prominent member of the Upper Hice."

"Upper...?"

"*Hice.*"

"Care to spell that for me, missus?"

"H...O...U...S...E," said Lady Hermione, swallowing back "you cretinous moron."

As you can see, this conversation wasn't going at all well, and continued in this vein for several more minutes, as each of its participants grew to loathe the other with the sort of venom lady rattlesnakes normally reserve for their cheating partners. Matters weren't improved by Lord Crossbar first staggering into the room—Lady Hermione's private boudoir—demanding to know who the sally butch was talking to then falling flat on his face, which led to Lady Hermione calling him a stupid old tosspot and Cynthia saying, "who the fuck're you calling a stupid old tosspot? I'll have you know I'm the Commissioner of P'lice, and you can go whistle for your soddin' son."

With that, the line went dead. Which was great news for Ringo/The Ring, albeit news of which he was, of course, ignorant—because it bought him the breathing space to play a few rapturously received gigs with Tosh at The King and Parrot.

Meanwhile, Lady Hermione resorted to the local constabulary for help but, as DI Malcolm Shufflebottom explained, he and his two officers were pretty busy with tracing the whereabouts of the local poacher and possible sheep shagger, Billy Bascombe.

"Little Piddlington In The Marsh ain't a big place, ma'am, narmean?" he elliptically replied to Lady Hermione's request for a search party. "An' what if young Fergus ain't 'ere anyhow? Could be bleedin' *any*where, couldn't 'e?"

"Bally police don't know what the world's coming to," Lady Hermione expostulated before tripping over the prone form of Lord Crossbar who had, yet again, staggered into her boudoir and fallen over.

What with one thing and another, it would be weeks before any copper anywhere in the land took the least interest in the disappearance of Fergus Ulysses Barr, which gave him all the time he needed to pop over to Dublin with Tosh and Mutt to meet Tosh's pal, Seamus O'Driscoll, the faux Irish passport dealer.

Four

Why go all the way to Dublin when Ringo was old enough to acquire his first full British passport in London, you will be asking. Because, given the Brexit baloney, he didn't *want* a British passport any more, that was why. What use would one of those be to a young man who wished to move freely around Europe in the new dark days? There would be visa problems, log jams in the Other Passport queues at airports and border crossings etc, etc... Plus, as an Englishman he would be likely to experience the well-deserved derision and/or pity from citizens of the twenty-seven EU countries who had watched on for the three years it had taken British politicians of all parties to argue each other into the ground over Brexit and come up with nothing resembling a coherent plan. Some dickwads *they* were. No, no, better by far to become an Irishman. Eire, after all, was still a fully-fledged member of the EU and intended so to remain. Tosh was in full agreement with this, having already negotiated his Irish passport in the name of Danny O'Milligan.

"No mileage in bein' a Brit no more," he'd agreed with Ringo. "Little bleedin' island in the middle of nowhere still reckonin' it's the bee's knees. A few more years in this joint and we'll all be out on the streets barterin' for food."

Ringo laughed. "Swap you a potato for a Rolex, Mister?"

"That's the kind've thing. Down the lav is where this place is goin'," said Tosh with the sort of acumen so signally lacking in British cabinet ministers and parliamentarians of all stripes. "So, yeah, over we go to Dublin Town and get you fitted up."

And how, you will also be asking, were two penniless runaways like Ringo and Tosh going to finance this trip, let alone buy a faux Irish passport? Trains to Liverpool and then the ferry over to Dublin didn't come cheap. Nor did the flights Tosh wouldn't take anyway because he refused to put Mutt in a crate in the hold. Back in the last century they might have hitchhiked, but that was no longer an option, so...?

Answer: they weren't penniless because the gigs at The King and Parrot had become sellouts in the month or so they worked there. Tosh was right...guys and gals were pissed off with robot music and looking for something different and "ethnic." And this was Camden Town after all, which was stuffed to the gills with one package tour after another of mainly French, German, Italian, and Spanish folks taking advantage of the plummeting value of sterling because of Brexit. It was mainly they who filled The King and Parrot to the rafters whenever Tosh and The Ring were playing and they who thereafter downloaded the songs in their thousands, "Outsider Blues" charting as their favourite. So because The King and Parrot's owner/landlord, Giorgio Delmardes—a pal of Tosh's from way back—was both grateful for the publicity and what Tosh called "a stand-up guy," he and Ringo received their share of the profits.

"Never earned so much dosh in all me life," Tosh commented one night in the copse encampment. And it's all down to you and your lyrics, sonny boy. Like I said, Clapton eat your heart out. He might've been God once, but now it's The Ring."

"Raaf, *raaf*," said Mutt, who'd taken part in all the performances, sitting on his best behaviour beside his master's drums, thereby becoming the most photographed dog in Camden Town history and a legend in his own right.

"Just give me the nod an' I'll book the tickets," said Tosh.

So it was that, unhindered by any police investigation but, nonetheless, disguised to the nines, Tosh, Ringo, and Mutt made their way to Euston Station for the trip up to Liverpool where, believe this or believe it not, such was the dissemination of their fame, they were destined to headline for one night only at the new Cavern Club at 10 Matthew Street. Perhaps the new Ringo would become a troubadour after all.

~ * ~

Seeing as School was a closed world behind its gilt gates, it took Dwayne Zobinski several weeks to figure out the truth of what had happened to Fergus Ulysses Barr. Naturally, in such a sealed environment, rumours abounded. Barr had gone insane overnight and been taken to an asylum in the highlands of Scotland. Barr had called Headmaster Quentin Fortesque a twat to his face, been expelled, and sent to a comprehensive school as punishment. Barr had been caught *in flagrante delicto* kissing a serving wench between the legs and died of an incurable infection...and so on. Such are the imaginations of teenage boys locked up together, especially when they're doing their damnedest to avoid any suspicion of involvement in another boy's escape. Omertà was thus the name of their game when it came to the real story. Not that School's teachers were any more helpful in Dwayne's researches, none of them agreeing to either confirm or deny the stories burgeoning by the day.

Niggling at Dwayne, however, was the first XV rugger team sheet with F.U. Bar down to play scrum half. Now he thought back, it had been *his* explanation of Fubar which had led to Fergie being dropped from the side, hadn't it? *And*—now Dwayne thought about it—to the *fooooo baaaaaing* around the dorms and corridors, after which the kid never showed up for much of anything. Kinda disappeared from sight...then he suddenly wasn't there at all. For the first time in his short, expensive, and star-studded life, Dwayne Zobinski started losing a little sleep, and then a little more sleep until he barely slept at all.

"Whadda fuck is going *down* here?" he would mutter, smacking himself around the head to keep the thoughts from coming. But keep coming they did, and this being Dwayne's first encounter with conscience, he had no idea why. And it wasn't as though the thoughts restricted themselves to the nighttime. Even in the daylight, they were still there swirling about beneath the surface, to the point even his rugger was starting to suffer.

"Wozza matter with ye, laddie?" Horrid Horace McIlroy would complain every time Dwayne fumbled a line-out ball he would normally catch with ease, or collapsed a scrum by not binding properly.

"Nudn, I'm okay."

"The hell you are."

And Horrid Horace was right. Dwayne *wasn't* okay. In the head, he was far from okay, and all because of an accidental freakin' fubar that wouldn't leave him alone. If only he'd kept his big mouth shut, but as his old man Dwayne Zobinski Snr always said, echoing the crazy dude in the White House, "If only's for dorks and shitkickers. You wanna get on in this world, son, you learn to forget, draw lines, never say sorry, and carry right on." Easily said from Zob Snr's super-rich perspective, not so easy for his son who, after all, had an ex-hippy painter for a mother. Shame she couldn't have come over for the London posting, but that had never been explained. CeCi stayed in NYC and that was that. At least they Skyped, though secretly at night on the phone he kept hidden under his pillow. Phones were forbidden in the dorms but for rugger star and Oxbridge candidate Zobinski, unseeing eyes had been turned. It was around three a.m. the same night Dwayne made the call that would change his life.

"Ma, I gotta problem," he whispered.

"Tell me about it, kiddo. Problem is my middle name." CeCi laughed.

So Dwayne told her.

"Poor kid," said CeCi.

"Me?"

"No, the other guy. And he disappeared, you say?"

"Gone with the wind. Nobody knows where."

"And it was you who came across with the *fucked up beyond all repair* line?"

"Yeah. I didn't mean no harm, Mom. It just…"

"Leaked out."

"Right."

"Kiddo, the times stuff leaked outta me, you…have…no…idea."

"And you just carried on, like Pops said?"

"Times I would, times I wouldn't. But a lot of folks get hurt that way. So…"

A pause while CeCi lit a cigarette.

"So?"

"Older I got, the more I tried to work stuff out. Like admit I was wrong? Stuff like that. You wanna know what I think about this story of yours?"

"It's why I called, Ma."

"Go find the kid. Make things better with him. Ooops, there's the bell at the door. Gotta go, kiddo. Love ya."

"How'm I gonna *find* him for crissakes?" Dwayne asked. But by then, CeCi was already in the arms of Josyanne La Jeune, her latest lover.

"Fuck," whispered Dwayne in case he awoke any of his slumbering, snoring dorm mates as dawn approached and sleep was now an impossibility. "Find him *how*?"

With nothing better to do than fiddle with his dick or his phone, Dwayne chose both. At least he could listen to some sounds while he played with himself. Randomly with his right hand, he therefore scrolled through his favourite sites, the ones playing the blues and old time music. Like Fergie Ringo, Tosh *and* CeCi—taught by her in fact—Dwayne's musical brain hurt when he heard twenty-first century jingle jangles with lyrics of ten words tops. It was as his eyelids were magically fluttering towards closure that a new song hit his eardrums. "Outsider Blues" it was called. Dwayne listened through the whole painful number to the last line. "No home to go to, never was one." then jolted awake and played the track through again. And not only because it was such a great song—which it was—but because there was something he recognized in that voice, a certain familiar inflection.

But where did it come from? Dwayne had no idea so he rewound and listened a third time.

Then suddenly, he had it. How or why he would never understand, but somewhere in his subconscious he was back on the rugger pitch scrumming down and awaiting the scrum half's voice to say, "Ball coming in...*now,*" as from the second-row he'd tightened his grip on the front-row forwards, the hooker especially, and heaved to ensure the team would get a clean strike, and the scrum half would get the backs into full flow. And who had that scrum half been? F.U. Bar, that was who.

Leaving his dick alone, Dwayne Zobinski spent the remaining hours of the night fiddling with his phone trying to locate the origin of the song. And, given its huge popularity, it didn't take him all that long to track it back to a pub called The King and Parrot in some place called Camden Town. Sung by a duo named Tosh and The Ring.

"Well now," he muttered, falling so deeply asleep for the first time in days, he had to be shaken awake by the dorm prefect, Norman Snodgrass, and told to get his arse in gear for classes.

Five

Tosh, Ringo, and Mutt didn't hang around in Dublin. Richer they were than they had ever expected, but that still wasn't rich enough to afford hotels and suchlike, so having done the business with Seamus O'Driscoll down by the docks, they took the next ferry back to Liverpool. Seamus would have offered to put them up for the night if he hadn't been married to Caitlin O'Driscoll, who knew nothing of her husband's illicit passport business and, if Seamus had anything to do with it, never would.

"Would like to help ye out, lads," he told Tosh and Ringo. "But…" he added peering down at his wedding band and twirling it meaningfully.

"No probs," said Tosh, who knew a thing or two about what he termed "hellcats."

"Some other time," said Ringo.

"Raaf," said Mutt, who'd enjoyed the ride across the Irish Sea and was looking forward to getting back on the boat.

And so it was that he and his two humans hit the high seas again and were back in Liverpool in the late evening, Ringo with his brand new Eire passport, and Tosh with an updated version of his old one.

"Train straight back to London Town?" said Tosh as they disembarked at the Pier Head.

But Ringo had heard a lot about Liverpool and fancied a look around. Nothing that would cost money, just a smell of the place would do. A person couldn't really ignore the city that had been home to the real Ringo plus John, Paul and George, could he? At least take a look at The Cavern. And Tosh was up for that. So, around the Pier Head Village with all its Beatles' memorabilia, the trio roamed, then up James Street to North John Street sniffing the air, which in The Fab Four's heyday had been bottled and sold all around the world. That plus partially distilled Mersey water. Nice little earners for the locals *they* had been. And, within ten or fifteen minutes, there they were at The Cavern's door in Matthew Street.

"Eh up, lads. Comin' in?" said Billy McKenzie, doorman for the night.

"Only if we could play yer a song," said Tosh, whose abiding lesson from the University of Life was brazenly to ask the impossible. Ringo was astonished at the bravado and shrank back.

Billy frowned behind his smile. "That's what all the wannabes say," he said. "Only I don't see you carryin' no instruments, narmean?"

"We could borrow some," said Tosh, pushing his luck.

"Yeah, yeah, yeah," Billy chorused She Loves You-ishly.

At which, Tosh pushed his luck to its limits by taking out his phone, selecting "Outsider Blues," and holding it to Billy's ear.

"That's us," he said. "Tosh and The Ring. You might have heard the tune before."

And such was the reach of the internet; Billy had. Pretty soon, he was tapping his feet and smiling.

"Come on in, lads," he said. "Let's see if we can't find you...what? A couple of guitars?"

"One guitar plus a drum kit are all we need. And the dog comes, too," said Tosh, ruffling Mutt's ruff. "He's our mascot. Like the His Master's Voice dog?"

Billy laughed. "Normally against the rules, woofers, but..."

And so it was that Tosh, The Ring, and Mutt, as the band had renamed itself, took the stage at the world's most famous venue and wowed the crowd. In addition to "Outsider Blues," they also played some Big Bill Broonzy numbers, their versions of Paul Simon's "Slip Slidin' Away" and a couple of Bob Dylan songs, and for a finale, Ringo's latest composition, "Tell Me It Ain't True," which bemoaned the fubar fates of the USA and the UK under their current leaderships.

A stunned audience whooped, applauded, and demanded the encores that paid for Tosh, Ringo, and Mutt to spend the night at the Adelphi Hotel right next door to Lime Street station from where they would catch their train back to Town the following afternoon.

~ * ~

Dwayne Zobinski was also riding the iron horse, having crept out of the dorm in the wee small hours, bribed the nighttime gatekeeper with fifty pounds and, unlike Ringo, careless of its tracking potential, paid off the pre-booked cabbie at the station with the Amex card his old man had given him. Using the same piece of plastic, he travelled first-class to Town where he arrived at much the same time as Tosh, Ringo and Mutt, although at a different station. Such is the nature of serendipity.

"Ookey, dokey," he said, peering about the environs of Victoria. NYC it wasn't, but after the confines of School, at least it was a city. Unlike Tosh, Ringo and Mutt who took a bus back to Hampstead, Dwayne headed straight for the taxi rank where, again flashing the Amex, he hopped into another cab and ordered the driver, Bogdan Kowalczyk, to get him to Camden Town and not to spare the horses, which caused Bogdan to wince for reasons Dwayne, obviously enough given his age, couldn't have understood. How could *he* have known his driver to be the grandson of a WW2 Pole interned in Wales, who on his return to Gdansk in 1945 had merrily told the tale of his English guards who had complained of Yanks being "overpaid, oversexed, and over here?" No way, that was how.

*Any*way, dissimulating such prejudices as best he could, Bogdan deposited Dwayne opposite Camden Town tube station ten minutes later, overcharged him by a mere five pounds, and wished him a happy stay in the UK. Bogdan might himself soon be having to leave if Brexiteers had their way with EU nationals. Sad, he mused as he headed back to Central London, to think the dumb Yank came from a country run by a psychopathic babyman not unlike the worst of the UK Brexiteers. Sometimes Bogdan wondered if the *whole* "populist" world was going to hell in a handcart, especially now that back home the Law and Justice Party was running Poland.

Meanwhile, Dwayne was asking a passerby where he could find a pub called The King and Parrot, only the passerby was an Italian tawdry trinket and bling hunter who spoke almost no English and, anyway, hadn't a clue where The King and Parrot was. So Dwayne asked another passerby, this time a Spanish tawdry trinket and bling hunter who had as little idea as his Italian predecessor. And so on through two Portuguese, three Germans, and two Japanese.

"Holy *shit*, what kinda place *is* this?" said Dwayne after each of these fruitless enquiries.

Then he spotted a black meter maid.

"Hey, babe," he said. "You wanna tell me how I find The King and Parrot?"

"Wid a map, honeychile," said Jamaican Jasmine Jonson in her favourite take-the-piss-out-of-whities-who-dissed-her Mississippi accent. "I'm busy."

"Fuck," said Dwayne.

"You should be so lucky," Jasmine called over her shoulder while ticketing a stationary Jeep with a German Shepherd at the wheel.

While Dwayne was lost in this way, Tosh, Ringo, and Mutt sailed past him on their Hampstead-bound number 24 bus.

~ * ~

In her Fifth Avenue apartment, CeCi—a derivative of Cecily since her teens—began to worry about her son Dwayne. Since they'd last spoken, she'd heard nothing more from him, and the messages she left on his phone went straight to voicemail because Dwayne, finally worrying about being tracked, had switched off his phone. But CeCi didn't know that, so she worried. If he had taken her advice and gone in search of the fubar kid, who knew *where* he could be by now. And calling his asswipe father would be pointless because all her soon-to-be-ex-husband Dwayne Zobinski Snr cared about was money. No way was he going to leave his desk and computer to go looking for the boy he'd insisted on bringing with him to the UK because CeCi was an "arty-farty liberal lesbian loser" who didn't know the difference between a wingback and a tight end. So no way José was *that* gonna happen. As a last resort, she called School, but all Quentin Fortesque BA, MA could tell her was that he was cross because the boy had disappeared, and such a disappearance might mean he would lose the big cheque Zobinski Snr had paid him to "make a man of the boy."

"So you called the cops, right?"

"Indeed we did, ma'am."

"And?"

"They said they would look into it, but they were somewhat busy at the moment."

"Too busy to look for my *son*?"

"Apparently so, ma'am."

"Some fuckin' country," CeCi told Fortesque before hanging up.

After that, she smoked some cigarettes, drank herself some beers, worried some more, then called her lover Josyanne to talk things through.

"It ain't like this is New York we're talking, Josy," she said, close to tears after explaining the situation. "This here is the U freakin' K."

"A little island one tenth the size of Texas but still thinking it can punch above its weight, even though it's even more screwed up than we are, and going down the tubes with the Brexit hoohah," said Josyanne, a fierce critic of the madman in the White House and keen observer of international current affairs. "The place right now is fucked up beyond all…"

"Yeah, yeah, I know. I hear the word fubar again, I am gonna start throwing things."

"Way to go, girl. You want I should come over? I'm kinda good at throwing stuff."

"That would be nice."

So it was that Josyanne hopped into a yellow cab and half an hour later she and CeCi were sharing a good bottle of Californian white and smoking a little grass.

"What d'you figure I should *do*, babe?" asked CeCi, still in her painter gear—a paint spattered smock over cut-off Levis.

"Go there."

"To the *UK*?" CeCi had only left NYC twice since her arrival there, once to visit her dying mother in Bangor, Maine, and the other time to attend her very own exhibition of New York street art in Los Angeles, on both occasions taking the train.

"Yeah. All you gotta do is jump a plane from JFK."

"And *fly*?"

"Yeah. A lotta people do that these days, hon. Also there're no trains across the ocean. There's the boat but that's gonna take, like, *weeks*."

"Aw, shit. Erica Jong I ain't, but..."

"I know, I know, you're afraid of flying. So take a pill before you go. Take ten pills. This is Dwayne we're talking about, right? Your son. Who is in some kinda trouble?"

"Deep shit could be."

"Sooo... All you gotta do is say yes, and I can book you a flight right now," said Josyanne, pulling from her purse a plastic-stuffed wallet and a phone. "Trust me, I fly Yurp all the time. Plus, I got air miles to burn."

CeCi knew it. Josy had travelled to France, Spain, Italy, all over the damn place to check out showings of some of her sculptures and always come home alive.

"Pass the grass," she said.

"And if I do, you'll agree?"

"Just pass the grass."

And so it was that, terrified though she was, CeCi Zoblinski was accompanied by Josyanne to JFK the following morning, shepherded through all the formalities with a special dispensation from British Airways, and six hours and forty-five minutes later, found herself at an airport called Heathrow. Sweating and faint, she managed to teeter out into the open air, breathe deeply, hail a cab, and tell the driver to take her to the hotel Josyanne had booked her into, The Ritz on some street called Peekadoolly.

Six

As darkness was gathering and, after several more fruitless encounters with clueless overseas visitors, Dwayne eventually found The King and Parrot by asking a bloke with a dog, figuring a bloke with a dog would be a local. And he was right in the sense that the bloke, Mickey McManus, and his raggedy bulldog Titan sold the Big Issue outside a local HSBC in the daytime and slept on the pavement at night. Some weird joint this Camden Town was, Dwayne figured, after peregrinations which had taken him off the main drag to some streets behind with big grand houses, like the superrich and the homeless lived side by side. Other hand, there were parts of NYC, Brooklyn for example, just the same, so...

Mickey didn't come across with the info Dwayne needed straight away. "What d'you take me for, sonny?" he said. "See a sign on my head saying 'Tourist Guide,' do yer?"

"Raaf, *raaf*," Titan emphasized.

"No, sir. I see no sign saying 'Tourist Guide.'"

"Bleedin' *tour*ists. Bringin' down the whole tone of the place," said Mickey paradoxically, seeing as Mickey made the only living he had from the very same tourists. "Time was, some years back now, when there was only yer regular English around the place. All right, some of yer Irish Paddys, but they was okay. Always slip yer a few bob they would. Proper shops there was, too…butchers, fish shop, betting shop, tailor's."

"Nice," Dwayne observed, patting Titan on his large head and almost being knocked over by the bulldog's response of planting both forepaws on his shoulders and slurping his face.

"It was. *Now* look at it. Bleedin' souvenir shops all over the place, Starbucks, Pret A soddin' Mangy, whole different class of cobblers," said Mickey ruefully, tapping his faux walking stick on the pavement for emphasis.

"Sorry about that. Shame. I wonder if you could tell me where—?"

"You're right there, sonny. *Bleedin'* shame. Yank, are yer?"

"Yeah."

"Never liked the Yanks much, but at least you spikka da English."

"Yup."

"Well, sort of," said Mickey, evidently a connoisseur of the world's differing versions of the language. "Kinda slangy but—"

"At least you can understand me."

"Raaf, raaf," said Titan. Muffledly, seeing as he'd taken to investigating his bottom.

"I like that new president you got now, though," Mickey opined. "Tough talker, huh?"

"Dougal Klank? He's an asshole," said Dwayne, causing Mickey to raise an eyebrow and swiftly change tack.

"Yeah, I s'pose there's a bit of the arsehole to 'im. *Any*how, sonny, been nice chattin' wiv yer. Don't s'pose you could see yer way to—?"

And so it was, that in exchange for five pounds—Mickey wouldn't take less—Dwayne came to find out where The King and Parrot was.

"Nice pub," Mickey muttered over his shoulder as he faux limped away with Titan at his heels. "Get some good bands in there, they do. Play the old time music, none of yer new-fangled bollocks."

"Heard of Tosh and The Ring?" Dwayne called after him.

"Yeah. Popular they are."

"Great. Fantastic. Looking forward to it," Dwayne shouted back, but Mickey was already deep in negotiations with a person bearing the legend *Allez Les Bleus* on the back of his blouson.

So it was that Dwayne finally found his way to The King and Parrot, which was already boasting the night's appearance of the newly named Tosh, The Ring and Mutt. FRESH FROM THE CAVERN WE ARE PROUD TO WELCOME BACK OUR LOCAL HEROES proclaimed a huge poster outside above a pic of the two lads and their dog.

"Wow," said Dwayne, running a forefinger down the image of the one who had to be called The Ring seeing as he was the only one who wasn't mixed race and wasn't a dog. With his moustache and shoulder-length black hair, the guy didn't look a whole lot like the scrum half Fergie he remembered, but...but now he looked harder; there *was* something in the eyes, a glint Dwayne couldn't quite put his finger on. Yet, as with his recognition of the guy's singing voice, he was pretty sure who it was.

"Oo*okay*, so here we go. And if it ain't him, it ain't him," Dwayne muttered, eyeing the queue that snaked all the way down the street and around into the next one, and hoping he could get a ticket.

But that's the ticket tout's role in life, isn't it? To sniff out wealthy last minute customers and fleece them. Not that Dwayne *looked* all that wealthy in his regulation blue jeans and sneakers, but the New York Yankees jacket pretty much gave the game away—at least to "Honest" Harry Harbottle, who still harboured the illusion *all* Americans were filthy rich.

"'Elp you out at all, mister?" said Harry. "Finest seats in the 'ouse an' all goin' like 'ot cakes so you'd better be quick, you want one."

"How much?"

"To *you*, mister, an 'alf price special knockdown offer. Big friend of you Yankees, I am. Cousins across the ocean an' all that."

"How much is *full* price."

"Hundred quid."

"*Quid*?"

"Pounds. Like *sterling*?"

"Right."

"Right, as in you want one?"

"Right, as in good to know what a quid is."

Harry nodded sympathetically. "Always 'appy to 'elp out. Now, the ticket?"

"Still kinda expensive," said Dwayne who, despite his best endeavours not to, had inherited at least a trace of Zobinski's Snr's haggling business acumen. "Fifty quids, eh?"

"Yeah but, hey, included in the deal you get to sit right up front next to Tosh an' whoever, *plus* you get free drinks all night."

"And if I don't have the drinks?"

Harry was getting irritated with this kid. On the other hand, he *was* big and muscly, and Harry wanted no trouble.

"Twenty-five quid," he muttered.

Which was also way over the top because regular concert tickets only cost ten pounds. Giorgio Dolmardes was scrupulous in never overcharging. "No good robbing the poor to pay the rich," was his motto.

"Man, that's *still* a lotta money," said Dwayne, who as yet knew nothing of Giorgio Dolmardes or his pricing policy but could spot a con artist when he saw one. Unless he was real dumb, a person didn't grow up in New York City without at least a sixth sense.

Honest Harry ground what was left of his teeth. "The price is twenty-five, take it or leave it," he grunted. "Only like I said, that's without the free drinks *and* the guaranteed good seat."

"Man, you sure drive a hard bargain," said Dwayne in the voice he'd learnt and practised from repeated viewings of *The Wire* and *Pulp Fiction*. Squaring his big shoulders as he said it. "Tell you whut, seein' as we're cousins across the ocean, how'd it be if you give me a freebie, an' I don't beat the shit outta you? How's that sound?"

Which was how it came to pass that Dwayne Zobinski joined the queue along with all the other Tosh, The Ring, and Mutt fans, made a lot of friends with the other guys and gals, and thoroughly enjoyed the show. When it was over, he would make his way through the crowd, introduce himself to The Ring—who he was still pretty sure *was* F.U. Bar, especially now he'd re-heard the singing voice—and offer his sincerest apologies for the misspeak back at School.

Of "Honest" Harry Harbottle nothing more was heard in Camden Town when Dwayne later mentioned his name to Giorgio Dolmardes. Persona *very* non grata *he* became with both fellow publicans and the cops once Giorgio had spread the news.

~ * ~

Chaos theory running amok as usual, it was in the downstairs lounge of The Ritz where the nouveaux riches went to sip tea that CeCi bumped into her soon-to-be-ex-husband, Dwayne Snr. In the background, a bloke in tails tinkled the ivories of a Steinway grand, smiled toothily like some latterday Liberace, and played mainly pre-WW2 numbers, although he also took *Casablanca*-type *"play it again, Sam"* requests. It was all very mock-historical as a reminder of Britain's once glorious past perhaps. CeCi didn't like it much but sipped at her tea anyway because there was nothing else for her to do. Being in London to look for her son was all fine and dandy, but talk about needles in haystacks when it came to taking the first step in the investigation. For all she knew, the boy could be in freaking *Scot*land by now.

It was an unusually antsy CeCi, therefore, who tipped her tea into its saucer when Dwayne Snr waltzed in, yacking thirteen to the dozen in the ear of some foreign looking dude, possibly Russian from the look of him, CeCi thought. She shrank down in her chair, hid behind her phone for a bit then, as in the old time movies, snatched up a copy of the day's *Times* newspaper and hid behind its pages.

"Holy fuck," she muttered to herself, as Dwayne Snr ushered what was evidently his guest to a neighbouring table and took to bullshitting in the familiar Dougal Klank manner CeCi had come to detest, while simultaneously clicking his fingers at a passing flunkey, and ordering "the usual" like he owned the place. Which, knowing Zobinski, wasn't beyond the bounds of possibility—a slice of the place anyhow.

"Jesus *pleasus*," she couldn't help herself whispering at this unfortunate turn of events as she speed read an article about the thing called Brexit, which even *The Times* reckoned was going to leave the UK up at the wrong end of shit creek without a paddle.

Dwayne Snr half turned his head and hissed, "Keep the noise down, sister."

Mind you, as coincidence would have it, Brexit was also the subject of the conversation with his guest, indeed a Russian named Anatoly Munchkov, who also owned a slice of The Ritz, only Zobinski's line was radically different to that in *The Times*, echoing as it did the same line as that of the madman in the White House.

"Man, that Brexit plays right into our ballpark," he was telling Munchkov, who to judge from the glazed eyes, spoke little American. But he nodded and muttered "*da*" a few times, nonetheless. Even CeCi knew what *da* meant and in what language.

"We break up the goddam European Union country by country and whadda we get?" Dwayne Snr continued. "And that ain't no rhetoricalistical question, right?"

Anatoly shrugged. CeCi winced.

"No more big bloc to fight with, that's whut. Just a whole lotta piddlin' liddle countries who can't tell their asses from their elbows. What we should be doin' right now is *thankin'* the UK for taking the lead and leavin' the stage open for your guys in Moscow and my guys in the US Man; some fortune we're gonna make. Fill your tea?" said Zobinski, finger-hooking a passing flunkey.

Anatoly nodded.

CeCi gripped her *Times* so hard she feared it might rip.

Which it did when Zobinski shouted out at Liberace to play "The Star Spangled Banner" and then "Midnight in Moscow."

That's when the tricky moment happened, the moment CeCi threw *The Times* in shreds to the floor, sprang out of her chair, took her soon-to-be-ex-husband by the throat, and told him he was the same old dumb ass-kissing Republican dickhead he'd always been, and now she had first-hand proof of the American/Russian conniving that had landed the dork of all dorks in the White House.

Either understanding more American than he had let on, or just fearful the crazy dame might go for his throat too, Anatoly Munchkov claimed another appointment and hustled out through the door into Piccadilly as fast as his stumpy little legs would carry him.

"*Cecily*?" Dwayne Snr gurgled, close to asphyxiation.

"The same, babe."

"You wuh-wanna let guh-go've muh-my fuh-fuckin' thuh-throat?"

"Not really."

On the other hand, she reflected, releasing her grip a fraction, who *else* was gonna help her find Dwayne Jnr? The asshole *was* the kid's father and still her husband after all. The biggest mistake of CeCi's life, despite the money that had come with the deal, but such was life. Maybe, however much it riled her, this was just one more opportunity she couldn't refuse. With his slimy background, Dwayne Snr was the very kind of guy to know some Sam Spade-type private eye who would help out. Which was when she fully released her soon-to-be ex, just slapped him around a bit more, ordered brandies, and then sat down with him for a powwow.

Seven

Lord Xavier Barr's phone took to playing Beethoven's Fifth in his pocket during the sixtieth re-reading of a complex government draft bill entitled, "Forty-Nine Ways of Either Agreeing or Disagreeing with Thirty-Six of the Government's Proposals about Either Leaving the European Union or Remaining in it Depending on Whether There is Another Referendum or Another General Erection [sic] or not," which had been sent up the Other Place for consideration.

Thrum, thrum, thrum, tinkety, tinky, tink went the instrument set as always on full volume, but Lord Barr showed no signs of hearing it except for some contrapuntal snores. He had to be nudged awake by Lord Keith McGear of Toxteth, Merseyside.

"Oi there, Barro, that's your bleedin' phone," said Lord Keith, prodding his neighbour in the ribs. "Shouldn't have turned on in here anyhow."

"Ungrr?" said Lord Xavier, emerging from his snooze and tossing his papers in the air.

"Shhhh over there," said Lord Speaker Arbuthnot.

"Sorry, milord," said Lord Keith, "Only the old fart here's left his phone on and it's ringing."

"*Which* old fart, pray?" said Arbuthnot, peering around the chamber.

"The one next to me. Barr."

"Ah-hah, *that* old fart. Tell him to leave his seat if he wants to answer it."

"Yes, milord," said Lord Keith, turning to whisper these instructions into Lord Xavier's ear. Only finding Barr's ear was tricky because of the swathes of bandages all around his head. So Lord Keith prodded him again, this time causing him to jump to his feet, fall face first across the three peers seated in front of him, scramble back to his feet and do a runner for the door from the upper chamber, whose occupants broke into spontaneous hoots of ribaldry.

"Order, order!" shouted Lord Speaker Arbuthnot, with little effect, seeing as the noble lords and ladies were bored shitless with the mindless U-turns and contradictions embedded in, "Forty-nine Ways of Either Agreeing or Disagreeing with Thirty-Six of the Government's Proposals about Either Leaving the European Union or Remaining in it Depending on Whether There is Another Referendum or a General Erection [sic] or not." Government gobbledygook they were well used to, but this took the biscuit, and they were grateful for any opportunity for light relief. So it was that the Lord Speaker called a comfort break, and they all sighed thankfully.

Meanwhile, Lord Xavier, forgetting his way around parliament and with Beethoven's Fifth still thrumming insistently in his pocket, stumbled into the grandiose zone separating the two Houses where he was greeted by a press phalanx sticking microphones in his face wanting to know his view on the progress of the latest Brexit draft bill so far.

Clearly, "Fock if ju winkers" was the wrong answer for Lord Xavier to have given, even though initially the media hounds were foxed by its meaning. It wasn't until he flipped them a V-sign as a visual aid, and baring his teeth, growled at them bestially that the message sank home, and they fell about laughing, their mirth being further fuelled by Lord Xavier inadvertently farting as he brushed past them and out into the open air. The following day's headlines, the double entendre-ish "FEISTY FLATULENCE IN THE LORDS" from *The Morning Snide* for example, were largely of a jocular nature, but they only faintly disguised the subtext of urgent need for the reform of the upper house or better still, its abolition. Lord Speaker Arbuthnot was, understandably, furious—but that's a whole different story.

Meanwhile, leaving the tittering press scrum in his wake and blocking traffic in Victoria Street, Lord Xavier finally dragged the phone from his pocket, but to no avail because just as he did so the "focking ding" finally went to the message Lady Hermione would have left earlier instead of persisting with Beethoven's Fifth in the knowledge her husband had little idea how to answer a smartphone and even less of an idea how to find a message.

"*FICK* JU, JU LOTTLE *BISTURD*," he exclaimed at the instrument, finally lurching onto Parliament Square and stumbling about, peering at the little screen wondering how to make it talk before giving up and hurling it up at the Winston Churchill statue.

A shame it was from Lord Barr's point of view this image had to be caught on camera by so many tourists and skulking paparazzi, and he was so quickly to be identified as a peer of the realm—albeit his name was mercifully withheld for reasons of his personal security. Also unfortunate that the picture should immediately thereafter have been blazoned across the internet, because it was to become *the* metonym for the general fucked-up-ness of latterday British parliamentary behavior, and served to add fire to both pro-and-anti-abolitionist arguments, especially with WW2 saviour-of-the-nation Winston Churchill in the picture. Clearly, too, it added impetus to the populists' jingoistic rhetoric.

"WHAT'S THE COUNTRY *COMING* TO?" asked the alt-right, pro-Brexit, *Daily Mole*, for example, above an article outlining the fears it had of subversively leftie peers seeking to besmirch the glorious past of GRRREAT BRITAIN through provocative acts suggestive of pro-European sentiment. A feverish conclusion indeed to draw merely from Lord Xavier Barr's addled brain no longer being able to handle simple issues like smartphone usage, but of such left-field assumptions is history often plagued (see Epilogue).

Anyway, *any*way, what, you will be wondering, was the message Lady Hermione had been wishing to communicate to the doolally father of their missing son?

It was: "Just heard from Chief Cop Cynthia Broadbent at the Met. At least she's got some Missing Person posters up around Town. Fingers crossed there will be a sighting."

~ * ~

When Tosh, Mutt, and The Ring had finished their King and Parrot gig with "Tell Me It Ain't True," Dwayne Zobinski was obliged to wait in line behind a gaggle of admiring girls before he, too, could make his way onto the little stage. He wasn't feeling confident about what he was about to do, but he knew he had to do it. It was that unusual-for-him conscience thing again. Meanwhile, the girls sought autographs and tried to touch Tosh and The Ring, who tolerated such behaviour for a while, then graciously asked to be left alone.

"Okay, girls, thanks for comin' an' see yer all again another time," said Tosh, who regarded himself as the bandleader.

"Raaf, raaf," emphasized Mutt, who reckoned the humans had been grabbing all the glory and he hadn't received *nearly* enough attention.

So it was that, blowing kisses and, in some cases, leaving addresses, the girls made their way back into the pub proper and Dwayne was left in full view. Ringo, decked out in his newly adopted *White Album*-type John Lennon look with brown hair to his shoulders, a middle parting and the famous round glasses, recognized him instantly, and drew a deep breath.

"Tosh," he said, "d'you wanna take Mutt for a pee or something? I need to talk to this bloke."

"He a friend of yours?"

"Dunno. That's what I've got to find out."

"Ookey dokey," said Tosh, reading the runes, whistling to Mutt and heading for the back door out to the street.

"Zobinski?" said Ringo.

"The same."

"What the fuck...?"

"Am I doin' here?"

Ringo nodded while bending to stow in its case the tenth-hand Fender he'd managed to buy from the band's earnings. "Yeah. Long time no see, Zobinski. How d'you find me, anyhow?"

"You're a famous guy now. Plus, I remember one of the songs from back at…"

"School."

"Right."

"Where you were the one who…"

"Fucked everything up for you. Yep, that's me. And trust me, I… am…sooo…sorry. If there's anything I can do to…"

"Re-write history?"

"Sumptn like that."

To Dwayne's surprise and relief, Ringo smiled. "The fubar business wasn't so great at the time, that's for sure, but let bygones be bygones, eh? No good looking back. In the long run, maybe you even did me a favour," he said with a wave around the now empty auditorium. "Funny how things can turn out."

"Glad you see it that way," said a humbled Dwayne.

"So is this School holidays or…?"

"Nope. Like you, I did a runner."

"And you came all the way here to apologize?"

"That's about the size of it."

Ringo pursed his lips and shook his head. "That took some guts."

"I felt I owed you."

"How d'you find me anyway?" Ringo repeated. "Can't have been easy."

So Dwayne explained.

"Wow, and all from a song. Come over here and give me a hug, brother," said Ringo, these days a much more confident if not much taller teenager than he had been only a few short weeks earlier.

Dwayne needed to bend from the waist and be careful not to lift F.U. Barr off his feet to reciprocate the hug, but he was happy it was happening at all. And this was a very new kind of happiness for Dwayne Zobinski.

"Buy you a beer?" he asked when the hugging was over.

"I'd like that."

Into the bar the pair therefore went, where they were joined by Tosh, Mutt, and Giorgio Dolmardes, who had obeyed the legal closing hour but was happy enough to keep the libations flowing for guys who had become his good friends, *and* be introduced to the American who had done him the favour of outing Honest Harry Harbottle. It turned into quite a little party, which lasted until four in the morning, by which time even Giorgio reckoned enough was enough.

Out on the street, there were no cabs around so Tosh called one with his special super-Uber app and, within the hour, the trio plus Mutt were back in their hidden Hampstead Heath copse. Before they bedded down—Dwayne had brought with him a roll-up US army sleeping bag in case of such an eventuality—they jammed a little and it turned out, borrowing Ringo's Fender, that Zobinski was a rhythm guitarist proficient enough for Mutt to raise an eyebrow and say, "raaf, *raaf.*"

Tosh and Ringo exchanged meaningful glances before exhaustion overcame the whole quartet and sleep became a priority.

Eight

Private eye Sam Snade met the Zobinskis in his client's tenth-floor office at the Thames's Canary Wharf, many of whose glittering buildings were facing desertion and dereliction after Brexit. In the glory days, London was *the* banking centre for Europe and the world, an axial conduit for money laundering and access to each other's countries, but now all the big banks were looking for new homes in Germany, France, Denmark, The Republic of Ireland, practically anywhere except London. Meanwhile Zobinski Snr clung on in the hope of building a new and thriving import/export bridge among Europe, America, and Russia. That's what he had been intending to discuss with Munchkov until CeCi got him by the throat over what she reckoned were nefarious business practices and cut the conversation short. Then there had been some bullshit over their idiot son whom Zobinski had parked at School and not seen in the flesh for several months. Nonetheless, he'd reluctantly agreed to a meet-up with Snade to see if something could be done to find the kid.

"Good of yer to come, Sam," he said, sweeping an arm towards a white leather couch. "Rest your ass. This can't take long 'cos I'm like busy, busy, busy. Coffee? Tea?"

"Coffee. Black, four sugars," said Snade.

From her white leather couch CeCi coughed meaningfully, both because in her book the meeting would take as long as freakin' necessary, and because her asshole soon-to-be-ex-husband hadn't so far bothered to introduce her. For all Snade knew, she could be the P.A.

"Comin' right up," said Zobinski after barking the order into an intercom. "Incidentally, this here is Dwayne Jnr's mother." Not "my wife," or "Cecily, my wife," just "Dwayne Jnr's *mother*." As if she were some professional child-bearer.

CeCi didn't like the look of Snade. Fat and weaselly was her take— if weasels could be fat, that was. Plus, he had sneaky little piggy eyes *and* a way-out-of-date Zapata-type droopy moustache. Didn't look to her like the kinda guy who could find his own ass with an ass map. All she therefore mumbled was, "Hi, there," while flicking dust off her silver hi-tops.

"Sooo," said Snade, stirring the coffee delivered by the real P.A. "Down to business. Like this son of yours who's missing?"

"Dwayne Junior," said Dwayne Senior.

"Right," said Snade, scribbling on a yellow lawyer-type pad.

Some private dick when he didn't even have a laptop or tablet, CeCi noted. Maybe just a *dick*.

"You have a photo, boss? Gonna need a photo."

Zobinski arched an eyebrow and stared at what he still thought of as his wife. He didn't know about the soon-to-be-ex bit yet. CeCi had come prepared for the meeting, however, even if dumbo Dwayne hadn't. Without looking at Snade for fear of visible nausea, she slid a relatively recent snapshot across the desk.

"Good looking kid," Snade remarked, nodding at the blond hair and the toothy grin above the high school football uniform.

"Takes after me," said Zobinski, at which Snade shrugged non-committally. It was the only thing CeCi liked him for.

"Ookay, so that's the photo," said Snade, stowing the pic in his bag. "The kid carrying, is he?"

Zobinski stared at CeCI, who said, "Carrying what?"

"A gun," said Snade.

"Hell, no." CeCi sighed, shook her head in disgust and flicked more dust from the silver hi-tops over the ripped flared Levi's she'd worn on purpose to embarrass Soon-To-Be-Ex.

"You're *sure*, honey?" said Dwayne Snr. "Like sure, sure, *sure*?"

"'Course I'm freakin' sure. Dwaney never touched a gun in his whole life. As you *should* know."

"You say so, honey."

CeCi stared off and swallowed hard. One more *honey*, and she would be at the asshole's throat again.

Snade swivel-eyed the Zobinskis as if he were at a tennis match, and sipped more coffee. "Couple not getting along too good," he scribbled on his pad.

"Okay, no gun," he said when the scribbling was over.

"So what else could he be carrying?" asked Zobinski. "Phone? Credit card? Anything I can trace?"

"By hacking?" said Zobinski, arching at CeCi an eyebrow she interpreted as meaning, "Some shit hot dick I got on *my* payroll, huh?"

Behind her back, she flipped him the finger.

"Hacking is right," Snade confirmed. Smugly. "Just gimme the numbers an' I'll have your guy in ten minutes. Tracking's kinda easy peasy these days. God bless technology, huh?"

"Yes siree," Zobinski yipped while checking his Rolex Submariner.

Despite herself, CeCi grudgingly agreed. Overweight, piggy-eyed, weaselly, with a droopy Zapata moustache and no laptop or tablet the creep might be, but if he could find Dwayne Jnr, well...

It was she who provided the info Snade needed, seeing as Zobinski had no clue.

"That be all, Sam?" he said.

"For now. Later I'll be in touch with the info and the bill," said Snade, levering himself off the white leather sofa and waddling to the door, soon to be followed by CeCi, who didn't plan to spend any more time than necessary in the company of Soon-To-Be-Ex. He'd find out soon enough once she'd filed the divorce papers.

~ * ~

It was a shame from Sam Snade's point of view that, only hours before this conversation, Tosh had persuaded Dwayne to take a phone-booked Amex-paid taxi trip to Wimbledon Common to mislead any possible hacker, then to ensure his phone was wiped of *all* previous information, and his Amex card was cancelled, and torn to shreds before both were buried deep underground.

"Hell, man, I can't do without my phone or my money," Dwayne had protested. "It's like...it's like...they're *me*."

"My point, bruv. You wanna new life, you got to tear up the old one. Plus, hey, you *want* to be found or dontcha? You know how it is with phones and plastic these days."

"But how'm I gonna live without *money*?"

Tosh laughed. "We have room in the band for a rhythm guitar player. Ain't that so, Ringo?"

"No question."

"Raaf, raaf, *raaaafff*," Mutt agreed.

"Plus," Tosh added. "I can get you a new throw-down phone any time you want. Apps, the whole bag of works."

And so it was that, unbeknownst to him, Sam Snade was thwarted before he'd even left Zobinski's office in the soon-to-be defunct Canary Wharf.

~ * ~

It was a week later that Tosh, Ringo, and Dwayne all fell in love—and not, as the syntax might suggest, with each other. With girls.

"*What*?" I hear you say. "They all fell in love with girls, all at... the...same...*time*? Stretching coincidence a bit far, isn't it?"

Well maybe, but the truth's the truth. No good dodging it. As a matter of fact, it wasn't even in the same *week,* but on the very same *day* that Tosh fell in love with a Polish girl called Maja, Ringo fell in love with a Japanese girl called Aika, and Dwayne fell in love with a super-posh English girl called Desdemona, whose father—unsurprisingly— was professor of Renaissance Drama at King's College, University of London.

"And how is this unlikely event supposed to have come to pass?" I hear you mutter. Dubiously.

At the first gig of the newly formed Tosh, The Ring, Mutt and Desmond at the King and Parrot, that was how. "Desmond" was

Dwayne's stage name adopted further to muddy the trail for any possible private dick his father might hire to try and find him. Going and falling in love with Desdemona was initially confusing for both of them, of course it was, but such an eventuality could not have been foreseen, and in the first instance, they made do with Des and Mona. When they fell even more deeply in love, however, they would return to their proper names, but that was all in the future.

*Any*way, back to the gig, which was a sell-out as usual and, for which Dwayne and the others had practised their hearts out. Some of the standards Dwayne knew already, but there were new ones, especially Ringo's, to familiarize himself with. And then there were some numbers of *his* composition for the *other* guys to figure out. Plus, everybody had to get used to playing with both rhythm and lead guitars for the first time. But the practising made pretty near perfect, as evinced by the tumultuous applause when the set was over, to be followed by the usual stage invasion.

Only this time it was different, or at least the girls who invaded it were. Not *all* of them, of course, but Maja, Aika, and Desdemona stood out, at least in the eyes of Tosh, Ringo, Dwayne—and Mutt, who fell in love with all of three of them. Let's just say love was in the air, and the band members' hearts all went boom even across a crowded room. What we are talking here is big time romance. And let us not disparage *that* with whimsical notions of coincidental improbabilities.

Tosh was the first to take the initiative by taking Maja's hand and staring into her limpid blue eyes as he mis-scribbled his name in her autograph book while she stared back into his brown orbs with unmistakable adoration.

Then came Ringo when approached by Aika who, apart from being the most beautiful girl he'd ever seen—he hadn't seen all that many, mind you—was exactly his size. So gobsmacked was he, that it was Aika who was obliged to take the lead by saying *"Kimi ga,"* which sounded magical to Ringo, even though he had no idea what it meant and Aika was obliged—very humbly—to say it meant, "I love you."

Which left Dwayne, who was still fiddling with an out-of-tune E-string when blonde goddess Desdemona marched up and told him he was the boy of her dreams and any time he felt like kissing her, she was ready and waiting. Which invitation, reckoning himself a pretty good kisser, Dwayne was only too happy to accept. Unlike Ringo, he *had* known a few girls—actually quite a lot of girls, football cheerleaders and so on—in his time, but this one was from *way* out of left field. So he French kissed her, and she French kissed back, and both of their knees trembled so much they had to sit down.

Meantime, Mutt hurried back and forth among the new lovers offering them canine slurp blessings. It was all unashamedly love-at-first-sight-ish...as I hope you are now convinced.

What was even better for all concerned—and let us be clear, this was predicated on ninety-nine percent passion and only one percent practicality—was the existence of the terraced house in Hackney belonging to the professor of Renaissance Drama, which was currently being occupied by the three girls. But it took only a few dates before Desdemona proposed a house-share expansion to include Dwayne, Ringo, Tosh and Mutt, who she invited to stay for as long as they liked. This after Tosh, under pressure from Maja, had been forced to admit he and the others had no fixed abode and were currently dossing on Hampstead Heath.

"Daddy won't know," Desdemona assured the quartet. "He's too busy poncing around plummy Plumstead with his new live-in lover and fiddling with his Shakespeare super-scholar image."

"Nah, it wouldn't be right." Tosh shrugged as they and the girls sat around the bar of The King and Parrot quaffing libations ahead of yet another gig. "Would it, lads?"

"Nah," the lads agreed.

"Be like spongin' an' I ain't never done that," Tosh continued. "Used to providin' for meself like."

The same could not be said for Ringo or Dwayne, but they saw where Tosh was coming from and felt obliged to support him.

It was Dwayne, however, who came up with the one percent practicality angle.

"Other hand, I guess we could, like, make a contribution to the bills, and food and suchlike," he said, squeezing Desdemona's hand under the table. "You gals all students, are you?"

"Sometimes," said Maja.

"Which means?" Ringo asked.

"We study as hard as we can," said Aika.

"Only we have McJobs too," Desdemona explained. "I do Starbucks. Aikie does Pret. And Maja just got the boot from Burger King."

Tosh nodded. "Tough life, huh? An' you with this rich prof daddy?"

"Yeah, sure. My rich prof daddy. You know where most of his recent money comes from? The money I wouldn't touch with a barge pole even if he offered it?"

Tosh and Ringo shook their heads. Mutt whimpered.

"From poncin' around being a prof?" said Dwayne.

"Yes, but there's worse."

Which was when Desdemona, a committed European, disclosed her father's "puke-making" contributions to the xenophobic hatred whipped up by the BeLeave campaign in the 2016 Brexit referendum. How he'd been on the phone daily to the "bastards" offering to write any chauvinistic slogan he could produce in exchange for shedloads of cash, which the myth-spreading campaign organizers had been only too happy to fork out. Nothing better, they reckoned, than a spot of history to add credibility to their lies. How they had just lapped up Daddy's reminder of Henry the Eighth's divorce from the papacy in Rome, "to set Britain free of foreign interference in its affairs." And how wonderful it had been in Queen Elizabeth the First's reign for Sir Walter Raleigh to, "sail the seven seas" in search of places and peoples England could colonize and make its own. All of this until, by the eighteenth, nineteenth, and twentieth centuries, Britain could boast an empire upon which the sun never set and to which its people regarded themselves as proud to belong.

"Even though they were in fact being raped, pillaged and exploited," Desdemona said.

But Professor Vincent Vinicombe—Daddy's name—had carefully sidestepped such scurrilous "misinterpretations," continuing to insist in a column he'd been granted by *The Daily Mole*, that all this power had been tossed down the toilet by the country's membership in the

European Union, and now was the time to make the break which would allow a return to full British sovereignty and a consequent revival of the nation's glorious past. Pages and pages of this crap he had written over the years, all laced with Shakespeare quotes stripped of their ironic context. And had the "non-reflective" Brexiteers bought it? Of course, they had. In...their...*droves* from both the left and right wings of politics.

On and on she ranted, until Giorgio Dolmades fetched her another gin and tonic to calm her down.

All of this went straight over the heads of Tosh, Ringo and Dwayne of course, Tosh because he'd heard of Brexit but had never bothered to find out what it meant, Ringo because all he knew was what he'd read in School's alt-right newspaper library, and Dwayne because he was American, and Americans generally pay little attention to what's happening outside America. Mind you, something in what Desdemona had said struck a chord in him, and that was the kind of populist shit spouting from the crazy man in the White House who wanted to build a Berlin-type wall all along the border with Mexico to "keep us (white folks) safe from those murdering criminals."

"Some shitkicker," Dwayne said after explaining he kinda *liked* Mexicans, at which Desdemona nodded and nestled her head against his muscly shoulder.

"Plus I know what you mean with daddies. You wanna meet *mine*," he added. "Second thoughts, you don't. My mom you might like, but my dad..."

*Any*way, long story short, it was as the result of a smidgeon of financial expediency, but mainly love, that Tosh, Ringo, and Dwayne agreed to an undefined experimental period chez Desdemona in her nasty father's house just off the high street in Hackney. The next day, they would all take a trip together back to Hampstead Heath and clean up the copse that had been home for so long.

"It was kind to us, so we'll be kind to it in return," said Tosh. "I'll miss it though."

A sentiment shared by Ringo and Dwayne. *And* Mutt who said, "Raaf, raaf, raaf, raaf, *RAAF,*" despite the little back garden Desdemona promised him in Hackney.

Nine

It was seventy-five year-old Willy Lightfoot, volunteer gardener specializing in the Kenwood House estate, who first spotted the Missing Persons photo of Fergus Ulysses posted on a tree by the Hampstead Heath police as part of the London-wide search and, doing what he saw as his citizen's duty, called the number provided by The Met. It wasn't Top Cop Cynthia Broadbent who answered the call, of course, but instead twenty-five year-old Marge McGuire who was so far down the food chain she was barely paid a living wage. Marge had wanted to be a proper policewoman but failed all the qualification tests—for example by objecting to black kids in Brixton still being stopped and searched so often. "Nice girl but dumb and politically dubious," her final report had read. And so, Marge had been drafted onto the phones instead, which was boring, but at least better than a zero-hours contract McJob. If she stuck it out for another forty-five years, she might even get a pension. Or, if all the foreign nurses got kicked out of the country after Brexit, she was pretty good with a bandage.

"You are through to The Metropolitan Police Missing Persons Hotline. Please state the reason for your call," she said, so robotically Willy reckoned it was probably a recorded message of the kind he'd become increasingly terrified by. Back in his day, real human beings answered the phone when he dialled. These days, there were all sorts of fraudsters out there trying to con you out of your savings. Normally, *they* called *you*, but it could also happen in reverse, Willy reckoned.

But this, seemingly, wasn't one of those. When Willy merely mumbled a bit, the human voice said, "Are you still there, sir?"

"Yuh-yes," said Willy. Tentatively.

"And the reason for your call?"

Which was when Willy told Marge he'd seen The Met's Missing Persons poster nailed to a tree—an elm, he reckoned…or it might have been an oak…or possibly a birch. Willy wasn't sure what particular *kind* of a tree it was, but…

"Could sir perhaps give the reason for his call?" said Marge in her best "patient" voice. Marge did patient well. Even her supervisor said so. "Our Missing Persons poster, you said?"

"I seen him," said Willy. "The kid who's missing. Leastways it looked a *bit* like him. Different hair, different clothes, different all sorts of things—but there was something in the eyes. Used to sit around with two other blokes and a dog playing guitars and drums in this copse of oaks…or willows…or pines…or…"

"Never mind about the trees, Mister…?

"Lightfoot. Wilfred Lightfoot."

"Mister Lightfoot. And if we was to invite you down to police station to take a closer look at our photo, would you be able to come?"

"Yeah, I s'pose. Couldn't you send a car though? I ain't too good on my pins these days. I could come on my bike, but…"

"We'll send a car, Mister Lightfoot. Just give me the address."

Willy reckoned the best place for a meet-up would be the Kenwood House car park, and it was that very afternoon he was whisked away to Kentish Town police station, the only one left in the Camden and Hampstead area after much-resented budget cuts. There he would more closely inspect the Missing Persons file on the Met's computer, which was all very exciting, especially after he had again identified Fergus Ulysses and was asked by P.C. Jennifer Grimes if the lad was still camped out on Hampstead Heath.

"Nah, last time I looked…which was yesterday…or maybe the day before…or maybe the day before that…or…" said Willy, patting what was left of his hair. "Find it a bit tricky remembering things these days. Member of the Craft Club I am."

"Craft Club? Artist are you?" asked Jennifer in her best nice-to-old-people manner, which wasn't *all* that nice but at least prevented her from saying, "C'mon, you daft old git, nobody gives a monkey's what bleedin' day it was."

"Nah, used to dabble in oils a bit but not anymore. Craft is the club for blokes who can't remember a fucking thing, excuse my French. 'Craft,' right?"

Jennifer pretended to laugh. "But you *can* remember the boy's face?"

"Yeah, I got a good memory for faces."

"And the last time you looked?"

"The copse of elders...or maybe ash...or oaks...*trees* anyway, was empty."

"So they'd gone," said Jennifer. Perceptively.

"Yeah. Three blokes. One was this Fergus you're on about, another one blackish with that long twisty hair they have down their backs."

"Jamaican?"

"Maybe. Only with bits of white mixed in, narmean?"

"Mixed race."

"Yeah."

"And the third guy?"

"A Yank. Loud talker, blond hair, blue eyes, the whole bag of works."

"And the dog? Was it called Mutt?" asked Jennifer, a keen patron of The King and Parrot on off-duty Saturdays when you would never have known she was a copper in her Goth outfit.

"Dunno, do I? Only, hang on a minute...now you're asking..."

"Yes?" said Jennifer, eyes widening.

"There was this one time..."

"*Yes*?"

"When the lads were playing' some bluesy stuff and the dog joined in yowling, and the Jamaican lad told it to shut up...hang on, hang on, it's coming to me...not Dog, he never called it Dog, but...yeah, you're right...Mutt, that was it. That matter, does it?"

"Mister Lightfoot, you just made my day," said P.C. Grimes. "Cup of tea before you go? A biscuit?"

"Cuppa would go down nicely, missus. With a digestive?"

"A chocolate one?"

"A chocolate one would be smashing."

"And one final question. You never moved them on, this Fergus, the Yank, and the mixed race guy?"

"Nah, not part of my job description."

Later, when Willy had been taken home in another cop car, Jennifer would call the Met at Scotland Yard to pass on her findings, of which she intended making the maximum use, seeing as this Fergus Ulysses was supposed to be the kid of some big noise in the House of Lords. How did *Detective* Constable Grimes sound? Nice, that was how.

It was a good job, in these circumstances, that Tosh & Co. had switched venues to The Queen and Carrot pub in Hackney getting Giorgio Dolmades to promise he'd tell nobody, especially not the police. Additionally, they had worked up a set of brand new songs, bought themselves freaky ghost outfits from Escapade in Camden Town, *and*—furthermore—at Ringo's witty suggestion, and to Dwayne's grateful amusement—re-named the band The Fubars. Mutt still featured in the line-up but was these days dressed in a catsuit, which he enjoyed.

So much for Jennifer Grimes's promotion any time soon, although she didn't know that yet.

~ * ~

Sam Snade's progress in tracing Dwayne was equally frustrated and, for similar reasons, namely the absence of *any* record of the phone or credit card numbers CeCi had given him. To all intents and purposes, Zobinski Jnr did not exist, which Sam was *very* pissed off about.

"Sheesh an' goddammit," he muttered, pacing up and down the box room "computer suite" of his King's Road Chelsea flatlet, chain smoking Marlboros and wondering what to do next. Except for the tobacco addiction, Sam wasn't Sam Spade after all, so he knew nothing of the gumshoe techniques of yesteryear, relying for his information solely on the legitimate internet and a number of sites on the deep dark web. But first, he would check with Zobinski Snr just to make sure the info he'd been given was correct.

"Yeah, Snade, you nailed him? Attaboy," said Dwayne Snr when the call was patched through to him after being filtered through his personal blacklist.

"Not exactly."

"Not ex*actly*? Whaddaya *mean* not ex*actly*? Either you nailed him or you didn't. You wanna earn money or dontcha?"

"Mebbe you gave me the wrong numbers for the phone and the Amex. Like, they don't ex*ist*?"

"And this is *my* fault?"

"I didn't say it was *your* fault. I'm just tellin' you is all."

"And you're expecting *me* to know the numbers? It was the kid's *mother* who gave you the gen, right?"

"Right," said Snade, who had forgotten that part.

"So call the kid's *mother*. I am, like...*busy* doin' my job."

Which was only true in the sense that Dwayne Snr spent most of his time these days tracking the byzantine workings of the British parliament, and its mentally disturbed prime minister, in relation to the endlessly delayed Brexit bullshit in order to know how to protect and further his interests with America and Russia if, and when, the EU divorce was finally realized. The rest of it he spent trying to check how long it would take the dude in the White House to make his election promises come true before he either got himself impeached or someone shot him. It wasn't an easy balance.

"I don't have her number," said Snade.

"Neither do I."

Snade sighed. "So...?"

"She's at The Ritz on Piccadooly. Go there. Ask for her. You're a freaking PI, ain't you?"

"A one-time NYC beat cop."

"So do...your...fucking...job and find my son or it's no dough for you," said Dwayne Snr cutting the call.

Sam Snade lit another Marlboro and paced his mini "computer suite" some more. He didn't like it when he had to leave the office. It was dangerous out there on the streets. He could get run over by a bus—or a cyclist. Sam hated cyclists. Briefly, he considered an internet phishing trip to see if that might yield the info he needed. He had the kid's photo after all. But with phishing trips there was always the risk of identity exposure and counter-hacking, which would be no good *at all*. Either that or you got a trillion replies from a trillion bozos from here to Hong Kong, who all swore blind they'd seen the guy and wanted money in advance for the info they would give, which was normally none. Sam knew as much having played the same game himself.

"Fuck it all to *fuck*," he said, stubbing out the fourteenth Marlboro of the morning in his specially enlarged, antique, Marlboro Man ashtray with its cool Stetson-wearing, moustachioed cowpoke picture on the side.

Thus emboldened by the myth of America's history, Snade dressed in his special Sam Spade detection clothes—the tweed overcoat and the dark grey fedora—rode the elevator down to the street, hailed a cab, and lit out into the wilds of London.

~ * ~

At Piddlington Hall, Lady Hermione Barr was fidgety with anticipation having heard from Chief Cop Cynthia Broadbent there had been a verified sighting of Fergus Ulysses on Hampstead Heath, and the police constable in charge of the case was confident he would very soon be found.

"Where? *Where*?" Lady Hermione had asked. Foolishly, in Cynthia's view.

"If we knew exactly *where*, we would have found him already, ma'am. Now *wouldn't* we?" she replied acidly. "As soon as we have any further information, we'll be in touch," she added before cutting the call.

Lady Hermione took to rushing around the mansion looking for Lord Crossbar to tell him the good-ish news, but he was nowhere to be found. Not in the bath, not in bed, not in the drawing room fiddling with what he termed his "pupers" (papers). Not *any*where. In the potting shed pottering possibly? But no, no sign of him there either. He *had* to be somewhere, for God's sake. After being banned from The House of Lords by Speaker Arbuthnot for rudeness to the media, public flatulence, and assaulting the Churchill statue thereby bringing the upper chamber into disrepute, he was, to all intents and purposes, under house arrest in the supervision of Lady Hermione.

"Oh *bugger*kins, where can he possibly *be*?" shrieked Lady H at full volume while Max and Milly Pratchett hid in their tiny quarters and feigned the "lesetcive duffness" (selective deafness) Lord Xavier had sworn them to in sign language—thumbs in his ears and a finger zipper drawn across his lips. If they were to mention *any*thing to do with his "boutywhores" (whereabouts) to the "woof manwo" (wife woman) he'd threatened, drawing a knife-type finger across his throat, they would soon be "mating" (meeting) their "Mookah" (Maker).

"COME OUT, COME OUT, WHEREVER YOU ARE, YOU OLD BASTARD," echoed Lady H's bellows throughout corridors of Piddlington Hall. To no response apart from deafening silence.

"Pissypots," she ululated. It wasn't as though she cared a toss for the old sod, but Lady H was a tidy-minded peeress, and to have lost a son *and* a husband in such a short space of time would amount to carelessness, as some playwright or another had put it. And when, as a last resort. she sank to her knees in a hydrangea patch and tried telephoning the braindead creep, all she got by way of response was a peculiar watery gurgling noise.

That was because, having made good his flight back to London in the repaired Roller with a new driver—a Romanian called Ionut Daniluc—Lord Xavier Barr had tossed his phone into the Thames. And even if Lady H *had* reached him with the good-ish news about Fergus Ulysses, he wouldn't have known who she was talking about because of his neurological problems.

And what was the reason for this precipitous escape? To repair the reputation so ungentlemanly sullied by Lord Speaker Arbuthnot, that was what. First off, the kerfuffle with the media morons, now banishment to "hume" (home), just because of a little "latuflunce" (flatulence) in the Hooce (House); latuflunce that hadn't even been defined in the letter he'd received from Arbuthnit. Was this actual "furtonk" (farting) the puffed-up creep had in "moond" (mind) or, worse still, an "hasperson" (aspersion) on his verbal contributions to "deboot" (debate)? As for the Wonsting Chargehool (Winston Churchill) accusation, Lord Xavier had no memory of that. Either way, he wasn't prepared to put up with *any* further "landersuss" (slanderous) "lusalts" (assaults) on his "porsing" (person). No way, Ésoj he wasn't.

It was with this slur on his reputation in mind that, once delivered by Ionut Daniluc to the very doorstep of the Houses of Parliament, Lord Xavier of Piddlington marched into the building, wandered the corridors for a while with vengeance in mind, then pounded on the door of the Lady Peers' private lavatory, burst through it when nobody answered, was surprised at the screams, and was consequently arrested by a beadle.

Ten

The Fubars were on their way to becoming an overnight sensation at The Queen and Carrot in Hackney. To begin with, they were seen as just another joke band in their ghost get-ups and with a dog in a catsuit, but the inclusion in the lineup of Maja, Aika and Desdemona dressed as masked fairies added an extra nuance of subtle glamour to the mix. Okay, all they mainly did first off was the bop-shoo-wop-a-bop-bop-shoo-wops, but they did them with such allure and glee, it was a pleasure to behold. And even more so on the occasions they graduated to fronting the band like the old-time American girl groups. It was a heady blend in anybody's book, every new appearance in some way adding a level of the unexpected to the last.

But, ultimately, it was the new song set that raised The Fubars to the heights of the cult status that was to spread way beyond the confines of Hackney. Never before much interested in their political environment, Tosh, Ringo, and Dwayne had listened to Desdemona's impassioned ideas about Brexit, particularly her fears—echoed by Aika and Maja—of the populism that appeared to be throwing down dangerous roots in all sorts of countries. These were to become the subtext of many of the songs the six of them wrote together. One of their and their audiences' favourites was, "Where Have All the

Protesters Gone?" Not sung to the same tune as the "flowers" version, and with an eclectic recognition of rock, blues, country and reggae influences, but the message was clear enough. So was their Bob Dylan tribute in, "Our Future's Blown in the Wind." Their human targets in Downing Street, the White House, the Kremlin and sundry other centres of government remained unnamed, but the inferences were clear, i.e. they were all dickheads making the world a more dangerous place. And the folk of Hackney, then the wider world, loved it. For how long had pop music made its living on silly love songs, repetitious computerized thumping, and mindless wailing? For...far...*too*...long, like half a century too long.

The band themselves were pleased but astonished at the interest they were garnering in the media, interest that was fed by their refusal to give interviews or indeed to identify themselves by name or in any other way.

"Best we stay a mystery," Tosh had insisted. "Not for the money, like. But just because."

With which sentiment, the rest had agreed without question. Clearly, neither Dwayne nor Ringo had *any* interest in being recognized, far from it. And, unlike most girls of their generation, Desdemona, Maja, and Aika didn't either.

"Fame's for fuckwits," said Desdemona, for example.

"Here today and gone tomorrow," Maja agreed.

"Me, I like to hide," said Aika. "That way I have more fun."

And so it was that the sextet could walk the streets of Hackney as free as birds. No autograph hunters, no hangers-on, just a gratifying sense of doing something useful whenever they overheard folk eulogizing their band or read local newspaper articles about the contribution of their songs to the educational health of kids in the neighbourhood, somebody finally giving them a chance in life, a reason to *be*, a sense of the possible. Later, there would be the national press picking up on what was to become Fubarmania, but Tosh & Co never responded. How could they when their address was unknown, they had no computers, and carried only throwdown phones. As far as they were concerned, their private lives were their own.

On which subject those lives were blossoming along with The Fubars' fame. Rule number one in the Hackney household was that no member was more equal than any other. Okay, Tosh was generally recognized as the leader of the band, and Ringo and Dwayne founder members, but when it came to domestic duties the boys played their part every bit as much as the girls. Not as efficiently as the girls to begin with, of course, given none of them could tell a domestic duty from a hole in the road. But they were trying, and Desdemona was glad to see it.

"Don't think I'm the one making the rules around here just because it's my sodding father's house," she had said in the early days of the share. "Far from it. And don't go thinking I'm some rabid feminist either. I'm not. It's just that…"

Tosh completed the sentence for her. "We're all in this together, and we all do the same work."

"Exactly. And never mind who's got tits and fannies and who's got balls."

Dwayne laughed at that and kissed her. "You know what?" he said when the kissing was over. "It's what my mom always said, and I figure she was right."

Maja and Aika laughed too, albeit a little less assuredly. In the homes they'd left behind in Gdansk and Tokyo, no such words had ever been spoken, but they were happy to hear them now. As was Ringo, whose house name had returned to Fergie. Having been at School practically all his life, he had little concept of inter-gender domestic responsibility, and whenever he went home for holidays neither Lord Xavier nor Lady Hermione ever did anything because that was what "The Help" were paid for. He was more than ready to do his bit though.

"Sounds like fun," said the lad who was to become bathroom attendant in chief, a master of toilet roll provision as well as tub and lavatory scrubbing, while Tosh was the vacuumer and window wiper, and Dwayne developed a passion for furniture polishing and looking after the bins, especially the one for recycling.

It wasn't even as though all the shopping and cooking were left to the girls either, although they played a major role. Within only a week or two, Tosh, Dwayne and Fergie had developed recipes for vegetarian curry and spaghetti bolognese they reckoned worthy of any dumb TV chef's. That was the other uniting force in the household: they were all veggies.

"And what about the sex?" I hear you ask. "Gender parity around the house is all very well, but there's no good telling a boy/girl story without a bedroom angle."

Fair comment.

Well, without entering the nauseous realms of *Ninety-Nine Shades of Blue*-type specifics, the breakdown between the new lovers went pretty much as follows: Dwayne and Desdemona were already pretty good at it, and together got even better, while Tosh and Maja were less experienced but soon learned to move beyond wham, bam, thank you ma'am, and indulge themselves in subtler pleasures. Which left Fergie and Aika, who were both untutored virgins with little or no idea who was meant to do what to whom or how.

"So what did *they* do?" you'll be eager to know, you nosey parker you. "Buy manuals, learn off the internet, what?"

To which the answer is neither of those things.

"So what *is* it then? They went on groping in the dark and being virgins? Quaint but improbable."

The answer is they had a little help from their more experienced friends. And before you start jumping to naughty two- or threesome conclusions, or Fergie and Aika watching on while the others did IT, the help we're talking about was verbally shared experience with some simple but explicit diagrams, although the importance of reciprocal love was always stressed as being of supreme importance.

"Self-gratification is one thing," Desdemona said, for example. "*Shared* sex is another thing altogether."

At which Fergie and Aika initially exchanged puzzled looks but, being fast learners and already in love, they began the experimentation with enthusiasm. It didn't click immediately, you understand. Took a few weeks of practice. But, pretty soon the deep dark Hackney nights began to echo with not only the sated moans of the already accomplished practitioners but also joyful squeals of discovery from the third bedroom.

So much for sex, okay? Just let us conclude this aspect of household balance by saying it soon became as harmonious as all the others.

~ * ~

Surprising himself, Sam Snade made it to The Ritz with no more hassle than being mocked by Norman Bradley, the cab driver, for thinking Piccadilly was Piccadooly.

"Don't they give you blokes geography lessons in Yankeeland?" said Norman as they ground their way around Hyde Park.

"Sure they do."

"So how come you never know where you are?" Norman chuckled.

Sam had no answer to that. "Just drive. And goose the gas if you have to."

"You're the boss," said Norman, slowing down and taking an extra loop around Hyde Park.

The bill came to twenty-five pounds when they finally reached The Ritz, which seemed like a lot to Sam. But he stuffed his plastic into the holder anyway, only it didn't work.

"Sumptn wrong wid your machine, man," he told Norman, who obliged by coming round to the back seat shrugging like he reckoned his passenger for a dope, and pressed the buttons that would ensure his twenty-five percent tip. Then he wished Sam a "nice day" in what he thought of as American and drove off leaving Snade teetering about on the pavement outside The Ritz.

"Some bozo cabbie," he muttered before pulling the brim of his grey fedora down over his eyes, marching into the hotel, and demanding at the desk to see a resident called CeCi Zobinski.

"Would that be Missus *Cecily* Zobinski sir is seeking?" asked Montmorency McCloud, desk guy for the day.

"Could be. I had her figured for CeCi."

"Sir would need to be a little more certain, sir. I am in no position to disturb a guest unless I am *absolutely* certain it is the correct guest I am disturbing," said Montmorency, whom Sam had already earmarked as a dork with his finger up his ass.

"Listen, dude," he said. "I ain't got time for no fooling around. Just try the Zobinski room and tell the dame I'm here, okay? I'm working for her husband who practically owns this damn place."

"Well, sir, even so I'm not *aw*fully sure I…"

It was the three twenty-pound notes slid across the desk under his nose that interfered with Montmorency's professionalism. In these crazy Brexit days, he wasn't sure whether sixty pounds were worth any more than *six* pounds, but it was better than a smack in the face with a dead haddock, so he said, "If sir would like to give me his name, I'll…"

"Tell her it's Sam Snade."

"Which is sir's *real* name or merely the name I should tell her?"

Sam was ready to smack this guy around the chops. First the freakin' cab driver, now this asswipe. Soon Sam would return to NYC and try his luck again there. Okay, he'd been kicked outta the police for what they'd called "negligence of duty" over the drug bust he'd fallen foul of by stealing and selling its product. But hey, all the other guys were doing it, and he was just unlucky to get caught was all. Ditto the little problem with the PI licence he'd lost for an upskirting case that was never proven anyhow.

"It's my real name," he growled.

"Only sir is dressed a little like Sam *Spade*," said Montmorency, who was a fan of the Dashiell Hammett stories.

Almost reaching his personal level of dipshit tolerance, a level which was in any case low, Sam leaned across the desk, looked as menacing as he was able—which wasn't *very* menacing—and said, "Just call the dame, buster, or you is in deep doo-doo."

Which threat, along with another worthless twenty-pound note, persuaded Montmorency to make the call while Sam huffed and puffed a lot. As an ex-all-in wrestler turned up-market desk clerk, Montmorency could have rebuffed Sam's posturing with ease, but for the sake of propriety—and his job— chose not to.

"Who?" said CeCi, picking up the phone.

"A Mister Sam Snade, madam. Apologies for the disturbance, but he claims to be working for your husband and…"

"Tell him to meet me in the downstairs lounge in ten minutes."

Which message Montmorency relayed to Sam word for word.

"Not in her room?"

"No sir, Mister Spade. In the lounge. In ten minutes. There's rather a good pianist on duty at all times. We call him Play-It-Again-Sam so he should be just up your alley, as I believe you Yankees have it. It's just over there and to your right," said Montmorency, picking up the newly ringing phone and starting to jabber into it.

"How nice to hear from you again, Lady Barr. She has a visitor currently, but I'll leave a message you called," he was saying as Sam Snade readjusted his fedora and duck-walked off in the direction of the lounge where, indeed, some throwback was thumping a piano.

"Sheeeesh," he said, sinking into a red leather armchair and ordering an Americano with biscuits from the floozy who turned up at his side.

He had drunk the best part of the coffee and eaten all the biscuits by the time CeCi arrived and stared at the Liberace lookalike whom she assumed to be some kind of a robot. Every time she came to the lounge with nothing better to do, he was sitting there churning out the oldies. Either the guy never slept or he *was* a robot.

"So we meet again, Mister Snade," she said, taking a seat opposite him. "I'm assuming you have good news for me about Dwayne Junior. You could have called, but I guess it's always better to do these things in person."

"Yeah, well, um..." said Sam, whose day was going from shitty to shittier.

It was when CeCi confirmed the phone and card numbers she'd given Snade *were* indeed the correct ones and Sam told her he'd tried to trace them, but they were dead, that she burst into tears, jumped back up from her chair, smacked Snade around the head, told him he was a scumbag posing as a PI, pointed a finger at him like *The Apprentice* asshole, now the president screwing up America, and shouted, "You're fired," which obviously enough caused concern in The Ritz lounge.

Much peering and muttering there was amongst the would-be genteel guests, especially after CeCi marched off to Montmorency's desk and told him to "throw the slimeball Sam Spade wannabe out onto the street" if he wanted to keep his job. Even Play-It-Again-Sam stopped tinkling the ivories and gawped, thereby proving his *was* human after all.

Montmorency—billed as Steve, "The Super Slam" back in his all-in wrestling days—smiled. "It is a task I shall enjoy, madam," he said in the posh voice he'd assumed for his retirement job at The Ritz. "Shall I follow you?"

"Damn right you will," said CeCi, drying her eyes. "Just pick him up and toss him right outta my sight."

"With pleasure, madam. No need for identification. I know the person you mean." Snade's eyes widened along with those of the would-be genteel guests and Play-It-Again-Sam's as they watched Montmorency, who was *much* bigger when he wasn't crouched behind his desk, stride up with both fists balled to the now visibly shaking, soon-to-be-unemployed-PI.

"Jolly good, Monters. See the blighter awf," called a number of guests. "He made the poor girl cry."

CeCi liked the "girl" part. She liked it even better when Monters lifted the offender off his seat by the lapels of his tweed overcoat, tossed his grey fedora into the crowd as a memento, and—to the accompaniment of tumultuous applause, and the theme tune to the movie *Dunkirk* from Play-It-Again-Sam—hoisted Sam Snade to the door of The Ritz, opened it, and tossed him out onto the street.

So much for Sam Snade, who will take no further part in this story because the next day, without notice to Zobinski Snr, he Airbnb-ed his Chelsea pad and boarded at Heathrow the plane that would take him to JFK, whence he took another one to Alaska where he'd heard PI pickings were still good.

Eleven

The main reason for CeCi Zobinski having Sam Snade turfed out of The Ritz was she thought him just the sort of a scumbag who *would* be working for her soon-to-be-ex and hoped they both rotted in hell. The other was that she had decided to take on the case herself, in pursuance of which she had again called Headmaster Fortesque BA, MA at School, this time explaining she knew of the fubar incident from her son Dwayne and would like to be put in touch with the mother of the other boy involved.

"Not at all sure I should disclose such confidential information, madam," Fortesque replied. Tersely. Quentin didn't like the rude American woman after her previous call. Not at all, he didn't.

CeCi put on her most caring maternal-type voice. "It's just that, as a mother myself, I can imagine what the poor woman must be going through."

Fortesque was unimpressed. "Even so, madam, School's rules make it perfectly clear that…"

Which was when CeCi told Quentin he could take School's rules and shove them up the place where the sun don't shine.

Quentin was on the very cusp of slamming the phone down when CeCi reminded him of her husband's promise of large sums of dollars for the construction of a new computer suite when Dwayne had been admitted to the institution.

"That money would sure as shit is Shinola be down...the...toobs," CeCi explained, "if you *don't* do as I tell you."

"Ah-hah, ho hum, so *that's* your game, is it? Filthy lucre and so on," Fortesque managed to splutter only seconds before reason reminded him of the requisite lure of such squalid earnings *and*, more crucially, the governors' insistence on acquiring as much of them as possible by any available means in these parlous Brexit days as the UK faced the distinct possibility of economic meltdown. It was Chair of the Governors, Sir Barney Chumsbury, who had made this clear at their last meeting.

"Keep the moolah gates open to any friend you can find, Forters, or you're fired," he said. Not one to mince his words, Sir Barney, obviously enough known as "Barmy" behind his back.

And so it was that Quentin Fortesque BA, MA spilled the beans CeCi had asked for, as a consequence of which she then came to phone Lady Hermione Barr, introduce herself, and propose the two of them put their heads together to find a way of locating their sons. To which Lady Hermione readily agreed. What with Lord Crossbar having gone bonkers and everything, it was indeed a pleasure to hear from somebody prepared to lend a helping hand. Plus, she rather liked Americans. Her favourite was Ingrid Bergman, although she also quite liked Greta Garbo.

Anyway, that was why Montmorency at The Ritz had been answering the phone to Lady Barr only moments before being requested by CeCi to perform his chucker-out duties on the luckless Sam Snade. What Hermione—she and CeCi were already on first-name terms—had been wanting to propose was a meet-up in Town soonest to plan a strategy. And, once satisfied Snade was out of her hair, CeCi took the message Montmorency had left on her phone and called back.

"Hi there, babe," she said brightly when Hermione picked up. "Any noos?"

Hermione liked being called "babe." It was sooo...sooo...Hermione couldn't find the right word for it. "A*meri*can," she finally decided.

"There is, and there isn't, my dear. On the one hand, the Met have at least deigned to put missing persons' posters up for young Fergus, and there's been a sighting…"

"Wow*eee*," said CeCi, opening her bedroom window, firing up a joint, and blowing the smoke out into the rancid London air where, she reckoned, it would do more good than harm.

"That's how I felt when I first heard, but the trail's gone dead, as I gather they say in the moving pictures."

"Shit."

"Quite. Plus Lord Crossbar's gone even *more* bonkers. Got himself arrested by a beadle at the hice."

"Not so great either," said CeCi, who had no idea was a beadle was—one of the remaining Beatles possibly—or where and what the "hice" was. But never mind, she was happy enough to put that down to Hermie's poor pronunciation.

"No," Hermie confirmed.

"So anyhow, about that meet-up? I could book you in at my place in Piccadooly for a night or two. How would that be?"

"Spiffing," said Hermie, which CeCi took for a yes.

"Oo*kay*, so I'll make the arrangements with Monty."

"*Monty*?" said Lady Hermione, thinking Lord Montgomery of El Alamein.

"The desk clerk?"

"Oh, Montmorency. *That* Monty."

"The same. Shall we say tomorrow at around noon? I sleep late."

"Tomorrow at around noon it shall be, CeCi, my dear," said Lady Hermione hanging up the phone before bidding Max and Milly Pratchett into her boudoir, telling them she'd be away for a few days and to be sure to look after the dogs.

~ * ~

Unsurprisingly, the unannounced visit of Professor Vincent Vinicombe to his old home in Hackney didn't go well. As noted, Desdemona's relations with her father were at a low ebb anyway because of his politics. But she hated him, too, because of having divorced her mother, Andrea, for what he termed "a newer model" when Desdemona was in her mid-teens. She also loathed the newer model, twenty-nine year-old Janine Humphreys, an ex-doctoral student of Vincent's who, with his connivance, had recently landed the job of editing exclusively his tomes at the little-known academic publishing house of Tickleton's in Oxford. Not that Andrea seemed to care that much.

"Silly old sod," she'd told Desdemona on her daughter's recent visit to the island of Anglesey, whither Andrea had decamped some years after the split. Now Desdemona made the Welsh trip regularly and was glad to find her mother "happy as a pig in shit."

Not that pigs *were* dirty creatures, Andrea insisted, that was just an urban myth. And she should know, given the drove of them and their regular farrows of piglets she kept, never allowing any of them to be turned into pork chops or bacon.

"Much higher IQs than they're given credit for, too," she'd told Desdemona on the most recent trip. "A site more intelligent than your fascist bloody father, if you ask me."

At which Desdemona laughed. Still, you know how it is with divorces. How they leave their mark whatever the circumstances. Yes, she detested her father as much as Andrea did…but he *was* still her father, which caused a person to wonder how many genes she'd inherited from him. How did the saying go? Like mother like son, like father like daughter. Desdemona just wished she could identify *which* of his genes were flowing through her body so she could zap them with a pill or maybe a ray gun and get Vincent Vinicombe out of her system forever. VV right? Like two fuck-off signs rolled into one. And yet, now here he was marching through the door with his own key like he *owned* the place, which sadly, he did.

"Hi there, Monie, just thought I'd pop in for a cuppa," he barked in the faux posh voice he'd acquired through elocution lessons in his late thirties, having hailed originally from the East End of London whose accent was not at all *comme il faut* for professors of Renaissance Drama at King's College. Desdemona hated it as much as she hated being called "Monie," which sounded a lot like Moany.

"Ah, DAD, wasn't expecting YOU," she said, waggling a warning hand behind her back at any of the boys who might be knocking around to get out of the way and quick. Vincent knew about the girls Desdemona shared with and, to her disgust, had tried advances with both of them. But of the boys, he knew nothing. Trouble was Tosh, Fergie and Dwayne were all upstairs struggling over a new song that would link the populist lies told by the psycho in the White House with those told by the Brit psychos who'd ushered in Brexit. Pro tem it was entitled "Liar Fire."

"What're you *shouting* for, girl?" Vincent wanted to know. "Just pop awf and put the kettle on, would you? Thirsty I am and a tad puckish, too, so a Hobnob or three would not go amiss. What's that damn faux music racket upstairs?"

"Um, radio probably. I'll go and tell Maja to turn it down."

"*Maja*?"

"Yes."

"But she's here with me," said Vincent who had already barged his way down the hall and through into the lounge.

"Aika then."

"She's here too."

"Ah."

"Doesn't *sound* like a bally radio, anyway. Keeps stopping and starting. And, if I am not very much mistaken, I can hear male voices. There's one of them now," said Vincent as Dwayne suddenly yelled, "Woweee, yeah, that's sooo cool, man," in response to a new Clapton-esque riff Fergie had been practising.

"Care to explain, young Monie?'

So Desdemona did. Not with the *full* story obviously, nothing to do with live-in lovers or anything like that. Which was hypocritical of her, she knew, given the way Vincent and Janine were shacked up together, but on the other hand, she didn't want the six of them plus Mutt to get thrown out onto the streets.

"Just some lads we know," she said. "They're in a band called The Fubars. I let them come round to jam sometimes."

"*Jam*?"

"Play together. Work up new songs."

Vincent hoisted his eyebrows and wrinkled his nose. "*Pop* songs?"

"Yes, they're rather good, actually," said Maja, alert to the problem and taking Desdemona's hand for reassurance.

"Famous even, around here," said Aika as Vincent pouted unpleasantly.

"Well, tell the blighters to unplug themselves right now and get their sorry arses down here so we can be introduced, and I can tell them a thing or two about *proper* music," said Vincent, who reckoned himself an expert on madrigals.

"No, Daddy, look, I don't think..." Desdemona was saying.

But too late, because that was when, stretching and grinning, all three ur-Fubars came scuttling downstairs to tell of their progress with "Liar Fire," read Desdemona's lips when, pointing, she whispered, "he's my fucking *father*" and prepared to scuttle right back where they'd come from. Too late however, because, madrigals on his mind, Vincent was already on his feet waiting to be introduced.

The awkward conversation that ensued might not have been *so* bad had Vincent stuck to his idea of expounding solely on madrigals. Tosh, Dwayne and Fergie might have handled that, smiled foolishly, nodded, yawned, and behaved themselves. But he didn't. You know how it is with academics, how once they've started spouting about their pet subject there's no stopping them. How it tends to expand into all manner of peripheral pathways until you're no longer certain *what* they're talking about. And such was the case on this occasion as Vincent moved on from a long list of cleverly counterpointed Renaissance songs to Renaissance plays, specifically *The Tempest* which he used as a springboard to illustrate Shakespeare's relevance to contemporary politics, specifically Brexit.

It was at this point that The Fubars' eyes widened, and Desdemona jumped up saying tea was ready, and would Daddy like a Hobnob. But in full spate, there was no stopping Professor Vincent Vinicombe, who was already making the analogy of "poor old Prospero, the purest of Englishmen" to the "bave" British Brexiteers in his handling of Caliban, the man of Inde.

"A man for our times, constantly struggling to reinforce his supremacy over the beastly foreigner when it would have been easier just to shoot him," he blithely continued, conveniently ignoring the fact that the island was Caliban's, and it was Prospero who was the foreign invader. "Just think how many wars we've fought against the bally Europeans down the centuries, and yet, *still* there are those in these isles who believe we should trust them and stay in their club. Many of them can barely speak English, you know."

Also untrue, of course, because most Europeans are taught English at school from an early age and have a better syntactical grasp of the language than most of the 52% of British referendum voters wanting foreigners banned from their land. Not the sort of message The Fubars wanted to hear, certainly not after having just composed "Liar Fire." Maja and Aika also exchanged uneasy glances.

It was Dwayne, enthused by recent discussions with Desdemona of politics on both sides of the Atlantic, who ploughed in first with objections to this stance by asking Vincent for his definition of a "pure" English person, at which the professor took to muttering about Anglo Saxons and so on, as if the answer were perfectly obvious.

"So kinda like our WASPs back home?" Dwayne countered.

Vincent supposed so, yes, although truth be told he wasn't awfully sure what a wasp *was* in this context. Some sort of insect native to the ex-colony, he assumed.

"Even though America is the melting pot of hundreds of different peoples?" said Dwayne. "Black ones, yellow ones, brown ones, *all* kindsa folks?"

Sensing opposition, against which he was normally protected by academic protocol, Vincent girned and sipped his tea.

"Just like the UK has been for years now," said Tosh, taking up the baton. Tosh very obviously wasn't pure white. "Caribbeans, Africans, Indians, all those guys from the old Commonwealth. And *we're* English, too."

Vincent spluttered into his teacup, preparing to mention Enoch Powell's rivers of blood speech.

"Plus there are loads of Europeans here, too," added Fergie who, like the other two ur-Fubars, had only recently come to think of these things. "Makes the place a lot more interesting I reckon."

"More cosmopolitan," said Maja.

"*Also*," added Aika, part of whose university course looked at the roots of what had come to be called *Britishness*, "what about the Celts and the Picts and the Jutes and the Romans and the Normans? Not like *they* were English, is it?"

Which was when Vincent could take no more, stood up, spilled his tea, and shouted, "I don't need to listen to any more of this bally hogwash from a bunch of juvenile leftie popsters." And, no longer able to contain herself, Desdemona called him a populist/fascist throwback typical of electorates in both the USA and the UK since 2016 and showed him to the door of his own house.

"And don't bother with any more unannounced visits," she called after him as he marched off down the street waving his eagle-headed cane in the air and fulminating in Early Modern English. "Because next time we won't be here. And if we still are, we won't let you in."

Twelve

The way CeCi tracked Dwayne down was by *him* calling *her*. And how did this come about? By Desdemona persuading him to, that was how.

"Don't you ever call your mother?" she said, lying back naked on a pillow amidst sheets tangled by a bout of athletic sex. "She'll probably be wondering how you're getting on with finding the Fubar Kid. It *was* her who got you going on that, wasn't it?"

"Sure."

"So she'll be wondering how you got on. Also, you did say I might like to meet her one day."

"Yeah, she's pretty cool," said Dwayne, stretching out beside her, also naked.

"So…"

"Kinda difficult seeing as Mom's back stateside."

"But you could still *talk* to her."

"And if she traces the call and tells Mister Master-of-the-freaking-Universe?"

"You have a throwdown phone, don't you?"

"Yeah, there is that to it."

"And you *like* your mother. You said so. An artist, you told me."

"Yeah, like I said, Mom's pretty cool. Did I tell you she was also bi?"

"Sexual or polar?"

Dwayne laughed. "Mebbe a bit of both, but mainly the first one. Like she kinda bounces back and forth between the guys and the gals."

"The gals can sometimes be more switched on emotionally than the guys."

"You got that right. She likes their bodies too, though. Paints 'em all the time."

"You could use *my* phone," said Desdemona. "Just *call* her. I talk with my mum every week and she appreciates it, I know she does. Each Sunday at lunchtime, I give her a ring. It's good to talk."

"It's late though and I'm tired."

"Not *too* late. It's only..." said Desdemona sitting up to peer at the bedside clock. "Just gone midnight here. What time in New York?"

"Seven o'clock, sumptn like that."

"S*ooo*," said Desdemona, slapping a phone into his hand. "*Call* her. Tell her how things are going. You don't have to say where you *are*. Just tell her you're okay. You have her number?"

"Sure I do."

"You won't regret it, trust me."

"Oookay," said Dwayne pulling on a shirt and pants. Talking to his mom naked would be a little weird, he figured. Then he jabbed the numbers into Desdemona's phone.

"Mom, it's me," he said when the connection was made.

"*Dwayne*, honey? *You*?" said CeCi.

"Me."

"Gimme a minute, willya?"

Dwayne shrugged at Desdemona and grinned. "Probably busy at her easel."

Which CeCi was. Well, not so much her easel as a Pollock-style canvas spread across the floor on which she was carefully stepping with ochre on one bare foot and purple on the other. The piece was to be entitled "Footsie." If The Ritz was famed for hiring suites to people with elephants so long as they could pay, she'd argued with

Montmorency, it sure as hell couldn't tell her not to paint in her room. And Montmorency had agreed.

"HON*EEEEEY*," she said when she came back on the line. "How *grrreat* to hear your voice. Where the fuck *are* you?"

"England."

"I figured as much, but where in…?"

"Right now, London. So how's it goin' over there in NYC?"

It was CeCi's reply that caused Dwayne's eyes to swivel in their sockets and Desdemona to reach out and prop him up.

"What? What *is* it?" she said.

"Muh-mom's huh-*here*. In London. Suh-staying at The Ruh-*Ritz*," he whispered.

"I *know* that, honey. I just told you," said CeCi. "And good to hear you're in London also," she added, scraping paint off her left foot. "What're you whispering for anyhow?"

"Nothing, I was just…"

"You got somebody there with you?"

"Yu-yeah."

"Don't tell me." CeCi laughed. "The Fubar kid."

"No, he's upstairs."

"Yeah, and I'm Princess Leia outta *Star Wars*. I was only foolin' around, Dwayney."

"No kidding, Mom."

"You *rilly* found him?"

"Like I said, he's upstairs."

"Holy shit, wow, that is *sooo* great. How'd you *do* that?"

"Wasn't so hard. Fill you in on the details some other time."

"Okay. Anyways bravo, kiddo. Who needs a PI when I got a son like you? Wait till I tell his mother!"

"You *know* his mother?"

"Sure I do. We got this hunt-a-son thing goin' together. She's gonna be so happy."

"Mom, look, maybe not yet? Maybe I should talk with Fergie first? He's like a runaway an' I don't know if he *wants* to be found."

"Fergie?"

"Yeah, like short for the Fergus Ulysses name I got him into all the trouble with?"

"Sure, sure, right. Dumb of me. And he doesn't want to see even his own mother?"

"Maybe, maybe not. I dunno. I should speak to him first about that."

"Ookay, whatever you think. Just let me know when. But make it soon. The cops already had a sighting…"

Dwayne's blood froze.

"But the trail went dead."

Dwayne's blood warmed up again.

"Anyways, *any*ways, you said you had someone there with you. If it ain't the Fubar kid then who…?

"My gal."

"You got a *gal* now? Well yippee an' another bravo, babe. You want I should say hello to her?"

Never one to take a back seat was CeCi Zobinski—who was soon to return to her original family name of Bodine. "Just pass me over. Her name is?"

"Desdemona."

"Desdemona like in *Shakes*peare? I don't remember which play."

"Like in Shakespeare. And it was *Othello*."

"Right, right, I saw the musical. Woweee. Give her the phone," said CeCi, the decibels increasing with every utterance.

Overhearing, Desdemona smiled. "So I get to meet your mum after all?"

"Saying no to CeCi ain't easy." Dwayne smiled, handing over the phone.

For the following ten minutes while his mother and girlfriend became best buddies, Dwayne just lay back and thought of nothing in particular. Well, not quite nothing. Clearly, before the call ended, he would need to be sure his mother wasn't in touch with his father, figuring *she* might understand his current situation, but *he* sure as hell wouldn't and cause ten kinds of trouble. When Desdemona passed back the phone with a big grin on her face, therefore, he put the question to CeCi who reassured him in her normal blunt manner.

"*That* asshole? You have to be kidding, son 'o mine. Also, I just fired his private dick, the one he hired to find you, so no worries there. Now, how about tomorrow for a meet-up at The Ritz? I am already in love with that gal of yours. She...is...a...*dia*mond. Bring her with you. Say around two. I sleep late."

"I remember, Mom. Two is good."

"You can find your way to Piccadooly?"

"I'm a big boy now, Mom."

"Gotta love you and leave you, babe. That's my other phone."

Anyway, that was the way CeCi tracked Dwayne down. By him calling her.

~ * ~

The way Lady Hermione traced her errant husband happened in much the same manner, although it was not *he* who called *her* in this instance but Sergeant Geoffrey Probert at The Victoria Embankment cop shop, where Lord Crossbar was being held in custody—"custard" as he called it—for causing grievous bodily harm to a beadle whilst being ejected from the House of Lords after breaking into the Ladies lavatory.

"Billy (bally) boodles (beadles)," he'd expostulated, struggling and kicking while being strong-armed to the door and out into Parliament Square.

"Now, now, sir, let's not be any more silly than we have been already," countered Johnny Frobisher (the beadle), who had no powers outside the House but plenty within it. "Frightening peeing ladies is bad enough, so let us not add badmouthing a beadle to your crimes, shall we?"

"Fecking bloodlums (beadles)," re-expostulated Lord Crossbar, biting one of the hands Frobisher was using to guide him out of the crumbling building, which was facing temporary closure for immediate and astronomically expensive repairs before it imploded on itself after centuries of being the "Mother of Parliaments."

"Nasty old bastard, aren't we?" said Frobisher, sucking at the bleeding hand.

Which gave Lord Crossbar the sudden freedom he needed to wriggle free, knee Frobisher in the nuts and, as the beadle said "ooommph" and folded over, to break his jaw with an uppercut—a move secretly admired by prime minister Penelope Pringle in The House of Commons who would have just loved to perform the same manoeuvre on all of her squabbling cabinet *and* the EU's chief negotiator in Brussels whenever he yet again said "*non*" to the latest of her fatuous Brexit proposals. But all she could do was watch the CCTV coverage, suck her thumb and wish.

*Any*way, when two passing lords—Lord George Brokenshire of Giggleswick and Lord Keith McGear of Toxteth—came to Frobisher's rescue, they were left with no alternative but to call the cops. They would have preferred not to and to have kept the matter entirely *sub rosa* in-house, of course they would. With its reputation running on zero amongst the masses over the Brexit fubar, there was nothing parliamentarians needed less in these dark days than even more bad press, especially not headlines like the following morning's "LOONY LORD KNEES BEADLE IN THE NUTS THEN BUSTS HIS JAW" in *The Daily Gripe*, but given Frobisher's whingeing about "justice being done," which took him three minutes to splutter given his jaw problem, they were left with little option.

While they conflabbed *sotto voce* for fear of attracting further attention, Lord Crossbar of Little Piddlington In The Marsh was doing a little dance more or less equivalent to the Haka and yelling, "Gitcha (gotcha), yu loddle (little) fickler (fucker)."

It was Lord Keith, who as a Scouser had little time for poncy lords even though he'd become one himself, that finally persuaded Lord Brokenshire they needed to call not only an ambulance, but also the boys or girls in blue.

"Only right, isn't it?" he told his fellow peer, who was blethering almost as incomprehensibly as Lord Crossbar.

So it was that, receiving no more of an answer than a series of non-committal shrugs from his colleague, Lord Keith did the right thing. So far as Lord Crossbar was concerned, it was quite the *wrong* thing but, as so often in the chamber, or anywhere else, he was unable to find the words to express his sentiments on the matter.

The squad car and ambulance arrived within minutes of each other, Lord Crossbar being carted off to the former and beadle Frobisher to the latter, both of them waggling V-signs at each other.

It was also unfortunate from Lord Crossbar's perspective that, yet again, in his time of distress there should have been a photographer present to witness the scene, but you know how it is with the paparazzi, how omnipresent they are. This one, Mike Delaney from *The Daily Snitch*, couldn't believe his luck, hence the following day's headline "LOONEY LORD CARTED OFF TO CLINK" *and* the worldwide internet exposure the pic received. In Brussels, EU chief negotiator Yves Bronsard chuckled and shook his head. *"Mon Dieu, ces Anglais,"* he said. In a number of different languages, and in different places— Paris, Berlin, Rome etc—parliamentarians chuckled, and shook their heads too, in much the same manner.

So that was how come Sergeant Probert was on the phone to Lady Hermione Barr who, when given details of her husband's latest *faux pas* uncharacteristically said, "Jesus sodding Christ on a bike."

"It is a somewhat tricky situation, ma'am," Probert agreed. "Seeing as we're a bit short on cells at the moment. Government cuts and so on. However, we are prepared to release Lord Barr into your custody on the assurance he will not be allowed to escape."

"*Again?*"

"Again, ma'am?"

"The old bastard's al*ready* under hice arrest for farting in the chamber. Couldn't you hold him a tad longer?"

"Afraid not, your ladyship. Pending any charges Mister Frobisher may or may not bring."

"Mister *Fro*bisher?"

"The beadle whose jaw your husband broke."

"Couldn't we buy him awf?"

"You could, ma'am, but then Lord Barr'd be free and back home, anyway."

"Bollockings."

"Indeed, ma'am. Now, when would you be able to come over to the Victoria Embankment police station and pick him up?"

"It has to be *me*?"

"Afraid so. You or a close member of the family."

"Shit," said Lady Hermione.

"No close family members?"

"There was a son, but he ran away and your blokes can't find him."

"So *you* then, ma'am. Soonest possible, if you please," said Sergeant Probert, tiring of this conversation and hanging up.

"Bloody lords and friggin' ladies," he muttered, ensuring the phone was properly disengaged. "It's the rich what gets the pleasure and the poor what gets the blame, eh?" he was adding as P.C. Jenny Mortenson, his latest squeeze, wandered into the office.

"You can say that again, Geoff."

So Sergeant Probert did.

There is, however, a happy ending to this messy episode because Lady Hermione's appointment with the police, unbeknownst to her till she checked, coincided with the very day she'd been scheduled to meet CeCi at The Ritz, which of course necessitated a postponement phone call.

"Soo sorry to hear it, darlin'," said CeCi, up to her eyes in paint as usual. "I was looking forward to it. You wanna hear some good news though?"

"About bally time, so the answer's a great big YES."

Which was when CeCi told of Dwayne Junior's call and the arrangement he'd made to come around with his beautiful babe.

"I'm so glad to hear it, my dear. Very good news for you."

"And *you*,"

"Excuse me?"

Despite her promise to Dwayne not to say anything on the subject until he'd had the chance to talk to Fergie, CeCi Zobinski/Bodine was unable to control her maternal empathies and said, "Because I just heard from *my* son, and he knows where *your* son is."

Well, that made Lady Hermione's day all right despite the recent marital setbacks.

"Yikes, yippee," she hollered. "In every cloud there's a silver lining. Thank *you*, and thank the Lord."

"You're right about the silver lining. As for the Lord part, I'm taking a rain cheque," said CeCi, a dedicated antitheist who reckoned you made your own luck. "Make another appointment with Monty at the desk, okay?"

"You...bet...your...*life* I shall."

Thirteen

Dwayne Zobinski Snr was having the worst day of his life since only narrowly escaping jail time over his contribution to the 2008 banking crash by selling dodgy mortgages and even dodgier futures—*and* consequently being fired from his lucrative Wall Street position.

"Just get the hell outta my office, outta this city, and outta this *country* if you know what's good for you," said his boss, Hank Laplanque, who had himself escaped US justice by buying off *any*body who accused him of *any*thing, and if they wouldn't take the bung "stiffing" them, which included the threat of all manner of nasty things such as hospitalization happening to either them or their nearest and dearest.

"But, and this is a *big* but, Zobinski, wherever you go never forget I got your balls in my pocket. Any time *I* call, you come running, right? Only *you* don't ever call *me, capice*?"

Dwayne Snr had *capiced* pretty quick. You didn't mess with Hank Laplanque.

"And the *only* reason I ever call you again is if I hear on the grapevine you've made shedloads of money someplace, and I want my share of what you owe me, which you pay into my account at this secret address," Hank added, slipping across his desk a to-the-naked-eye blank piece of purple paper. "All you gotta do is shine a blue light on it an' the numbers'll come up. Once you've used it, you eat it. Now beat it."

Dwayne didn't owe Hank a red cent but didn't say anything about that. He knew guys who Hank had stiffed, and it wasn't pleasant, so he just walked out of the office, down into Wall Street, and out into the big bad world, some days later leaving behind him in New York City his arty-farty wife and his little kid. No kind of a mother was bi-sexy CeCi, but until Dwayne Snr found a new base she'd have to manage. And to pay the bills, she would just have to start selling her freakin' "paintings."

Which arrangement had suited CeCi just fine. A little quality time with Dwayne Jnr, and also the chance to test the art market, what could be cooler? Especially when the dealers lapped up her work, and the big bucks started to flow. With her back turned, "Bye, bye," was all she said to Soon-To-Be-Ex on the day he hit the road.

Other American cities were out of the question for Zobinski Snr because Hank had tentacles every place, so Dwayne first tried South America (too unstable) then Yurp (too foreign) before landing up in the City of London where he found banking to be booming and after making friends with the Ruskies, began to accrue through such dodgy deals a tidy fortune, none of which was ever transferred stateside to Hank fuckin' Laplanque.

It was only then he demanded the now much bigger Dwayne Jnr be sent over to join him and, albeit reluctantly, CeCi agreed. After all, she was busy with her art and, maybe, the trip would do the kid good, broaden his mind, she figured. Not that Zobinski Snr ever spent any time with boy. Just packed him off to School to keep clear the space *he* needed to do what he liked doing best—screwing dopes out of their money. How proud he had been the day the guy after his own heart had been elected to the White House. Now things would *really* take off, he'd assumed. A shame, three years on, that Klank was mired in so much shit, but hey, like Zobinski, he was a fighter and he would survive. Hadn't the attorney general himself said he'd been exonerated of the Ruskie collusion charges? Sure he had, although Zobinski knew it to be a PR scam, but schtum was the word for him and all the other good ol' boys on that score, so business could continue as usual. Soon, the whole thing would be wiped off of the map, anyhow. That was Klank's greatest skill. This was what he'd been trying to explain to Anatoly Munchkov at The Ritz before CeCi did her best to throttle him, and Munchkov got outta Dodge faster than a fox with a hound on his ass.

But now, here he was facing a day potentially even worse than that in the wake of 2008. It was from the first of the two unpleasant special delivery letters he received in the day's mail that Zobinski was beginning to see why Munchkov had been so antsy. It was from Scotland Yard's Special/Anti-Terrorist branch.

> "Dear Sir," it said, "We have reason to believe you have or have had a "business relationship" with a certain Russian named Anatoly Munchkov who, amongst other misdemeanours, is currently under investigation for his suspected role in the recent spate of Kremlin-inspired poisonings in our cities. Please respond within twenty-four hours and in person to this letter by attending our offices at the address on the letterhead. We are open 24/7. Failure to do so may lead to serious consequences.
> Yours faithfully,
> Scribbled signature,
> Chief Superintendent Marvin Matheson."

Well, that had put the shits up the normally John Wayne-ish Dwayne Zobinski Snr all right. His hand shook as he read and re-read the letter. He'd seen news of the poisonings on TV, but never given them a second thought. Killing exiled critics of the Kremlin was par for the course for the Ruskies, he figured. Just a sensible way of killing history. Not that they ever admitted to it, even when internationally accused.

"Nothing to do with us, pal, fake news," would come the well-rehearsed response from Igor Ripurpantzov, Russian president for life. "Don't know nothing about it, do I?" And when pressed for further elucidation, he'd fulminate: "Quit it with the accusations if you know what's good for you. Like I said, we're innocent of any crime. *If* the doer *was* Russian, and you can prove it, he sure as shit wasn't ex-KGB like you're saying, but probably some criminal gang member. Now cut the crap or we'll retaliate. Which...you...would...not...*like*, trust me."

The same sorts of response came whenever Ripurpantzov was accused of cyber fixing the 2016 US elections for Zobinski's hero in the White House. But the bad news was Klank had *not* been fully exonerated even by his very own attorney general appointee on the matter of obstructing justice when it came to burying the Russian matter. Plus, he was still under so many FBI investigations for not only his dealings with Moscow but a string of other crimes—tax fraud and evasion, libel, slander, sexual harassment, mendacity, shutting down government on a whim etc, etc—that his remaining days as president looked doomed. Which pissed Dwayne Zobinski off. But he was a whole lot *more* pissed off that *he* should be tarred with the same brush of links to Russian terrorism just when he was hoping to do the sorts of deals with the Ruskies that would increase his fortune post-Brexit. Easy to see *those* going straight down the tubes.

And then there was the second letter, this one from the Home Office, which, in conjunction with the Munchkov one, had him hurrying to the toilet.

"Dear Mr Zobinski," it said. "It has come to our attention that you are a foreign national currently resident in the UK for less than five years. In our preparations for the UK's exit from the European Union, we would be obliged if you would fill out the enclosed ninety-page form in the next forty-eight hours, and return it to us in the enclosed envelope. Failure to do so may lead to serious consequences.

Yours sincerely,

Scribbled signature.

Dame Nora Milburn."

"What the *fuck*?" said Zobinski to the toilet roll dispenser. "That kinda crap is for the Yurpeans, not the good guys, guys who fought in two world wars against the bad guys over in Japan and Yurp. Holy *shit*."

As usual, Dwayne Snr hadn't done his homework. Mind you, even if he had, his perspective on foreign nationals resident in the UK wouldn't have been any clearer. One minute the prime minster was saying everybody could stay, the next she would ship them *all* off back to where they'd come from, depending on who was saying what in opposition to her in cabinet and Brussels. Result: like Zobinski, nobody knew what the fuck was going on. For all *he* knew, it could be Americans as well as Europeans who were shown the door.

*Any*way, it was these two time bombs placed under him that pretty quickly reduced Dwayne Snr to nervousness of a kind to which he was unaccustomed. If he *were* to be deported from the UK, the first hiding place that came to mind would be back stateside, but how welcome would he be *there* for crissakes? Not very, he concluded. Not by Hank Laplanque, that was for sure, unless he came with truckloads of money. And not without investigation by the feebs or the CIA either, if his name, like Klank's still, was linked to complicity with Russian atrocities. So where to? Russia itself? No way, José. Not so long ago, Dwayne would have billed them "damn commoonists," plus they spoke a real weird language. So to *no*where civilized, that was where. And man was that some *bad* feeling. Those in the psych business might have termed it "existential angst," but Dwayne Snr didn't know any hard words like that. All he knew was he was one worried American.

Although he wouldn't admit it to *any*one, so was his hero in the White House. But Klank was better protected than Zobinski. Not by the truth but by the psychopathy that allowed him to believe he'd never done anything wrong in his whole life and was only ever blamed by ignorant, jealous, "witch-hunting" enemy liberals for the success he continued to have in all aspects of his life: sex, golf, and self-publicity.

~ * ~

Pacing up and down her office at 10 Downing Street, occasionally headbutting a wall, Penelope Pringle was as much a worried prime minister as Zobinski was a worried American and for similar reasons, namely where could *she* run when the UK collapsed out of the EU with no deal, facing a future of economic meltdown and she was finally given the boot? Unlike Dwayne, she could possibly go to America, but wher*ever* she went, she would be followed by the spectre of Brexit whispering in her ear she had been the worst prime minister in British history with the possible exception of her predecessor, the one who'd called the 2016 referendum in the first place. Already some of the more cerebral journos in Fleet Street were naming *her* as the thing that was rotten in the state of the UK.

"Aaaagghh, ggrrrr, ouch!" she mumbled as the wall got fed up with being headbutted and headbutted back.

"Fickle bastards," she grumbled, undeterred by the reverse headbutting which she assumed she'd imagined, anyway. Was she finally going crazy? God alone knew she'd done her best with the bally cabinet and the bally Irish, the idiots in parliament, *and* most of all the brainless, dimwitted, objectionable Europeans in Brussels—and derision was all the reward she got.

Like Klank in the White House, however, she displayed none of this distress in public. But unlike Klank, this wasn't because she was at best a sociopath and at worst a psychopath, but because she been trained at School and Girton College Cambridge to behave Britishly at all times in all aspects of public life, in other words robotically. In every speech she ever made, in every pic taken by even the most daring of paparazzi, she is seen dolled up in quasi-sexy outfits smiling gormlessly in the face of barrages of criticism. During the early Brexit negotiations, this absence of gorm was taken as a sign of willpower and strength, but now time was running out, it was increasingly being recognised as some form of hitherto undiagnosed neural deficiency.

"IS THE PM BONKERS?" screamed the *Daily Groan*'s most recent banner headline, for example, before reporting the recent poll it had conducted of erstwhile convinced Brexiters who had since boned up on their economics, watched on as bank after bank and business after business relocated to pastures greener, concluded that leaving the EU would leave them penniless, and had thus at the eleventh hour switched their allegiance to the Remain campaign.

"We want another referendum," they were chanting on the streets of all major English cities. "When do we want it? *NOW*."

And that was just in England. In Scotland, Wales, and Northern Ireland similar protests were being heard, but added to them were calls for separate referenda on the independence question which, if answered as predicted by the pollsters, could lead to the breakup of the United Kingdom and lead to England being left all alone to face the ridicule of a colonized world it had once dominated. But had Penelope paid any attention to any of that? Of course not. Instead, she had ploughed on regardless with her finagling fantasies of a Brexit that delivered "the will of the people."

And so it was on this occasion, as she dabbed her damaged head with TCP, swept her dyed hair over the bruises, and marched defiantly out onto the steps of Number Ten to deliver her latest Plan B—actually Plan Z—to a waiting press. For any other similarly deluded person, there might have been sympathy, but how to sympathize with a robot, that was the question.

"Hello there, good to see you all again," said Penelope, grinning moronically through her plastered-on red lipstick for maybe the thousandth time.

The congregated hacks took out their notebooks and dutifully took to scribbling while the TV and radio ones took out their microphones and asked the usual questions to which they'd become accustomed to receiving answers so garbled as to be meaningless. Then off Penelope marched towards the waiting limo that would take her just down the road to parliament to answer Prime Minister's Questions so ambiguously that nobody would have a clue what she was talking about.

Buoyed by her customary mask of public hubris, however, Penelope barely noticed the grumbling and muttering from even those on the front bench right alongside her, never mind the one opposite. On the whole, she thought it a pretty good performance and she was doing a jolly good job.

~ * ~

This was not a view shared by The Fubars who, with their newfound interest in the political scene, reckoned she was full of shit.

"Man, I had Klank figured for dumb, but this dame beats him into...whadda you English guys call that?" said Dwayne.

"A cocked hat," said Desdemona.

"That's the baby. A hat full of cock."

But mock her though they would, The Fubars also feared the impact of her mindless meanderings on their own futures. Unlike Zobinski Snr, his son was yet to receive the Home Office letter because nobody, bar CeCi, knew where he was and she wouldn't be telling, but he feared it could happen. As did Aika and Maja, again as yet unnotified of the need to pack their bags, but aware, along with the three million other foreign nationals in the UK, that the awful repatriation demand might one day drop through their letterbox. As proper Brits, Josh, Fergie, and Desdemona were unaffected, of course, but were damned if such a fate was going to be allowed to befall their lovers.

Fergie was the first to voice this concern. "Hat full of cock she might be," he said, "but I've been reading up on her. When she was Home Secretary, she was already hellbent on kicking out as many immigrants as she could. Now, through Brexit, she can do so to her heart's content. But she lays a finger on Aika, it will be over my dead body."

This sentiment was echoed and embellished by Tosh and Desdemona, both of whom declared not only that they were prepared to die for the sakes of Maja and Dwayne but also, and most significantly, they would "break the balls of any arsehole in a uniform who tries to take them away," as Tosh put it.

"Even at four o'clock in the morning, the kind of time the Gestapo would come calling," said Desdemona.

"Nice goin,' and thanks, babe," said Dwayne. "Me, I'll just sleep with one eye open, and a pistol in my hand like a good cowpoke. But let's hope it *don't* happen. This is twenny-nineteen, right? Other hand, back stateside Klank is spouting the same crap against the Mexicans and the Muslims, and anybody who ain't white, right?"

"So are the populist fascists all across Europe. Immigration is at the root of all this. Believe me, I know," said Maja. "And, would you bel*ieve* it, using Brexit Britain as the example they all should follow."

"The Britain that was the home of freedoms when I came here," said Aika, tears in her eyes.

"As was The States when my granddaddy sailed into Ellis Island. Now, it's the Statue of Liberty, my sweet ass. So much for taking in the tired and the poor and the tempest tossed," said Dwayne.

Sitting in a ring on the lounge carpet and holding hands, they talked on and on into the small hours. How maybe they would run away to The Republic of Ireland, which, as they understood it, still welcomed newcomers and showed no signs of the civil war dividing the UK. Seamus O'Driscoll in Dublin would be only too happy to see them right with new passports, Tosh promised.

"They do speak English over there, don't they?" said Maja.

Tosh laughed. "Yeah sure, kind've. It helps to learn a bit of Gaelic, though. The big bonus is you get smiles wherever you go."

"Not like London then," said Desdemona, who'd lived her whole life in the impersonal capital.

"Like London *not*," Tosh assured her.

So escape was one aspect of the conversation, but the core of it was affirmation of their feelings for each other *and,* of course, The Fubars.

"No freakin' government is gonna split up the band," said Dwayne to vigorous nodding all around.

Then, running on adrenalin (and a little weed), they took to juggling with lyrics for a new song, which sure as hell was hot would not be some silly boy-meets-girl ditty.

Fourteen

At least Lady Hermione Barr was granted the privilege of a police van to take her deviant husband back from Victoria Embankment cop shop to Piddlington Hall.

"Just to be on the safe side," said Sergeant Probert. "Wouldn't want our boy escaping on the way home, now would we? A bit frisky he is."

Lady Hermione nodded grateful assent. "Thank you so much, my man. I have to admit I was somewhat fearful of the journey all alone on the train."

"No problem, ma'am, give me a minute while I pop down to the cells to fetch him, then we'll be on our way."

"You'll come, too?"

"No, sorry, on duty here, aren't I? You'll have a couple of my best blokes with you, though, the ones who normally ferry murderers to court. Bert and Jim know what they're doing so you'll be safe as houses. Just hang on a mo."

And with that, Probert was gone, leaving Lady Hermione in the squad room to survey posters of violent criminals wanted for a range of heinous offences. Which chilled her to the bone. To *think* that the once almost lovable Lord Xavier had fallen so low, it beggared belief.

How ashamed she was. How ashamed his father Lord Clarence would have been. How *amused* on the other hand poor little Fergus Ulysses would be after the treatment he'd received at the hands of his absentee father and, indeed, as Lady Hermione ruefully reflected, his absentee mother. So many fences would need mending when she finally found the lad. She could hardly wait for her meeting with the American at The Ritz.

Such were her ruminations as Probert returned, pulling behind him a handcuffed, glassy- and black-eyed Lord Crossbar who was making ursine grunting noises and had spittle running down his chin.

"Doesn't look too pretty, I'm afraid," said Probert. "Only he was a bit of a naughty boy last night so we had to calm him down with sedatives. Then he fell over on his face, which is how he got his black eye."

"I see," said Lady Hermione, buying the black-eye lie because it was convenient. She knew as well as the next person it was pretty hard to get a black eye by falling over on one's face, but this was no time to file a police brutality complaint. And frankly, she rather hoped it had been Probert who'd administered the blow. She was starting quite to like Probert.

"Lastbed (blasted) pockeps (coppers)," gurgled Lord Crossbar, eyeing Lady Hermione suspiciously. "Ooz zis loodby (bloody) wimmon?"

"Your wife, Lord Xavier."

"*Waif?*"

"Hello, darling. Come to take you home," said Hermione.

"Fuck off," said Lord Crossbar with one of the sudden and unpredictable returns to fluency his neurologist, Doctor Jonathon Grimhausen, had outlined at his first assessment.

"Some days our patient will muddle syllables and consonants in the manner of the normal aphasic," had said Doctor Jonathon. "Some days he won't."

"And can we foresee when this might happen?" Lady Hermione had asked.

"No," was the unhelpful medical answer. "The science has not thus far developed sufficiently. Have a nice day."

*Any*way, today was one of those rare moments of lucidity, albeit it only lasted for two words. Once they'd been said, Lord Crossbar returned to ursine grunting. Plus foot stamping and trying to throttle Sergeant Probert with his handcuff chains.

"Okey dokey, Lord Whatsit, enough of that," said Probert, finger hooking Officers Bert and Jim (no second names) into the squad room and giving them orders to accompany Lord and Lady Thingummy downstairs to the garage where the van and its driver would be awaiting them.

"Any bother from him, you know what to," he told Bert and Jim, who nodded knowingly.

Lady Hermione was reassured. Bert and Jim didn't look like the sorts of chappies for Lord Crossbar to win a fight against. Big, muscly, and tattooed with fiery symbols they were.

And so it was, with sirens wah-wah-wahing all the way, that Lord Xavier Barr of Little Piddlington In The Marsh was safely delivered back to his mansion. Well, not to the mansion it*self*, Bert and Jim considered that far too comfortable. Instead, he was consigned to a courtyard stable he would share with a horse called Nemesis who under normal conditions was sweetness and light but who, if he sensed any form of disruption to his quarters or daily routine, had a double hind leg kick capable of flooring an elephant.

Lady Hermione sighed with relief as the police van sped away having disgorged its prisoner. Then, alerting Max and Milly Prachett to their additional responsibilities—i.e. feeding Lord Crossbar as well as Nemesis and the dogs—she hurried to the phone to confirm the longed-for appointment with CeCi Zobinski.

~ * ~

Dwayne Jnr's visit to The Ritz with Desdemona went wonderfully. No sitting around in the lounge listening to Play-It-Again-Sam *this* time, no siree. Montmorency was under strict instructions to show the pair straight upstairs to CeCi's suite.

"Madam Zobinski will be *so* glad to see you," he said, tactfully showing no signs of knowing any of the backstory to the recent separation, despite CeCi having confided in him after sex one drunken evening. Yes, folks, sex. Paying no attention to her soon-to-be-defunct marriage vows, Mrs happy-to-be-bi Zobinski had made no bones about her desires where Montmorency was concerned. If she fancied a romp with an ex- wrestler she'd damn well have one, hence her appearance in a diaphanous jade negligée on the occasion of his being invited to her room on the pretext of fixing a window hinge, and her goosing him as he was bending to inspect it. After that, what with the champagne and everything, it had all been pretty passionate—and, of course, strictly secret.

*Any*way, with her son and his lady friend, Montmorency was naturally professionalism incarnate. "Lift to the second floor, and first door on your left," he said. "I shall call ahead to alert the lady of your coming."

Which was why the door was wide open when Dwayne and Desdemona arrived, each of them immediately to be smothered in a tight embrace then kissed. First Desdemona then Dwayne.

"Babies, my babies, come...on...*in*," CeCi cried, bowing from the waist and wafting an arm behind her thespianly when the embracing and kissing were over. "Make yourselves right at home."

Just the lounge of "home" was many square metres larger than the sum of all the rooms in Desdemona's entire terraced house in Hackney, a vast space decorated in an anomalous style somewhere between high Victoriana and Hollywood, which CeCi had rendered yet weirder with the inclusion of several of her Jackson Pollock-esque canvases. To Dwayne, remembering the NYC apartment, such a space was familiar enough. But Desdemona was gobsmacked and showed it.

"You okay, honey?" said CeCi, taking her arm and steering her to a white leather couch spattered with the usual spectrum of colours plus some of CeCi's invention. As noted, if Ritz clients could have elephants in their rooms, CeCi could have paint. When she'd gone, they could redecorate was her idea.

"Don't worry, babe, it's all dry now. Ain't gonna stick to your pants or anything," she said as Desdemona wiped at the sofa's surface. "If it does, I got plenty more your size in the closet."

So Desdemona sat and Dwayne sat next to her.

"Same old Mom," he said.

"Old I ain't, babe. Old enough to have had you, but that's the size of it. Old is only a number, like Clint Eastwood said. And what was it Bobby Dylan said in one of his songs?"

"That he used to be so much older, but he's gotten younger now. Sumptn like that."

"Right on, Dwayney. He bought one of my pictures, you know?"

"Bob Dylan?"

"Yeah, he was in Greenwich Village one time doin' a gig. Talk about old, the guy never gives up. He's still on the road. Anyhow, he sees one of my pictures, likes it, and buys it."

Dwayne smiled. Such talk brought back memories. It wasn't as though he'd had all that much contact with his artist mother, but at least she was there for him when his father wasn't—when he broke a leg playing football, when his latest date blew him off, when all kindsa stuff. Sure, she was a little bit crazy but always fun to be around. Made a person feel life was worth living.

"You want I should order sumptn up?" she said. "Don't know what you guys have this time of day. Coffee? Tea? Ice creams?"

"We ain't kids, Mom."

"Sure enough," said CeCi, cuddling Desdemona. "This gal is *sooo* cute. I want her for mine."

Uncharacteristically, Desdemona gave herself to the cuddle. She wasn't normally a cuddly person, but this one reminded her of Andrea on one of her visits to Anglesey. Maybe CeCi and Andrea could meet one day. She reckoned they would get along.

"How about beers and a little weed, Mom?" said Dwayne. "Wine, if you'd prefer."

"Wine would be sooo good. I'm gonna order it up," said CeCi, hoisting the intercom phone to Montmorency. "Yeah, Monty? Three bottles of your finest white, the French," she said.

"Coming right up, ma'am," said Montmorency to the guest who'd shagged him senseless only three nights earlier.

"You *knew* about the weed, my baby?" she then asked Dwayne.

"Mom, I know a lotta stuff. I always have."

"Oo*kay* then, so I got me a nice new stash. Don't ask how."

Dwayne pulled a zipper across his lips.

"And your gal?"

Desdemona smiled.

"I'm taking that for a yes, darlin'."

And so it was that the afternoon at The Ritz passed in a dreamy haze during which CeCi learned the details of how Dwayne had tracked down Fergie, and then become a key member of the well-known rock band he played in.

"*Wow-eee*," said CeCi. "An *art*ist. Like mother like son, huh?"

"And Desi is one of the backup girls, but she writes the songs, too. We write them all together."

"Fan*tast*ic. Not just a pretty face, huh, sweetheart?"

"I do my bit," said Desdemona.

"I'm sure you do," said CeCi, going on to ask about the other band members. "Fergie you already told me about. And the others?"

It was Desdemona who filled her in on Tosh, Maja, Aika.

CeCi slapped her cheeks. "Man, that's sooo great," she said. "Boy, oh *boy*. You guys and gals must get along real good."

"We do. There's more though," said Dwayne, going on to explain how the guys and gals had met, fallen in love, and now all lived together in the Hackney house.

"Wow*eee*," said CeCi slapping her cheeks. "That is sooo, how'm I gonna say? Like ro*man*tic only in the real old meaning of that word. Like romance as in fabulous story? Not one of those smoochy gooey numbers we got today. Man, it must have been so *fun*."

Dwayne nodded. "It sure turned out good," he said, running a hand through Desdemona's blonde tresses.

"You can say that again. And this Fergie, he forgave you for what you did to him?"

"I never meant him no harm, Mom. Just goofing off as usual. The word came out without me thinking, and next I knew all hell broke loose."

"Sure, but did he forgive you?"

"Yeah, he's the sweetest guy. We're best buddies now. His gal's called Aika."

"Wow, some *name*."

"She's Japanese."

"Cool. Like Yoko Ono."

"You could say so."

"Well, good for him. Which leaves Tosh and Maja, right? They hooked up, too?"

"In one, Mom. Plus, there's also Mutt."

"Mutt?"

"Is Tosh's dawg."

"Don't tell me. He's in the band, too."

"He sits right next to Tosh while he's drumming," said Desdemona. "Only he doesn't write any songs."

CeCi fell about laughing. "Geez, you couldn't *make* it up."

"It's all true, Mom."

Which was when CeCi told of her recent connection with Hermione Barr and how happy she would be to be reunited with her boy.

"You figure he would be up for that, Dwayney?"

"I guess. Like I said, we'd need to talk with him about that, but I figure so."

Glossing over the fact she'd already told Lady Hermione Fergie had been found, CeCi went for reassurance about the fathers in both Fergie's and Dwayne's cases.

"And if you're wondering about what the kid's old man might have to say about it," she said, "like me with *your* dipshit father, Hermie won't be telling him nothing. He wouldn't understand in any case 'cos he's like crazier than a shithouse rat. Not playing with a full deck since he banged his head when your guy Fergie was being taken away from school, and keeps getting himself arrested all the time so no problemo there."

"Should be okay then. And you'll tell *my* dad nothing?"

"Like I said, zilch, nada. Soon as I can, me an' your dad are gonna be history anyhow."

"You're divorcing?"

"Yup. He don't know it yet, but yup. You wanna see him again that's your business, kiddo. Me, I've had it up to here." CeCi raised a hand to her hairline.

"Anything we can do to help, all you have to do is ask," said Desdemona.

"You are a sweetheart, babe. But you don't need my problems on your young shoulders. Now, this band of yours. Its name is?"

Which was when Dwayne explained it had been Fergie of all people who'd proposed The Fubars.

"Some great kid he must be. I wanna meet with him too. And his gal. And the dawg. And Tosh. And his gal, Maja. She ain't British, huh?"

"She's from Poland," said Desdemona.

"Great to see so many guys and gals from so many countries getting along together."

"It is," said Desdemona, before giving CeCi a thumbnail breakdown of the UK's current Brexit problems and the dangers of deportation implicit in them.

"Holy hooley, I hadn't figured it was *so* bad," said CeCi who'd begun to take an interest in the subject dividing the nation. "Sounds like you guys got another civil war comin' on just like we do stateside since the criminal dork got himself elected to the White House. Just hope your foreign gals don't get hit too hard. I can help, you only gotta ask."

"Thanks, Mom. One helluva big ask it would be, though. Right now, nobody's knows what the hell's going down."

CeCi rolled a fresh joint, fired it up, and passed it around. "You want my advice, meantime, just keep your heads below the parapet and get on with your art. Art can never hurt you, but mess with politics, and all you'll get is pain. Too many me-me-mine bullshitting assholes in *that* game."

"I remember you saying that when I was a kid. Didn't know what you meant by it back then, but now I've learnt."

"Sooner or later we all have to, kiddo. Mebbe that was why Bobby Dylan and me got on so well. What was he said in that song?"

"Which one, Mom?"

"The one about the artist dame."

"I know it. 'She Belongs to Me,'" said Desdemona, "Don't

remember all the words but the idea was she had everything she needed and didn't look back. Never stumbled because she had no place to fall."

"That's the baby," said CeCi, humming the tune. "Well, let us all remember the wisdom of it. Had to be a reason Bobby got his Nobel Prize."

"Although he took his own good time accepting it," said Dwayne.

"Precisely. Who needs prizes from doofuses who never wrote a song in their lives? Now sing me one of The Fubars' numbers."

"Difficult, Mom. No band, no instruments, no..."

"Aw, *c'mon*. Just a little taste?"

So Dwayne and Desdemona improvised with the one the band had penned only the other night. "Screwed Up Brexit Blues" it was provisionally called.

"Fan*tastic*." CeCi clapped and hollered when it was over. "I love you sooo much. Next time, I hear the *whole* band version."

The party split up in the early evening when the wine ran out. CeCi wanted to order up more she was having so much fun, but leaving their address and current phone numbers, Dwayne and Desdemona called it a day.

"At least let me pay your cab fare," CeCi insisted.

Which, having come by bus, her son and his "best gal" were only too glad to accept.

Fifteen

Now that King's College London, like many British universities, had cut its teaching costs by putting lectures on the internet and conducting tutorials via Skype, Professor Vincent Vinicombe had plenty of time on his hands to pursue his research interests as long as they were guaranteed to enhance the institution's standings in the league tables, and bring in a tidy income via the Research Assessment Exercise. These days, Higher Education was *all* about money. Cuts to courses, cuts to staff, but increases in student fees to in excess of nine thousand pounds per annum for the privilege of rarely seeing a lecturer in the flesh and needing to find the sorts of McJobs Desdemona, Aika, and Maja did in order to pay the rent and eat. Gone were the lazy, hazy days of indolence and flâneuring—except at Oxbridge where all the rich kids went before becoming prime minister, or foreign secretary, or something else important they weren't unqualified for.

Not that Vincent minded. He'd never liked students much anyhow. Smelly and ignorant, he'd reckoned the majority of them to be. And if they now all got the upper- second-class degrees they'd paid for, well, that was market economics for you, wasn't it? He did get cross, mind you, when the little bastards became litigious if they *didn't* receive the degree they felt they deserved.

"Nasty little ratbags," he would tell Janine over supper whenever his dander was up, which was regularly. "Can barely spell their blasted names, and they want top marks. What's the world coming to, one wonders."

"Indeed, Vincent," Janine would agree because arguing with Vinicombe was about as effective as cleaning a lavatory with a toothbrush.

"So much better in my day when only eight percent of the very top brains went to varsity. Nowadays, it's any Tom, Dick or Janet. No wonder they can't get jobs when they graduate. Bally market's flooded with the morons. Plus, a lot of them are *foreign*. How're *they* supposed to understand Early Modern English, for God's sake, when they can't even speak the Queen's English properly?"

"Quite so, Vincent," Janine would comment, pouring herself a fresh glass of Châteauneuf du Pape. She was no longer the sex slave she had once been because, latterly, Vincent found himself less potent than in his younger days, which infuriated him. She remained in his thrall, however, and, given the chance, would have escaped at the earliest opportunity. Had Desdemona known this, she might have been more sympathetic to her mother's replacement and offered assistance. But she didn't because she never spoke to Janine, "the arse-licking snotty little bitch," even on the phone.

"Just imagine how much better it shall be when we finally shuck off the shackles of Europe," Vincent would blithely continue on his hobbyhorse subject of conversation. "No more of those overhyped Erasmus exchange cretins sitting in classes giggling and gawping because they can't tell Thomas Kyd from Billy the Kid."

"You don't actually *have* classes anymore," Janine occasionally dared intervene. "And when I was at uni some of the French students, especially the Sorbonne ones, were pretty much on the ball. Knew all about poststructuralism and everything. Derrida, Barthes, Foucault…" Her voice would trail off as Vincent took to glowering.

"Bah, baloney, just wishy-washy, arty-farty, continental bullshit masquerading as philosophy. No wonder they spoke through their bottoms, *when* they dared speak. I shut them up sharpish when they tried that gobbledygook on *me*, I can tell you."

"Yes, Vincent. I remember. I was *in* some of your classes, if you recall."

"Indeed I do, my dear. And how lucky you were to have me as a lecturer, otherwise you might never have achieved your first-class degree and moved on to postgrad. Jolly fortunate too to have had me for supervisor of your thesis, of course."

"In exchange for sex. Talk about conflict of interest," Janine muttered so sotto voce Vincent couldn't hear through his increasingly deaf ears. Just as well he was too proud to have learnt to lip-read. He saw them move, though, despite Janine lowering her head as she topped up the Châteauneuf du Pape glass that was giving her a smidgeon of Dutch/French courage as usual.

"*What*? What did you say?" said Vincent, cupping his ears.

"Such a range of interesting texts."

"Texts?"

"You taught us."

"Indeed, my dear. Now *if* you'd excuse me? Bladder playing up again."

"With pleasure. I'll wash up as usual."

"So wonderful to have you around," said Vincent, a telltale patch of piss appearing at the crotch of his brown corduroy trousers.

As always Janine shook her head as she cleared the table. How easy it would have been to report Professor Vincent fucking Vinicombe to the authorities for the sorts of sexual harassment now making headlines on both sides of the Atlantic, where women were finally standing up for themselves against the monstrous regiment of men. But now it was too late...or *was* it?

On the occasion Vincent had come storming home screaming blue murder after a visit to the Hackney house, she had dutifully agreed to his assessment of his daughter as an "ungrateful bitch just like her mother," and listened sympathetically to his account of the other people present including the "three total Neanderthals who played in some rock 'n' roll band called The Fubars and couldn't tell a madrigal from magpie. Horrid, repulsive, op*ini*onated young fools," he'd declaimed, stamping up and down the lounge kicking at waste paper baskets. "If I ever find out Desdemona has linked up amorously with one of them and the bastard is *living* there, I'll have his balls for breakfast. Then I'll take back the house and kick them *all* out."

Reflecting on this while Vincent was off persuading his pesky pecker to be personable, and she was, yet again, squirting washing-up liquid onto dirty dishes, Janine reckoned now might be a *very* good time to mend fences with Desdemona. Apart from anything, she'd heard a number of Fubar tracks on the internet and really liked them. Plus, she'd heard they had a dog in the band, and Janine liked dogs. She'd grown up with a Shetland collie called Shep and grieved for years after he died of rat poison sprayed around the park where she took him for his walkies.

~ * ~

Desdemona's mother Andrea lived in a grey-brick cottage in the tiny village of Llanddeusant near Holyhead on the island of Anglesey and never returned to "The Smoke" as she and her neighbours referred to London. Too much pain she had left behind her in the big city, but that wasn't the only reason she'd headed off to North Wales and then across the Menai Strait to Anglesey. Raised at Grange in Borrowdale near Keswick in The Lake District, she was, by nature, a country girl used to open spaces and had never accustomed herself to the anonymity of London. Young and very foolish she must have been, she often reflected, to have sought the bright lights that promised so much but never delivered. If she hadn't been so bloody clever and got those excellent A-level grades, she never would have gone to King's College, met the youthful Vincent Vinicombe, been swept off her feet, got herself pregnant, and then been locked up in his house in horrid Hackney. Still, she had to be grateful for Desdemona, perhaps the only good thing to have come from those dismal days and still the light of her life.

Apart from the pigs, of course: John, Sylvia, Herbert, and Harriette. They and their offspring lived in one of the barns built as adjuncts to the cottage and were a great source of comfort, as were her two golden retrievers, Barry and Hyacinth, to whom she confided all her secrets as they sat before the log fire during the long winter evenings. She had a TV but never watched it. Too much soapy rubbish for her tastes. And currently, *far* too many programmes about Brexit, none of which were conclusive. How could they be when all they did was recount the latest opinions on reports of other reports of what politicians had or had not said in London and Brussels? It made Andrea's brain hurt. So following her grandmother's dictum that "if you don't use your legs you lose them, and if you don't use your head you lose it," after giving the pigs their breakfast in the mornings, she would walk Barry and Hyacinth across the meadows, and, sometimes take them in the car further afield to the sea. The afternoons she would spend on her only concession to modernity: her computer. Not to surf the Web or blether asininely on Facebook with false friends, but to write her poems or work on the re-re-revisions of the paranormal romance novel she expected never to finish. But that was okay. Nobody would publish the thing anyway in these days of fiction sales plummeting because books had been replaced by smartphones. But it was fun to think she was making something. Other folk in the village made tables or chairs or pullovers or garden ornaments or whatever. Andrea made poems and books.

Then once a week, she would speak on the phone to Desdemona who, bless her, would come to visit whenever she could. Nothing like a nice cuddle with Desdie. The latest she'd heard, the girl was still in the old Hackney house and singing in a rock band called The Fubars. Some *name* when you thought of its derivation but Andrea liked the irony, particularly as she gathered from Desdie it might also double up to be used to refer to Brexit.

Speaking of which, should it finally become clear the UK had succumbed to the will of a dangerously growing bunch of alt-right citizens brainwashed into blind xenophobia by fork-tongued, power-hungry Westminster bandits who were also denying Wales the chance of disentangling itself from them via an independence referendum, she could always hop on a ferry to Dublin. Only took a couple of hours. Pack up the pigs and the dogs and off she would go, reckoning the Irish would be only too happy to welcome her. And she wouldn't be the only one from the village. Plenty of folk she'd talked to were considering the same trip. The majority in Wales had voted Leave in the 2016 referendum but had begun to change their minds once they realized what Brexit would actually mean.

"Not much point in hanging around here and watching the ship sink," had said her nearest neighbour, seventy-six year-old widower George Meredith, who had children and grandchildren in Normandy. "Want to keep visiting the kids, don't I? And not bother with queues and visas and all that bollocks. Want to take Bertie with me, too, like I always do."

Bertie was George's twelve-year-old cocker spaniel.

"Way things are going, he'd have to get special permission and go into quarantine for months, and I ain't having none of *that* bollocks either."

"Blimey, I hadn't thought of that," said Andrea, sipping at her half pint of shandy at a table outside The Green Lion.

"All sorts of nastiness are going to happen we haven't even thought of yet. Plane delays, ferry delays, you name it, it'll be delayed. Stockpiling everywhere there'll be because ships won't be able to get in and out of European ports fast enough," said George, tamping tobacco into his pipe. "Not that I blame the Frenchies or any of the other Euros. Not their fault the bleeding UK went barmy in 2016, was it? What was it that Polish EU president geezer said about the liar politicians who rigged the vote without any proper plan?"

"A special place in hell should be found for them."

"That's it. And so it should be."

And George wasn't the only one of the same mind. Myfanwy at the post office already had her bags packed and at the ready.

"Things ain't what they used to be, girl," she'd told Andrea. "Love Llanddeusant I do. Love *Angl*esey I do. Born and bred here I was. But proper pissed off I am with those bastards in London. Let *them* pick up the shit they're leaving behind, not us poor folk, especially not us poor *Welsh* folk. No Henry bloody Tudor and there never would've been no Act of Union in 1536 anyway."

Myfanwy knew her history.

"And look where it's got us. Second rate country all along and now *this*. Sorry, Andrea love, you being English an' all."

"And thoroughly ashamed of it."

"So you should be, girl, still not your fault. Anyhow, you're part of our family now."

Such were the feelings of all the folk around Llanddeusant Andrea had spoken to on the subject. She imagined the same was true of the whole of Anglesey and, she hoped, of mainland Wales. And Northern Ireland. And Scotland. Maybe the Celts could form a whole new alliance all of their own and eventually find a way of leaving the Anglo-Saxons to wallow in the mire of their own making. The new country, including The Republic of Ireland, could be called Celtland, which would be only too happy to rejoin its European neighbours and friends. A happy thought indeed, which she communicated to John, Samantha, Herbert, Harriette, Barry and Hyacinth one evening in early March and, in their own idiolectal manner, they all agreed.

"Oink, oink, oink, oink, *raaf, raaf*," they said.

Which cheered Andrea. It was good to know the animals were on board.

Sixteen

Had Dwayne Zobinski Snr not been murdered by a poisoned umbrella ferrule jabbed into his thigh as he walked across Westminster bridge, The Fubars and their various family members might only have come together slowly over time in individual dribs and drabs. But you know how it is with murders, the catalytic effect they can have on otherwise mundane circumstances. And such was the outcome of Zobinski Snr's unfortunate demise. Hermione and CeCi were already pals because of the shared knowledge of their sons' whereabouts but with Hermione's offers of help, this event brought them even closer. And once CeCi had contacted Dwayne with the bad news and it was passed on to the other Fubars, they too became involved, Desdemona because she loved Dwayne Jnr, Fergie because he too loved Dwayne Jnr, and the other Fubars, particularly Tosh, because as a group they sympathized with the whole traumatic situation. And, breaking with all tradition, even Andrea made the trip to The Smoke to be with her daughter at the time of her lover's bereavement.

The only folk to buck the trend of this sudden togetherness were Lord Crossbar because he was under house arrest and, anyway, too doolally to understand what had happened, Vincent Vinicombe because he remained "insulted" by his previous contact with The

Fubars, and Janine Humphreys whom Vincent had forbidden from having any contact with his daughter. Mind you, Janine pretty quickly found a way around this ban by marching out of the Plumstead home flipping the finger behind her and taking a bus over to Hackney to offer the sincerest condolences to Desdemona and her young, now fatherless, lover. And you know what? Desdemona accepted them.

And so it was that Zobinski Snr's passing had the sort of unpredictably harmonizing effect of which he would most certainly have disapproved, seeing as harmony wasn't his idea of good business. But, being dead, he had no say in the matter either at the family-only cremation once the police had completed the postmortem and released the body or at the memorial event CeCi organised for what she had begun to think of as her extended family. With Montmorency's help, she commandeered The Ritz's lounge for an afternoon and evening and, on this occasion, it wasn't Play-It-Again-Sam who provided the music, it was The Fubars, who couldn't play a dirge to save their lives and so filled the room with fortissimo rock 'n' roll. There was dancing, there was laughter, and there was inebriation given the amounts of champagne on tap. Even Andrea and Janine buried hatchets deeper during the event by getting very drunk indeed and swapping stories of Vincent Vinicombe, "The Vile" as they named him. In other words, just the sort of party CeCi liked. Okay, she could have been accused—with some justification—of *cele*brating the expiry of her now, very clearly, ex-husband, but that was just CeCi's way. Why weep when you could laugh? A case of no good crying over spilt milk. Hey, in some religions she'd heard of, the dead themselves were happy to be sent off to a better afterlife. In Heaven or Akanistha, for example. Not that Zobinski Snr was likely to be destined for such places. Or would have liked them anyway, unless they could offer some means of making a quick buck, which CeCi deemed improbable.

"Hope you didn't think I did the wrong thing though, guys," she nonetheless told Dwayne and Desdemona back in her suite after all the other guests, including Andrea, Janine, and Hermione had returned to the little Hackney house. Where they were all going to sleep was anybody's guess, but nobody was up for separation just yet, especially not Hermione who needed the opportunity for a *long* talk with Fergie before going home to Piddlington Hall and his crazy father.

"Wrong how, Mom?" said Dwayne.

"Ya know, by having a rock 'n' roll party instead of sumptn serious with readings and speeches an' suchlike. Like they do at proper memorials so folk can get all gloomy."

"It was just you, Mom. The way you are. Plus, how many guys are there who would've stood up and said *good* things about Pop? Like… none? Did he have any friends around here?"

"Some jerk I figured for a Russian, mebbe. I saw him with your father one time here at The Ritz. Zobinski was yackin' thirteen to the dozen about trade deals the pair of them could do with Russia after this Brexit thing, but the Ruskie beat it fast when me'n your old man had a little fight. Otherwise, how should I know about friends? I was home in New York."

"Exactly," said Desdemona. "So don't beat yourself up over it."

"I ain't sweetheart. I just wanted to be clear with you guys is all."

"You're clear," said Desdemona.

"Gimme a hug, babe."

So Desdemona did.

"You want one from me, too, Mom?"

"That would be so great, Dwayney. Let's have us a hugfest."

"Other thing you should be happy about," he said when the all the hugging was over, "is how everybody came together like that."

"Even Janine and me. Even Janine and my *mother*," said Desdemona, rolling a fresh joint and handing it over to CeCi. "Clouds and silver linings and all that. You should be happy about it."

"I am. Hubby would've been pissed as hell seeing us all laughing an' dancin' an' all instead of weeping over his loss, but hey, he wasn't around to see. Not unless you believe in reincarnation, which I don't."

It was Dwayne who returned to Zobinski Snr's only apparent pal. "A Russian guy, you said."

"That's whut it sounded like. I ain't good with foreign languages, you know that. Only the guy did say *da* a few times. Even *I* know that means 'yes' in Russian. Elsewise, he didn't say a whole lot and scooted pretty damn quick when I started beating on Zobinski."

"Who'd been talking about trade deals with Russia."

"Right."

"So it's most likely he *was* Russian. You catch his name?"

"Nope, but you can ask Monty on reception. All guests gotta register with Monty. Why'd you care anyhow?"

Dwayne shrugged. "Just a hunch is all. Only seems to me I heard about Russian agents killing enemies over here with poisons sometimes from umbrellas. Ex-KGB guys and the like under orders from The Kremlin."

"Holy fuck. Zobinski was a lotta things, but an enemy of the *Ruskies?*"

Dwayne shrugged. "Weird stuff's been going down between the US and Moscow for some years, the media tell us. All the way up to the White House, even though Klank is hollering he's been 'exonericated' of the whole deal."

"Yeah, I heard about that. Some lying asshole."

"You got that right, Mom. Only Klank don't care about lies. In his fake world, they only make him stronger."

"On the button, kiddo. So you want I should call Monty right now? I could do that."

"Sure, why not? Can't hurt."

Which was how Dwayne came to be apprised of the identity of Anatoly Munchkov and was the following day to pass on the name and his, albeit possibly tenuous, suspicions to Scotland Yard's Special/ Anti-Terrorist branch.

~ * ~

It was around ten p.m. when Dwayne and Desdemona left The Ritz and again headed back to Hackney in the cab CeCi had insisted on at her expense.

"Fuck knows how much money Zobinski'll leave us in his will, *if* he ever bothered making one," she'd told Dwayne. "Knowing him, damn likely none. Good chance he was stony broke and we'll find all *we'll* get left is a shitstorm of bills. Meanwhile I ain't poor, so take… the…cab fare, or I'll disown you."

"Some mother you have there," said Desdemona as they sat in traffic around Piccadilly Circus.

"She is kinda unique, but I like her. Looking forward to meeting yours. I was too busy playing in the band for conversation. Looked cute, though."

"Whoa there, big boy," said Desdemona in a pretty decent American accent. "*I'm* your gal, right? No glad eyes for my *mom.*"

Dwayne shrugged and grinned as they phutted along another few hundred yards. "Good to know how *you'll* look when you get to her age though."

Hiatus while Desdemona digested this comment.

"Meaning?" she said when the hiatus was over.

Dwayne shrugged again, smiled, and took an unnatural interest in a jewellers' shop window.

"Tell the lady it's a proposal," advised Jerry O'Driscoll, the cab driver, through the intercom. "You don't, I will. And let me tell you, I'm competition for any guy."

Dwayne laughed. "I was only foolin' around. It was just a throwaway remark."

"To such a beautiful young lady? I don't think so. And don't go telling me about slips of the tongue," said Jerry, who knew his Freud. "You might never find another…"

Jerry's voice tailed off, his attention distracted by a Rolls Royce cutting in ahead of him. "Watch it, tosser, or I'll scratch your paintwork," he yelled, evidently enjoying himself.

Dwayne took Desdemona's hand and squeezed it. "The guy has a point."

Desdemona squeezed right back. "About the Rolls?"

"About slips of the tongue."

Desdemona squeezed a little harder.

"But let's just wait a while, huh? We're kinda young and all sorts of stuff could happen meantime," Dwayne said as the taxi lurched around the Roller with Jerry tapping his forehead meaningfully at the driver.

The trip to Hackney that would have taken maybe half an hour as the crow flew, in fact took an hour and fifteen minutes during which Jerry told Dwayne and Desdemona how he'd been brought up the eldest of eight kids in Belfast during The Troubles and come to London to seek his fortune, but "what with Brexit and all that shit" was now thinking of going back home then slipping over to the Republic before the border closed and joining up with a brother of his called Seamus in Dublin.

You know how it is with cab drivers, how if you make any kind of verbal contact with them they'll tell you their life stories? So it was with Jerry. Not that Dwayne and Desdemona minded. Just snuggled up together and watched as images of the richest part of London slowly morphed into the very different vistas of its northeastern outposts. Desdemona leaned through the driver's window and kissed Jerry when they finally arrived at her front door and he offered to cut the, by now, ludicrous cost of the trip by ten percent "in the interests of true love."

"Not on your nelly, my friend," she told him. "Traffic isn't *your* fault, is it? Dwayne, give the man his money, would you?"

Which Dwayne did from the wad of notes CeCi had given him, in the process adding a fifteen percent tip.

"Nah, nah, man I *couldn't*," Jerry protested.

"Sure you could, sounds like life's been tough enough already. And hey, good luck with the Dublin deal. Who knows, one day we might see you there."

Taking the money, Jerry said, "Wouldn't want you fellas thinking I was tellin' you sob stories just for the money. As God is my witness, I..."

"Never mind God. I'll always remember you as the guy I could have married if I didn't marry *this* guy. Think of yourself as Cupid," said Desdemona, elbowing Dwayne in the ribs. "And if it doesn't work out, I'll come looking for *you*."

Dwayne frowned and pouted comedically.

Smiling, Jerry hit the accelerator and returned to trawling the streets for clients.

Meanwhile, Desdemona already had her key in the door, behind which she could already hear a low-thrumming hubbub of voices.

Seventeen

Hank Laplanque was pleased with Anatoly Munchkov's work.

"Nice goin', Ana," he told him over cognacs and burgers at his NYC office.

Anatoly didn't like being called Ana, but there wasn't a lot he could do about it. Laplanque paid his wages, which gave him the right to call him anything he liked.

"Thanks, a pleasure," he said in English a lot better than he'd ever allowed Zobinski to believe. What Zobinski had needed to think was he was dumb.

"An' not just the killin', though that was pretty neat. You done good with the research, too. Findin' out about Zobbo's little plans to make his megabucks with Moscow after the Brexit screw up. I needed to know that. None of those ideas in his head an' the guy wouldn't be dead."

"Now we have to be careful though, Mister Laplanque. Nothing must lead back to us. Already the story is all over your newspapers. Russia suspected of killing US citizen in the UK? What did Klank know about it?" Munchkov raised both eyebrows.

"You got that right, Ana. Inneresting he ain't said *nothing* about it though."

"Never going to happen, Mister Laplanque. Still up to his neck in Russia shit he is, never mind the AG's whitewash. Also Zobinski's plans have Klank's worldview all over them. Nothing he would like better for the US economy than the UK, all on its ownsome, to deal with trade tariffs without the protection of the Europe market. How he'd love it if the same happened to Germany and France and all the rest of the EU countries so they could *all* be picked off. Schtum is gonna be his most likely policy. Mebbe call the murder a terrible crime or some such shit, otherwise just wait, watch, and hope there're *no* links to him, right? And if some surface, he'll start bitching about fake news and change the story like always."

"Good thinking, Ana. Which leaves us home free to do all the deals we want."

"It's how I see it. The cops may poke around for a while, but they'll find nothing. I'm a guy who don't leave traces, and no way is Moscow gonna get involved. Anybody asks, my guys'll deny I even exist."

Laplanque laughed. "Nothing so good for business as a first-class fubar, huh? While the cat's away the mice will play."

"Fubar?" asked Munchkov, whose American vocabulary didn't stretch that far.

"Situation 'Fucked Up Beyond All Repair.' Or 'Fouled Up Beyond All Recognition' you wanna be polite about it. It's one of the military's old World War Two sayings."

"When the US and the Soviets were *also* on the same side."

"You got that right, Ana. Top up your cognac?"

Munchkov smiled and passed over his glass.

"Now how about we get down to stealing Zobbo's little plan," said Laplanque. "Like how we make big time money from this nice new market. A whole *load* of goods those Brits are gonna need when they can't get them cheap from Yurp no more. Already, they're stockpiling pharmaceuticals so's folks don't die in hospitals and on the streets, right?"

"And that's not all. Soon it'll be food, and booze, and car parts, and Christ only knows what else."

"Which we will find a way to provide."

"*Zazdarovje*," said Munchkov, raising his glass.

"Huh?"

"Cheers."

"Ah, ookay, right. Here's to us," said Laplanque, clinking his glass against Munchkov's. "And to money. Gazillions of greenbacks."

"Money," Munchkov agreed. "Lovely, lovely, *money*."

~ * ~

As noted (see above), given King's College's cost-cutting yet profitable self-teaching programmes, Professor Vincent Vinicombe had plenty of time on his hands. And this he used not only to do his Renaissance drama research and write his drum-thumping pro-Brexit articles for the highest bidder on Fleet Street, but also to spy on his Hackney house. Why? Because he nurtured dark suspicions Desdemona had something far deeper going on with one of the frightful rock 'n' rollers he'd met there than she admitted and, should he be able to prove it, Vincent intended to turf the whole bunch out onto the street. With the exception of Desdemona, that was. *That* little leftie whore he would drag over to the Plumstead house newly vacated by the ingrate Janine where he would teach her a few lessons about proper daughterly behaviour including shopping, cooking, cleaning, clothes-washing and ironing. A man needed a woman around the house.

So it was that, disguised as a policeman, Vincent took to lurking and skulking in the vicinity of the Hackney address, hiding behind the few sparse trees, the garden walls of a derelict house, and anywhere else he could find shelter from prying eyes. In one hand, there would always be either a police-type notebook in which he pretended to jot notes or a smartphone with "Police" written on it which he used for urgent faux conversations. If ever questioned as to the reason for his presence by a passerby, he would tell them he was on a top-secret mission and to mind their own bloody business or he'd arrest them for interfering with police matters.

Vincent's suspicions of filial misbehaviour were confirmed on only the fifth day of these research activities when he espied Desdemona and the American Fubar oaf waltzing down the street together hand-in-hand, stopping every few steps to off-load their shopping bags, then falling into each other's arms and kissing before picking up the bags again and letting themselves into *his* house.

"Ah, *hah*," said Vincent Sherlockly. "Swine, vermin, de*fol*iator," he spat, confusing a deflowerer with a defoliator, which is a leaf-trimming machine. "Begad, I'll see the young devil in Hades."

On this occasion there was, however, little PC Vinicombe was able to do about it, except of course, to return on a quotidian basis to Hackney to confirm his suspicions. Which was how it came to pass that, on the occasion of Zobinski Snr's memorial bash, Vincent in his phony uniform was again stationed in the proximity of the house doing his lurking and skulking. But this time, it wasn't the appearance of Desdemona and Dwayne that got his dander up. *This* time it was the fleet of cabs in the early evening that had disgorged more of the detestable Fubars, Desdemona's girl tenants, and after they'd staggered into the house, three other women, a willowy posh-looking one, then two others, one of whom was his ex-wife, and the other his ex-girlfriend.

It would certainly have been better for Professor Vincent Vinicombe's professorial and journalistic credibility had he *not* then lost what remained of his mind, rushed across the street and confronted Andrea and Janine with bestial grunting noises, vicious Early Modern English oaths, and intimations about what he intended to do to them for their treachery. Certainly it would have been preferable for his reputation had he not also taken first Andrea then Janine by their throats and started shaking them about. *In*finitely better it would have been for him to slink off quietly and lick his wounds, particularly when Andrea resorted to the Women's Protection skills she'd secretly learnt at a Hackney gym before leaving the marital home. Nasty indeed, but effective, were the kidney chops and testicle kicks she administered while he was trying to strangle Janine.

"Oooofffff, aaaaggghh, grrrrerch," he said as a result, before collapsing to the pavement groaning. Adroit with witty ripostes, trenchant rejoinders, and acid putdowns professors of Renaissance Drama may be when under verbal attack, they're normally crap at proper fighting.

Anyway, it was these scenes of male on female violence that caused next-door neighbour Maggie McPherson to dial 999 and call the cops.

"One of yours is down and moaning," Maggie told PC Susan Rankin. "And bleedin' well deserved it he did. It was him what started it. Threatenin' the two women with death and worse he was. Lucky they let him go with only a bloody good bollockin'. Me, I'd've gouged his eyes out."

"One of *ours*?" said Susan.

"Got a copper's uniform on. Had both of them by their throats he did, only the older one gave as good as she got. Better, as a matter of fact."

"Okay, I'm sending a car," said Susan. "This better not be a hoax."

"No hoax, missus, as God is my witness."

"All right then," said Susan, reckoning God would have worse things to witness, like global climate change in the world he was supposed to have created, for example. Also, which god was the woman on about? Hackney boasted loads of gods. Still, the woman seemed kosher enough, so off the car was dispatched, sirens screaming and blue lights flashing. PCs Janet Robertson and Norman Jenkins were on the scene in ten minutes, by which time the Hackney house had emptied of its occupants, all of them out on the street wondering what was going on. All minus Desdemona and Dwayne, of course. They were still at The Ritz with CeCi.

"What's all the bother then?" asked Norman, as Janet checked whether Vincent needed CPR and was pleased to find he didn't but displeased when he sat up, groaned, and puked on her trousers.

"Fuck's *sake*," she said. Then to Norman, "This ain't one of ours, Norm. Not even a proper copper, I reckon. Fancy dress is what he's got on. I'm taking it off to get a better look."

"Not his pants, Jan. Leave his pants on."

"Just his jacket and his helmet, Norm."

"Good, right, *okay*," said Norman, turning to the crowd around him. "Anybody recognize this geezer, do they?"

And, of course, with the exception of Hermione, they *all* did. Andrea and Janine obviously, both of them still nursing bruised throats, but also the three Fubars plus Aika and Maja. Identification was pretty straightforward. This was Desdemona's dad, professor of Renaissance Drama at King's College, Vincent Vinicombe.

"Bleedin' *prof*, eh?" said Janet, who had little time for academics.

"Wanker," muttered Norman, who had no time at all for them.

And so it was, after statements had been taken from all those out on the pavement, that Vincent was arrested on two counts: attempted grievous bodily harm and impersonating a policeman, the latter an even more serious charge than the former.

"Get him on his feet, Jan, and we'll stick him in the car," said Norman.

"Gonna need a hand there, Norm."

"You got it, babe," said Norman, who'd seen a lot of NYC cop shows.

Then having ducked Vincent's head and dumped him in the back seat, off they sped, sirens and blue lights again on full blast. Not the sort of exit from his Hackney vigil Vincent would have wished for, but you know how it is with hubris. How nemesis is always prowling around the next corner.

Unsurprising it was that Desdemona should have heard such a hubbub behind the front door when she inserted her key in the lock after she and Dwayne had been dropped off by Jerry O'Driscoll.

Eighteen

As far as they went, Anatoly Munchkov's assumptions about Dougal Klank's silence over the Zobinski case were spot on. The president *was* still up to his neck over allegations of both collusion and obstruction of justice as regards his relations with Russia and in no mood for yet further aspersions, especially not one that linked him, however distantly, to a murder even his pals at Fox News were uneasy about. So omertà *was* the best plan plus, as Munchkov had predicted, a few crocodile tears over the tragic loss of a US citizen on shores thousands of miles away if push came to shove. Otherwise wait and watch.

Trouble was the story wouldn't go away because "enemies of the people" like *The Daily Washingtonian* and *The New York Insider* inter alia across the nation wouldn't let it. Pissed off at the AG's four-page partial absolution, they were still in the hunt—"witch hunt" as Klank dubbed it—for *any* evidence that would link him to criminal practices. As was the Justice Department's Special Counsel, Richard Michaels, who, like the rational press, was angered by the Klank-appointed AG's virtual dismissal of his findings and continuing to sniff here and there and everywhere for evidential material. On top of all that, there were the bitches in the House of Representatives who wouldn't give the president *any* money for *any*thing, let alone building a wall across the country to keep even more enemies out. There were even Republicans in the Senate who were losing the faith, for crissakes. Plus, of course, there was the bullshit chatter all across the Twitterzone as a consequence of all of which, despite the accustomed bravado, even psycho Klank was beginning to feel the icy chill of potential presidential lame duckness; a prospect he relished about as much as eating a turd-filled burger. And now this fucking murder! How many more lies did he have to tell till *all* the people believed he was the saviour of the nation?

"Goddammit to hell and back, Jacko," he hollered at his latest Chief of Staff, Jackson Truman whose parents, as the name suggests, had had presidential ambitions for their son, only to see them dashed by a series of nefarious business dealings before and after the 2008 crash and, like Zobinski and Laplanque, a neatly sidestepped jail term. Just the sort of guy Klank needed to cover his ass after all his predecessors had so signally failed.

"You gotta get *all* of these dingbats off've…my…*back* like to*morrow*. Elsewise, Jacko, no more pay checks for *you*. No more dinner parties at the White House, no more insider schmoozing, no more *no*thing for you. You heard how guys can get themselves stiffed around here, right? And nobody does it better than me. Nobody does *no*thing better than me."

"I hear you," said droopy jowelled Jackson, peering forlornly around what was once the Oval Office but had become the Round Office since Klank refurbished it with mini tees and fairways to reflect his prowess at golf. "Only…"

"Only *whut*?"

"Nudn."

"You were goin' to say sumptn, Jacko."

"Only," said Jackson, in a moment of mind-blowing epiphany opting to tell the truth for once and fuck the consequences. He'd screwed up so many times, how could one more make a difference? "Way I heard it, the dead guy texted you over some plans he had for US trade in Europe after the Brit Brexit deal. Some kinda approval he wanted for that. Any truth in the story? Could be bad news we'd have to eliminate if you gave any reply."

That's when puce-faced Klank climbed out of his presidential chair behind his presidential desk and hissed, "*More* fake news, where the fuck d'you get this from?"

"Sources," said Jackson, starting to wish he'd never had his epiphany.

"Sources horses, horses for courses. *What* sources?"

Jackson shrugged. "Just...sources."

"What're you hiding, Jacko? Who're you protecting?"

"Nudn, no one. Just trying to cover your back is all, Mister President."

"You got one minute to fess up, bozo, or you are *his*tory."

Once the minute was over, and Jackson continued to withhold the name of Janice Madely, the girl in the Special Ops office who checked all the internet correspondence, Klank went apeshit.

"TELL ME," he shrieked. "OR YOU'RE *FIRED*."

Jackson sucked in his cheeks and stared off as Klank took to hurling golf sticks and balls at walls, pictures, and statuettes of past presidents—and Jackson Truman's head. Unsurprisingly, given how bad Klank was at golf, none of them hit its target. But Jackson was, nonetheless, shaken *and* stirred.

"Holy *shit*, Mister President," he ululated, ducking and diving as Klank stumped around the Round Office picking up objects and smashing them.

While this was happening, Jackson Truman made what was possibly the best decision of his saddo life so far, namely to yell, "I *QUIT*, anyway," head for the door, advise Klank's personal shrink Doctor Fritz Finkelstein his patient needed urgent treatment, then do a runner back onto Pennsylvania Avenue, hail the cab that would take him to Ronald Reagan airport, and buy the ticket that would fly him to Missoula, Montana, where his parents had lived so far from the madding crowd for so long they'd become nonagenarians. Jackson reckoned his chances of reaching *that* age were minimal, but better to give it a shot than fester forever in the mire of the White House

~ * ~

Chief Superintendent Marvin Matheson at Scotland Yard's Special/Anti-Terrorist branch was interested in Dwayne Zobinski Jnr's suspicions about Anatoly Munchkov's potential involvement in the killing of Dwayne Zobinski Snr.

"And you're sure, sure, *sure* it was Munchkov your dad was meeting at The Ritz," said Marvin, twiddling a Special/Anti-Terrorist branch biro between a thumb and an index finger.

"My mom saw them together in the lounge. My old man was doing all the talking about some Brexit deal, and the dude wasn't saying much, but she was pretty sure the guy was Russian."

"From the accent?"

"Plus some Russian word she understood. But then we asked the desk guy. Who has to check all the guest names."

Matheson nodded. "And."

"He said the name was Munchkov. Anatoly Munchkov."

"Pretty stupid of him to use *that* name."

"Huh? It's not his real one?"

"One of them. Also known as Vassily Kuznutsov, Alyoshenka Popovski, and Pavushenka Kazychansky amongst many others. But Munchkov was the one known to us when we sent your dad a letter telling him to pay us a visit."

"Because?"

"We'd heard a lot of rumours of some Americano/Ruskie business deal they were cooking up together. Plus Munchkov was suspect numero uno for offing two ex-KGB spies turned informers to the Yanks and the Brits."

"And Pop showed up?"

"No. Maybe he'd been warned off. Who knows? But then he got dead, so it was too late anyway."

"But Munchkov, or whatever else you call him, is still the one you reckon did it?"

"Makes the most sense. Some kind of a disagreement between partners maybe. Who was the boss and who was just the runner, that kind of thing. My info, such as it is, tells me Munchkov was sick with only ever playing second fiddle. Possibly that was his motive for taking your old man out of the picture."

Matheson shrugged, splayed his hands, and stared at the ceiling. "Not that we can *prove* it, of course. That or anything else. Look, kid, I shouldn't be telling you any of this. If you weren't Zobinski's son, I wouldn't have, but..."

"I get it. I just thought it might help."

"And in a way it has. Is there anything else you think I should know? Like, did your dad still have contacts in the US, or was he just a loner playing his own game?"

Dwayne shook his head. "I dunno. I was locked away in school over here. Me and Pop were never close, anyhow. He was a very secretive person."

"Maybe I should speak to your mother?"

"You could, but I doubt she knows more than I do."

"So no names we could link up with in New York? Like who your dad worked with before he made the switch to the UK?"

Distant bells rang in Dwayne's head.

"Well there was one guy, lemme think."

"Take all the time you want. Coffee?"

"That would be great."

Maybe it was the caffeine that jerked Dwayne Jnr's memory, or just some random collision of otherwise disjunctive neurons, but whatever it was he then said, "There was some Wall Street guy called Leplank, Hank Leplank. Kept coming around to the house saying the firm wasn't making enough money and it was all Pop's fault. Mom hated the guy. Called him Hank the Plank, and said he was full of shit."

"And he's still in New York?"

"Far as I know. Everything went quiet after Pop quit. Or better was fired. According to Mom, anyhow. Sorry I can't be more helpful."

"Maybe you have been. Who knows? In the spook world, every little helps. In any case, thanks for your time. I'll check out the Leplank angle. Meanwhile, I'll call a car to take you home."

~ * ~

As a result of Dwayne Zobinski Snr's sudden and premature demise, Lady Hermione Barr had also missed her second attempt at a protracted mother-to-mother appointment with his widow, but that no longer mattered because at The Ritz memorial party she had both been reunited with Fergus Ulysses and had the opportunity for a brief chinwag with CeCi—a case of two birds with one stone.

"So sorry for your loss," she began, but CeCi waved that away.

"No need to be. There's loss, then there's gain," she said, at which Hermione nodded empathetically. Some day she would tell her new American friend about Lord Crossbar's latest humiliation from which she currently could see no prospect of gain. But today wasn't the time. The pair of them were sitting at a table relatively secluded from the din made by The Fubars.

"Anyway, now finally you might tell me how you came to find out where my Fergus was."

"It was all down to my son Dwayne, honey. Seemed he owed it to the kid."

"For?"

"You don't know?"

"Not the full story. There were whispers from the headmaster, but no more than that. More than his job was worth and so on."

"Some asshole, huh?"

"You could put it that way. Care to fill me in?"

So CeCi told the full fubar tale while Hermione's eyes widened.

"Gosh," she said, as CeCi poured them both champagne refills. "And all because of Fergus's initials?"

"Yup. I guess you guys don't speak too much American."

Hermione laughed. "I suppose not. But I'm perfectly sure young Dwayne meant no harm."

"I believed him when he said so. He just misspoke, the way he tells it, and I believed him. Okay, so I'm biased but even so, I know the kid ain't got a bad bone in his body. *Any*how, all I did was suggest he might follow the trail and say sorry."

"Which he clearly did with great success. Just look at the pair of them now," said Hermione, turning in her chair to look at The Fubars' lead and rhythm guitarists.

"Yeah, ain't that so great?"

"It surely is. And how...?"

"Don't ask, honey. I don't know all the details myself. Dwayney can be a little cagey like his dad. I guess we should just both be happy they are where they are. Dwayney is also in love with a wonderful gal by the way. Desdemona her name is. You see the blondie in the backing group?"

Hermione turned to peer. "*Very* pretty," she said.

"Indeed. A great kid, lemme tell you. I met her already. And she could just be my new daughter-in-law."

"Gosh, you must be so happy."

"I am. And," said CeCi, "you gotta keep this all to yourself, Hermie okay? Say *nudn* to Fergie when you finally meet up again."

"Keep what to...?"

"You see the little Japanese babe next to Dezi. Aika is her name?"

"Yes. So?"

"So rumour is she's the new light of your Fergie's life."

"Fergus is in *love*, too?"

"Can't you see it in his eyes when he turns around to her when he's playing a good riff? Look, he's doin' it now."

Hermione watched as her son's fingers raced up and down his guitar neck, and his eyes swivelled around to glitter at Aika, who smiled back while bop-shoo-wopping her heart out.

"My son...in love," she said. "Whoever would have thought it?"

CeCi smiled. "There's still some good in the world. Don't always look that way but..."

"There's still hope."

"A little, but yes."

The optimism of this conversation stayed with Hermione for the duration of the cab ride back to Hackney, although much of it drained away when she alighted and watched on aghast during the assault on Andrea and Janine. So much for good in the world when such things could happen, she reflected. Nonetheless, once justice was done and Vincent Vinicombe had been driven away kicking and screaming by the police, there remained sufficient positivity running through her veins to want to set matters straight with her long-lost son. So it was that after she and The Fubars had settled Andrea and Janine in the lounge and comforted them as best they could, she took Fergus Ulysses to one side and asked if they might have a little chat.

"It's been *such* a long time, darling," she said, "and there are *so* many things I want to tell you. Could you perhaps spare me a few minutes?"

"Um, erm, well…" said Fergie, unsurprisingly hesitant given the more or less total absence of a past relationship with the mother now addressing him as "darling."

"It's just that I need you to…"

"Forgive you?"

"N-no, it's just that…"

"Because it's too late. Too much has happened. I'm different now and…"

"Fergus, is there not somewhere more private we could go?" said Hermione, looking over her shoulder at the still shaken Andrea and Janine. "Just the two of us."

Fergie sighed. "Come with me upstairs. I have a room there."

Which was where the normally resolute Hermione, steeled in sangfroid since her quasi-noble birth, collapsed on the bed, broke down, wept, and left Fergie with little option but to pat her on the back and say, "There, there, what is it?"

And through the tears out it all spilled, the whole bag of works: the barely clandestine relationship with Sir George "Ginger" Wigglesworth in Hampstead, her lack of love for Lord Xavier whom she'd dubbed "Crossbar" even before Fergus had become "Fubar," her deep regret for having spent so little time with her son, but her gladness now she had found him again.

"Juh-just suh-so you're in the picture," she said when she stuttered to a halt. "And it's *not* your forgiveness I'm asking for," she added pulling herself together. "Such should not be the burden for a son. For God maybe, if there is one, but not for a son."

"What then?"

"Understanding perhaps? I was rich, I was lonely, and I made mistakes. Yes, I am your mother, but I am also a woman."

Fergie nodded and laid a hand on her quivering shoulder. "It's okay. Dad was always a bit of a tosser," was the best he could manage verbally, untutored as he was in consoling mothers for their past peccadilloes. Hermione took the hand and squeezed it.

"And this Ginger bloke?"

"Is history, Fergus, you have my word. But what I want you to know is that through all the years we were apart I always thought of you. Always knew I should have been there for you, but..."

Hermione's tears came again.

"'Should have' doesn't count, Mum. I've learnt that. The past is gone and there's no good looking back. You can't change it."

"Thu-hat's wu-what CeCi says."

"Dwayne's mum? You've been speaking to her?"

"Yes. We're friends, or almost. It was through *her* I found *you*."

"How?"

So Hermione outlined the manner in which she and CeCi Zobinski had come together.

"She's a wise woman," said Fergie when Hermione drew to a close with details of the recent Ritz conversation. "And if you're worried about your chequered past, don't be. CeCi's beats everyone's into a cocked hat. And you know what? She couldn't give a monkey's."

Hermione squeezed Fergie's hand even harder and laughed. "Wise woman, eh?"

"Dwayne thinks she's the bee's knees."

A pause while Hermione took her son's other proffered hand and squeezed that too.

"And is it possible that you might...?" she said when the pause was over.

"Feel the same way about you? Why not? Let's forget the past and look to the future, shall we? Draw the famous line underneath what's gone and can't be re-lived."

"So you *do* forgive me?"

"Mum, I thought we'd been through that."

Hermione climbed off the bed and hugged her son, who hugged her right back. "Clean slate?" she said in mid-hug.

"The cleanest."

"You are an angel. Now, tell me all about your new life, The Fubars and all that," said Hermione, taking care not to break her promise to CeCi by mentioning her son's new lover.

So Fergie obliged, telling the whole tale from the moment he ran away, which took the better part of ten minutes.

"Gosh," said Hermione.

"And Dad?" Fergie asked when the story—including Aika's part in it—was over. "Sorry about making him bang his head on the windscreen, but I was cross."

"And with every justification."

"Got better afterwards, did he?"

"Not exactly," said Hermione, outlining the current state of Lord Xavier Barr's mental health and the reasons for which he was incarcerated in a stable with a horse called Nemesis at Her Majesty's pleasure.

"Ooops, sorry," said Fergie.

"Don't be. As you said, he was always a bit of a tosser. What goes around comes around."

"Ain't that the truth," said Fergie in Dwaynespeak, taking his mother by the hand and suggesting they go back downstairs so she could be properly introduced to his new friends, particularly Tosh to whom he owed so much, but also to his girlfriend Aika. And of course Mutt, who was the best dog he'd known since Woofer and Barkie, aka William and Lucy.

Nineteen

Stuck between a piece of granite and a hard place, Prime Minister Penelope Pringle would dearly have loved a son of hers to be as understanding as Fergus was towards his mother. But Penelope didn't have a son, or a daughter, in whom she could confide. She didn't even have a dog or a cat to stroke on those dark nights after yet another day of being mocked and battered by the media, the eurocrats of Brussels and members of her own party who were divided between those who hated her for not delivering a hard enough Brexit, and those who hated her for delivering Brexit at all. She *did* have a husband called Percy, but a fat lot of good *he* was when it came to offering comfort.

"So sorry, sweetie, just popping out for a meal with the chaps," was his standard line whenever she returned to Downing Street after a hard day's battering. "Speak later, p'raps. Toodle pip till then. Meanwhile, chin up, fight the good fight and so on, eh?"

Ironically, although he didn't exactly offer comfort either, one of the least effective of her enemies in parliament was Opposition Labour leader Jeffrey Creasey—*Greasy* to his many detractors. In principle, he should have been one of her fiercest critics on the Brexit issue but, mercifully for Penelope, rarely mentioned the subject in case he offended his Trotskyite handlers who were just as xenophobic as the alt-right populist battalions but wouldn't admit to it. Jeffrey did his best to pummel her during Prime Minister's Questions on social issues irrelevant to the worst disaster to befall the country since WW2, but she never understood what he was talking about and could rebuff him with ease.

Anyway, so it was that Penelope spent much of her time out of the spotlight of politics headbutting the same wall (see above), which was getting pretty fed up with it.

Mind you, Mister "Silent on Brexit" Greasy didn't fare much better when he went home at night after yet another ideological day proclaiming the virtues of British socialism circa 1945. Once the darling of the loony left and the recipient of such adulation as "Oooh, Oooh, Jeff-er-ey" during his Trot-handlers-scripted appearance on stage at a Glastonbury festival, Greasy was beginning to feel he was losing his grip on his own party. What his puppet masters were happy to term "constructive ambiguity" on the Brexit question wasn't paying nearly the dividends he'd expected. Far from it. About time he came out of the closet and fessed up to hating foreigners practically as much as Dougal Klank, in which case he should be given the boot, many colleagues believed. Or if he truly *wanted* to win an election, he should forget his "principles" and proclaim long and loudly he was a convinced EU Remainer, in which case, he could expect backing from the majority of his MPs and the party membership. Riven between these two extremes, however, Greasy merely dithered, which was causing splits in the parliamentary party and an increasing number of ex-supporters in the country to quit the party altogether.

Like Penelope Pringle, the public face remained brazenly solipsistic, but in private, he quivered. Back home there were the vegetables in his garden to discuss matters with, and his bicycle to talk to, but that was about the size of it. He had a wife, his third one, but as a Mexican she was pretty pissed off at her husband's "lily-livered" refusal to come clean on an issue which could see so many overseas citizens, possibly including *her*, being summarily deported as non-Brits. Trotsky first or *her* first was his ex-banker wife Lana's main topic of conversation these days. And, just as in parliament, Greasy had no clear answer to that, which produced a lot of domestic Mexican fury.

*Any*way, such was the state of leadership in the main political parties as the time approached when Britain dumped itself out of Europe with no plan for a better deal anywhere else in the world. The Tory party at war with itself, ditto the Labour party. No wonder the nation felt itself leader*less*. Talk about fubars!

Sitting around the Hackney house lounge, the eponymous rock band penned two new songs on this theme, one called "Muppets," the other "Bye Bye Britain."

~ * ~

The equanimity in Hermione Barr's mind after her fruitful reunion with Fergie and the meeting with his lover and new-found friends, only lasted until her return to Piddlington Hall, from which Lord Crossbar had escaped.

"Escaped?" she shrieked at Max and Milly Pratchett when she alighted from the taxi and they came hurrying out to fetch her bags. "*ESCAPED*?"

"'Fraid so, Your Ladyship," said Max while Milly fiddled with the luggage.

"How in the name of *God* did you let *that* happen? He's under hice arrest, or didn't you know? All *sorts* of trouble I could be in now. For heaven's *sake*, I take my eye off the ball for two days and..."

"He just disappeared in the middle of the night, ma'am. Nuffink we could do about it. We was asleep in our quarters."

"And you hadn't set the alarms?"

"'Course we had. As usual. Only he must've turned 'em off before he did the runner."

"Turned them *off*? In his state of mind, the old bastard couldn't have *found* the switch let alone turned it off."

Milly tut tutted at the "old bastard" and went back to her luggage duties.

"Well he must have, mustn't he?" said Max. "Either that or he had an accomplice."

"Of course. *Just who would that be,* Nemesis?" said Hermione. Sarcastically.

"Nah, the horse must've been drugged or sunnink," replied Max. Factually. Max didn't do sarcasm, let alone irony.

"So if not the horse, then *who*?"

"Dunno, do I? Been chattering a lot on the phone recently though, hasn't he, Mill?"

Milly nodded her assent.

"Phone? *Phone*? I left explicit instructions he was to have no *phone*. Doesn't know how to use the bally thing anyway. Where did he get a *phone* from?"

Max and Milly shrugged.

"Mystery innit?" said Max.

"And even if he *had* somehow learnt to use it, what kind of language could he have '*chat*tered' in? Crossbarese? And to *whom*? Pull the other one, Max. Oh God, oh God, what am I to *do*?" cried an increasingly desperate Lady Hermione, tearing at her auburn-dyed hair and peering skywards.

Silence from God.

"Had he been behaving funnily *prior* to the escape?" she continued, pulling herself together. 'Never look foolish in front of The Help' was a golden rule. "I mean, even more funnily than normal?"

Max took an unnatural interest in a shoelace.

"Well, my man?"

Max looked over at Milly, who was carefully arranging the bags on the gravel by the portico to Piddlington Hall. But then, she put them down and came over to support her husband.

"Well, Milly. If you have something to say, now's the time to say it," said Hermione.

Milly looked at Max who nodded, then back at the mistress.

"He did tell me the other day he'd like to be a fairy," she admitted. "Took me a while to work out what he meant when he said 'rifary' was 'fairy,' but when he took to flapping his arms and doing a little dance and looking kinda fairy-like, I got it."

"You mean he's become a homosexual?"

"No ma'am. Fairy as in, like pixie or sunnink," Max corrected. "Reckoned he had wings what would take him away to... um... *Fairy*land."

"So he *flew* away?" said Hermione, patting at her cheeks distractedly.

"No," said Max. "I know that because his bike's gone from the garage."

"The old sit-up-and-beg one?"

"That's it, the ladies' one with the basket on the handlebars. Maybe he'd found a hole in the fence somewhere away from the gates and..."

"Just pedaled away," said Milly, the secret horse doper and gate-opener with whom Lord Xavier had been enjoying regular paid sex until the recent dementia, which had left him uncertain as to where his willy was, let alone how to use it. So much in Xavy's thrall had Milly been that when he'd garbledly asked her to set him free, she'd obliged just as she always had when asked to perform unusual sex acts. And despite the short-term loss of extra income, Max had agreed, reckoning the master would be back soon enough and up to his old tricks.

"So," said Hermione taking out her phone. "And what am I supposed to tell the police they should be looking for? A fairy on a ladies' bike?"

"Well, not an *actual* fairy," Max clarified. "More like an old fat doolally bloke on a ladies' bike who *thinks* he's a fairy."

That was when Lady Hermione went puce in the face and from her lips spilled words not normally associated with her class of person.

"Who the *fuck* d'you think you're taking the *piss* out of?" were the words to which the astonished Max and Milly Pratchett had no ready answer.

"Well?"

Still no answer, only what Lady Hermione read as insolent smirks. Which was how it came to pass that, for their "gross dereliction of duty," the pair were told they could pack their belongings and get the hell as far as possible out of her sight in the next ten minutes, after which Lady Hermione would personally see to it they would remain unemployable as "Help" in Little Piddlington In The Marsh or anywhere else.

A brutal decision on the basis of such paltry evidence, you may say, and with some justification, but like her new friend CeCi Zobinski, Hermione Barr was tired of being fooled around with. Whatever it was the Pratchetts were hiding from her she didn't want to know. And as for finding her demented "fairy" husband, she'd worry about that after six gin and tonics and a good night's oblivion.

~ * ~

At Scotland Yard, Chief Superintendent Marvin Matheson spent some hours mulling over his conversation with Dwayne Zobinski Jnr. Laplanque's and Munchkov's potential involvement in Zobinski Snr's killing was an interesting and persuasive one, but Matheson was still wondering whom the killer had been working for. The Russians? The Americans? Unlikely he was a loner, Matheson reckoned. Over this conundrum and with no evidence on the table, he hummed and hawed long and hard before deciding to take a closer look at the computer files taken from Zobinski's office which, needless to say, were mainly so encrypted as to be more or less meaningless. Until his IT nerds could crack the codes, that was, which would take time unless he gave the breakdown high priority. But murder was murder, even if not of a British citizen, so Matheson was quickly on the blower to super-nerd/hacker Willy Higginsbottom (not his real name) with instructions to pick out any recurrent names, particularly Russian or American sounding ones. And being the super-nerd/hacker he was paid for being, Willy was in Matheson's office within two hours.

"Fast work, Willy. Thanks," said Matheson. "Anything interesting?"

"Most of it's crap, boss. Usual stuff. Bills, lawyers, contacts at the CBI, contacts with UK politicians and Unions et-cet-er-a."

"All of them kosher?"

"They check out, put it that way. Guys and gals with their hands stretched out for the money Zobinski was promising them when his post-Brexit deals went through."

"Preparing the turf."

"Exactly."

"And the Ruskies and Yanks?"

"A sprinkling of those, too."

"Any repetitives?"

That's when Willy's face creased into an ear-to-ear grin. "There're three. You're going to love this, boss."

"Stop it with the loony face and tell me, Willy."

"Okay. So, name numero uno, Dougal Klank."

"The *prez*?"

"Unless he changed his name recently, which I wouldn't put past him. Dumb of him to use his real name though."

"Wow. And what was *he* asking about?"

"Zobinski's progress with the Ruskie deal. Looks like he wanted to build a tower block in Moscow and wanted Zobinski's contacts to help with it."

"It figures. And the other two?"

"The Anatoly Munchkov bloke, the Russian we already have eyes on, right?"

"Right. I'm glad he's in there. And he wanted?"

"The usual, money up front for this and that. Each time Zobinski tells him to go and suck his dick until after Brexit, then they'll talk again."

Matheson nodded and jotted. "And the third?"

"A guy in New York called Hank Laplanque. First of all, I reckoned he had to be some Frenchie with a funny first name."

"But?"

"I made a few calls to pals of mine in the NYPD and FBI."

"And?"

"It turns out he's known to them for money laundering. Originally from New Orleans where there's all kinds of French names."

"Mmm, that's interesting," said Matheson, thinking back to the conversation with Dwayne Jnr and the Hank the Plank who'd kept coming around to the house. The one CeCi had dubbed "full of shit."

"And what was he on about?"

"Looks like news of Zobinski's deals had reached him, and he wanted his cut. Said Zobinski still owed him money from the time he'd worked on Wall Street and if he didn't pay up soon he could look forward to getting stiffed."

"Stiffed?"

"It's an American term, boss. Can mean all kinds of Mafia-type revenge punishments."

"Including murder?"

"It has been known."

"Willy, you are a genius," said Matheson. "Thank you so much."

Higgingsbottom just shrugged, asked if that was all, and headed for the door, leaving Marvin Matheson to mull over the new information he was starting to like. The question was how to use it?

Twenty

Both of them, having been the victims of Vincent Vinicombe's crazed attack, had brought Andrea and Janine even closer together than they had been at The Ritz party. The physical wounds would heal soon enough, but the psychological ones remained. Desdemona suggested counselling, but Andrea, the oldest in the cramped Hackney house, was reluctant.

"I'm sure they're good people and mean well," she said, "but I tried it once after the break-up and good though it was to talk, in the end it was up to me to get my own head straight. Plus, these days there're such long waiting lists that by the time you see somebody you're probably feeling better anyway."

Desdemona had to agree to the second part of this argument. "Yeah, I know. I've heard that. Even teenage kids with serious identity issues having to wait eighteen months for an appointment."

Janine agreed. "Same all across the NHS. Quick fixes they can do, but the long term…forget it. Not their fault. They're understaffed and struggling to provide a service at all."

"Damn government too fixated with Brexit to worry about anything else," said Tosh, who'd had experiences of his own with the social services before taking matters into his own hands and hitting the road.

Nods all around.

"And the Opposition too stuck up its own commie arse to produce anything but platitudes about austerity," said Fergie. "Grand ideas about social welfare, but who's ever seen the plan to pay for them?"

Andrea smiled. These kids were so great. Sure, she and Janine could talk through the Vinicombe madness together and that was already bearing fruit, but she also admired and cherished the support the young ones were offering. That was as helpful as anything a counsellor could give. And not just to her and Janine. They also took good care of each other. The political world could learn a thing or two from them all, Andrea thought. And then, of course, there was Mutt. Animals, dogs in particular, always knew when there was something wrong with their humans, and Mutt was no exception. Every time she and Janine looked sad, up he would come with his big brown eyes and proffer paws on knees and licks, the canine nostrum for all ills, which was impossible to resist. Andrea blessed the day she'd taken the trip from Anglesey and only hoped she'd done her bit to reciprocate the kindness she had been shown in Hackney.

Mind you, she needn't have worried on that score. Janine was "over the moon" at her invitation to stay at the Llanddeusant cottage for as long as she wanted until she found her way again. And she wasn't the only one to appreciate the generosity of Andrea's heart. Speaking for the whole household, perhaps even the normally taciturn Tosh, who had never known his father and begun to forget what his mother even looked like, found his own understated but allusive way of expressing it. Hence the song he wrote called, "Andrea," modeled on John Lennon's, "Julia" but with distinctively up-tempo Fubar additives. Andrea snuffled when she heard Dwayne's first strummed version, but was pretty soon inveigled into a happier mood by a singalong with the whole band. The occasional whispered bop-bop-shoo-wops she and Janine joined in with Desdemona, Aika, and Maja were a tonic in themselves and practically brought the tiny Hackney house down.

Ditto The Fubars' appearance at the Hackney Empire where Andrea and Janine, nervous as kittens, also joined in for Tosh's tribute song. After that, they waved to the crowd and left the stage to tumultuous applause while the band carried on with "Muppets," "Bye Bye Britain," "Liar Fire," and the rest of the set. The encores continued for a full ten minutes with the audience on its feet, so Tosh called Andrea and Janine back on stage for a reprise of her song. *Very* happy was emcee Mikey Lemonde (not his real name). As was ex-EMI record producer Johnny Jimson who, in the dressing room after the show, offered The Fubars contracts for his New Stars label.

"Who would have thought," Andrea said back in the Hackney house at two o'clock in the morning, "that an old biddy like me would find herself in a *pop* group?"

Tosh smiled. "What is it they say? Learning never ends, right?"

That's when Andrea kissed him, and he kissed her right back.

Desdemona shook her head and laughed. "The best mother a person could have," she said.

~ * ~

Unsurprisingly, since he hadn't ridden a bike since childhood, Lord "Fairy" Crossbar didn't get very far along the unmade road outside Piddlington Hall before wobbling uncontrollably and falling headfirst into a ditch. The darkness hadn't helped, nor had riding no hands and flapping the wings he misguidedly trusted would see him on his way to Fairyland.

"Aaaagghh," he said twice, the first time on initial impact, and the second when the bike landed on top of him enclosing his head in the handlebar basket.

His screams were not the only noise in his vicinity, however. Pretty soon they were joined by irritated and perplexed baaing from a ewe called Samantha and her three lambs called Bertie, Florence, and Jennifer, who had lost their way in the adjacent field and bedded down for the night in the ditch.

"Humans!" said Samantha in Sheepish, "what more can they do to us? They eat us, they make our wool into pullovers, and now there's one disturbing our rest."

"And *they* think they're the master race," said Florence, the eldest and most gifted of the lambs.

"You can say that again," said Bertie, who was great at frolicking but not so hot in the brain department.

So Florence did.

"Let's give him a big baa," said Jennifer.

"A protest baa," their mother agreed. "Okay, after three. One... two...and..."

"BAAAAAAAA!"

Having with difficulty managed to extricate his head from the handlebar basket, Lord Crossbar sat up and peered around him, fascinated by what he took to be the voices of fairies.

"Hello, chaps, it's me. Sorry, it is *I*," he said in proper syntactical English.

Why? Because the headlong fall into the ditch had magically reversed the brain injury sustained by banging his head on the Roller windscreen and re-introduced him to the joys of meaningful speech. Not that he noticed the difference, having always believed himself to be making perfect sense even when he wasn't.

"Hang on a mo, I'm coming over to join you," he added, crawling along the muddy ditch towards Samantha and the lambs, who weren't best pleased.

"Oh, for Dolly the sheep's *sake*, he's getting closer. There's no peace with these cretins around," said Florence, for example. "Let's give him another blast. After three again, okay? A-one, and a-two, and a..."

"BAAAAAAAAAAAA."

"Gosh, thanks for the directions," called Lord Crossbar. "How *won*derful it must be to be a fairy. Mind you," he added on reflection. "You *do* sound a bit like sheep. P'raps you're in disguise."

"Silly fucker," said Bertie, who was rebuked by Samantha for his language albeit she agreed with the sentiment.

Bertie stood his ground though. "All the other boy lambs say it."

"I don't *care* what all the *other* boy lambs say, I'm not having a son of mine..." Samantha was continuing in the usual way of mothers, when Lord Crossbar of Little Piddlington In The Marsh suddenly appeared only a few yards away along the ditch.

"By God, you *are* sheep," he said.

"Twat," said Bertie. Giggling while Samantha's attention was diverted.

It was Jennifer who was first to address this meddlesome human in joined-up language. "No we're not, we're wolves in sheep's clothing so watch out or we'll eat you," she said. To no avail, however, even when she bared her teeth, you know how it is when threatened by a sheep in its own language. How hard it is to feel fear.

"There there, nice little sheepie. And baa, baa baadie baa to you, too," was Lord Crossbar's understandably unterrified response.

"Prick," said Florence but, except for Samantha's *malocchio*, that cut no ice either. What with one thing and another, the little sheep family was pretty much at a loss as to what to do next.

Mind you, this potentially tense situation was eased once Crossbar finally reached the ovine family and showed no signs of wishing either to shear or to eat them. Just snuggled up next to Samantha, curled into a foetal ball, and closed his eyes.

"Curiouser and curiouser," said Florence. "Still, if the creature means us no harm..."

Her mother shrugged agreement, licked the peculiar human a bit, and sang it a lullaby.

"Can't do any harm, I s'pose," she told Bertie, Jennifer and Florence, who shrugged and took to nibbling at clumps of ditch grass.

And so it was that Lord Xavier Barr of Little Piddlington In The Marsh spent the most blissful night of his whole life so far and woke up a new man. Call it a dream, call it a bestial epiphany, call it anything you want, but when at daybreak he was awoken by the search party conducted by PCs Bartlett and Tomlinson (no first names) he followed them home as meek as—okay, a lamb.

By then, of course, Samantha and her children were long gone, back to their field waiting to be herded by their pal Colin the Collie.

~ * ~

The US Justice Department's Special Counsel Richard Michaels was the second American official to be alerted in the chain of information regarding Laplanque's, Munchkov's and, at a stretch, even the president's potential involvement in the Zobinski killing. Chief Superintendent Marvin Matheson's first point of call had been his counterpart at the NYPD, Carlos Benitez, who promised an investigation and also said to keep him in the loop, he would be sure to contact Michaels.

"You reckon it could go that far up, Carlos?" said Matheson on the triply encrypted secure line. "It is after all a very long shot. All kinds of dots would need connecting."

"Sure, sure, but anything with Ruskies involved, Dicky Michaels needs to know about, Marv. Guy was on the horn to me only the other day saying anything interesting I heard he wanted to hear, too. Saying the same to PD chiefs all across the country, only to me he was a little more open. Me'n Dicky go back a ways, right?"

"Right. And?"

"This is top secret, Marv, okay? Between you and me only. No media leaks, no telling the wife..."

"I don't have a wife, Carlos."

"Me neither. Best guarantee for a happy life."

"I couldn't agree more. So Dicky Michaels told you...?"

"He'd had a text from Klank's last fired Chief of Staff, Truman Jackson. You heard of him?"

"No," said Marvin who'd lost interest in Klank's shenanigans on the basis the bloke was a psycho who needed impeaching at the earliest opportunity if America wished to remain a democracy.

"*Any*how, what this Truman Jackson dude told Dicky was the reason he quit..."

"Or got fired. Klank normally fires people. He enjoys it."

"Whatever. Anyhow, the reason was he knew the prez and Zobinski swapped texts over the Brexit deal. Which kinda adds weight to what *you're* telling me."

"Holy shit. Conformation of what I told you."

"Holy shit is right. That's why it goes so far up."

"And if we add Hank Laplanque and Anatoly Munchkov to the mix?"

"Then maybe we gonna have us a story, a big *time* story. Great speaking with you, Marv, you've been a big help. I'll pass this up to Dicky soon as we get off the phone."

"Always a pleasure, Carlos," said Marvin, but already the super encrypted line had gone dead.

Twenty-one

During his hearing for common assault at Woolwich Magistrate's Court, Professor Vincent Vinicombe was anything but contrite. It didn't help his mood or case, mind you, to find himself faced by three steely-white-haired, gimlet-eyed female Justices of the Peace all noted for their local and national contributions to matters of women's rights. Three male magistrates he might have cajoled into some form of acquiescence, but in Mesdames Chalmers, Cuthbert and Galsworthy, he met more than his match. It wasn't as though his defence counsel Jonathan Peabody hadn't warned him prior to the appearance to behave himself in court either.

"Look, old chap," he'd told Vincent. "Play your cards *very* carefully in front of the ladies on the bench. You were caught *in flagrante delicto* trying to throttle your ex-wife and your ex-girlfriend, so don't piss around with any claims of false arrest or 'it weren't me, guv, I was nowhere in the vicinity' okay? Apart from eye witness assault statements, the prosecution also has evidence from locals you'd been seen lurking and skulking in the area before."

"Bitches," said Vincent.

"Who?"

"The ex-missus and the ex-girl. Ungrateful bitches."

"I doubt that. They very possibly may be, but you...must...not...say...that...in...court, Vincent. Chalmers and company will have your balls for breakfast."

"Drove me to it, they did. Allowed them the honour of loving me, put a roof over their heads, gave them everything money could buy..."

"A case of money not buying them love possibly?" said Jonathan.

"Took them to King's College parties. Introduced them to other world-renowned academics like me as if they were equals. But were they thankful to be seen in the same room as somebody as prestigious as me? Were they hell as like. No sense of values, just scaredy-cat bitches who ran away at the first opportunity. A man has his honour to think of, you know."

"The sort of thing you should say in court—*not*. Because according to victim statements both A and B, you treated them as skivvies and sex-slaves, Vincent."

"Bollocks, fake fucking news!" spat Vincent, straining at the handcuffs holding him in his chair, thereby pulling it forwards and falling flat on his face.

"Everything okay in there?" shouted PC Janet Robinson from the next room in the cop shop.

"Yes, sort of," Jonathan replied. "But I reckon diminished responsibility's the only way I'll get this bloke off."

"Doesn't deserve to get off," said Janet, marching into the holding cell. "Deserves banging up and the key to be thrown away."

"I...am...not...dim*in*ished," said Vincent once he'd been set back upright. "I am a man who acted entirely within his *rights*."

"Bullshit," Janet called over her shoulder as she headed back to her desk.

Jonathan raised an eyebrow at Vincent, shrugged and headed for the door. "See what I mean about the ladies," he said. "Best watch your Ps and Qs when we get to court, that's my advice.

But did Vincent take Jonathan's advice? No, of course not. Precisely the opposite, just went on and on and *on* about male rights with what he thought of as poignant reminders of the subordinate place of women in the sixteenth century which had Jonathan writhing on his chair for the duration of the half-hour session, while his opposite number, counsel for the prosecution Mack McGinity, smirked contentedly. Six months in pokey without remission, Mack would be asking for and given the way Vinicombe kept glaring at the bench muttering about hags, and "double, double, toil and trouble," he looked sure to get it. Especially with Chalmers, Cuthbert and Galsworthy in charge. Shakespeare scholars they may not be, but they could tell a misogynist from a milkshake any day of the week. Throw the book at him they would if he went on that way.

Which, having taken over his own defence, Vinicombe did in spades, citing the wisdom of mediaeval dunking stools as punishment for adulteresses who'd cuckolded their poor innocent husbands who'd done nothing worse than beat them around a bit to keep them in order.

"Damnable witches of women," he declared triumphantly while Chalmers et al ground their teeth. "Same as the bitches in the US House of Representatives giving dear old Dougal Klank so much trouble."

And so on...and on...and *on*. How women should know their place in society as the sensible Victorians had known only too well, as had the Germans in the same sort of period. Where was it they said women belonged? In the *Kirche und Küche*, that was where, in church and in the kitchen.

More teeth grinding, this time sufficient for prolonged dentistry.

"Bit of a dork, your boy," whispered Mack to Jonathan, who nodded. What else could he do in the face of a diminished responsibility plea that had already bitten the dust? Vinicombe was clearly barking, not through psychological illness, but in a manner too sadly in tune with too many frustrated macho male members of the population to count as abnormal.

"Book throwing imminent," he had to admit. "I did warn him."

But, having convened in the magistrates' room for fifteen minutes, during which Vinicombe had to be restrained from following them by two burly coppers, Chalmers, Cuthbert and Galsworthy returned with a much more subtle punishment than a mere six months in pokey as requested, reckoning that would achieve nothing in terms of reform, in fact might render the accused even more of a recidivist. They knew only too well what male jails were like.

It was Marianne Chalmers who delivered the verdict of "guilty as charged" before announcing the court's requirement of a five thousand pound fine—two thousand five hundred pounds per victim—and a period of six months community service during which Vincent, wearing an orange jump suit bearing the logo "Spouse Abuser," would be required daily to clean the male and female lavatories of King's College. Nothing better than humiliation and ignominy in his very own playground would there be, Chalmers, Cuthbert and Galsworthy reckoned, to bring the old bastard to his knees. And indeed, on hearing the sentence, Vincent quivered satisfyingly before being led away.

It was on their way out of court for lunch at The Horse and Rabbit that Mack McGinity reminded Jonathan Peabody of the old joke about the overworked lavatory attendant who asks his boss if he could take a few days off and the boss says, "Anytime, son. Take them at your own convenience."

Jonathan laughed at that. "No time off for our Vinicombe, though. Got to hand it to the ladies, he got what he deserved."

"Certainly a nifty judgement," said Mack. "Shepherd's pie and pints as usual?"

"Would be very welcome, pal."

~ * ~

Hank Laplanque didn't fare much better than Vincent Vinicombe in his brush with justice. When Carlos Benitez called him at his Wall Street office with an invitation to NYPD HQ at 1 Police Plaza to clarify "certain matters" relating to his relationship with Dwayne Zobinski Snr, Laplanque refused, claiming he'd had nothing to do with Zobinski for years and Carlos could go whistle. "I paid my dues over little misunderstandings in the past and you ain't got nothing more you can hang on me. I ain't got nothing to say about Zobinski, okay? I'm taking the Fifth on this whole issue."

"And the Anatoly Munchkov guy? You never heard of him either, right?"

"Who?"

"The Russian dude the Brits are thinking killed Zobinski."

"Okay, *that* Munchkov. Sure. I read the papers. Only, same as everyone else, that's the *only* way I heard of him."

Benitez sucked at his NYPD special issue pencil. "Only see, we have evidence you were repeatedly in touch with Zobinski over his trade ideas with Russia, wanting your cut. And seeing as Munchkov was in cahoots with Zobinski, I was kinda wondering if..."

That's when Laplanque hung up, booked a flight to Honolulu, and called the cab service to take him to JFK. He was on the cusp of calling Munchkov to warn him to get out of town too, but figuring the Russian's line would be tapped and not wanting *his* call overheard, thought better of the idea.

"Let him stew in his own juice," he muttered, packing an overnighting bag.

Listening in to this call back at 1 Police Plaza, Carlos Benitez smiled.

"He took the bait, Harry," he told his favourite sergeant, "Get your favourite black and white down to Wall Street, willya? Our friend Laplanque needs a ride."

"Hank the Plank like you called him?" said Sergeant Hawkins.

"The same. And make it fast unless you wanna car chase to JFK."

"I kinda like car chases, boss."

"I know you do, Harry. Only you know how they fuck up the traffic. Great for Bruce Willis movies, but..."

"Yeah, yeah, I got it. On my way."

Which was how only three quarters of an hour later Hank Laplanque came to be sitting across the desk from bureau chief Carlos Benitez at 1 Police Plaza.

"You can't do this to me, an innocent citizen," he growled, writhing on his chair.

Carlos shrugged. "I already did. These things can happen when I rilly wanna talk with a person who hangs up on me."

"You have no right. I'm taking the Fifth."

Carlos sighed. "Mister Laplanque, just so we're straight on this, you can't take the Fifth unless you're already in court, okay? And I'm not even reading you your rights because you ain't been accused of anything...yet."

"I ain't *done* nothing."

"So you say, but you might like to take a look at these," said Carlos, sliding across the desk a file of the correspondence from Zobinski's computer in which Laplanque is repeatedly seen demanding cuts from the Russia deal.

Hank blanched as he flicked through the document. "I can explain this. The guy owed me big time, right? All I was doing was asking for what was due me."

"And the Russia deal that keeps coming up? You knew nothing of the details or who the guy was Zobinski was working with?"

"Not a goddam thing. It was his business. All I wanted was the money."

Carlos winced *and* sighed. "All I'm asking, Hank, is you tell me the truth. It's gonna come out anyways, believe me. You can take your Fifth in court all you want, and you *will* be going to court, but you can bet your ass there's gonna be more evidence coming your way. You know how these things go...we guys don't give up easy. Only, look, you quit lying right now and tell me *all* you know, and mebbe further down the line we could be talking plea bargains."

Laplanque chewed at a hangnail, took a deep breath, then sold Anatoly Munchov down the river claiming the whole Zobinski murder idea had been the Russian's.

Carlos nodded. "And you had nothing to do with it."

"Nudn. He was just a guy I happened to come across. I told him he could go fuck an elephant when he told me his plans."

"And there was nobody else involved?"

A pause while Hank chewed at a different hangnail.

"Well?"

"He did say there was some deal goin' down between the prez..."

"The *prez*?"

"Klank. Who *else* is prez?"

"Deal between him and?"

"Ripurpantzov. To build some towers in Moscow. Munchkov and Zobinski were oiling the wheels on that deal. That's *all* I know."

"Holy shit."

"Holy shit is right. Can I go now?"

Benitez nodded. "Only don't try to leave town again, okay? Wouldn't be no use anyhow. From here on in you're under surveillance twenty-four-seven, and you'll be wearing one of those little gizmos on your ankle. The kind that tells us each time you take a piss?"

Laplanque twitched and scowled.

"Harry?" Carlos called out to Sergeant Hawkins. "Gimme some more of your time to fit this guy up and take him home, would you?"

And so it was that Hank the Plank was handed over to the care of Harry Hawkins, who strapped the tracking monitor on Laplanque's left ankle before taking him downstairs to a waiting black and white, ducked his head as he shoved him into the back seat, then slapped the car's roof to signal Officer O'Malley to hit the road.

While this was happening Carlos Benitez was on the phone to Dicky Michaels with a little extra tidbit of info regarding Klank and the Russian connection he figured the Special Counsel might be interested in. And Dicky was interested, *very* interested.

"Nice work, Carlos," he said. "Could get you a big promotion one of these fine days."

"Aw, shucks it was nothing. Just kinda fell into my lap from the Brits at Scotland Yard."

"The special relationship up and running, huh?"

Between the psycho in the White House and the crazy Brexit dame in Downing Street, Carlos didn't think so, at least until they were both removed from office. But this was no time for further fubar speculation. Carlos knew Dicky was doing his best from this side of the pond.

"Let's just hope," was all he therefore said.

Mind you he was pleased at the chuckle he heard down the line before Michaels hung up. If there was anybody who could nail Klank's ass it was Dicky. Clever guy biding his time, picking up any little detail he could, even after the still-contested AG's "exoneration" whitewash, until wham bam end of story Mister President, how about thirty years in jail with no money? Carlos was just glad to have added one more little shred of evidence to the ever growing pile of accusations.

Twenty-two

Once Dwayne Snr was out of the picture, and Dwayne Jnr had been found, CeCi might have been expected to head back to New York and pick up her old life there, but she was starting to like London. She had her painting to keep her busy and was already making connections with art galleries and dealers around town to make a start on UK sales. But she had other projects on her mind too, like being a better mom to Dwayne, for example. Plus she figured she could help out with poor Hermione's situation and offer help to Andrea and Janine should they still need it after Vinicombe's attack. An agony aunt she surely *wasn't* going to be, but a friend she already was and, hey, seeing as she was okay, why not give a little help to those who might not be? CeCi had always been a person with many irons in many fires and she sure as hell wasn't going to stop now. Sooo, a little more time at The Ritz? Why not, especially now she could use Zobinski Snr's shares in the company to negotiate down her suite fees. Plus there was the sex with Montmorency McCloud to take into account. No strings attached, just straight, honest to goodness, heavy sex. There was poor old Josyanne back in NYC to think of, but CeCi figured a gal like Josyanne would understand well enough. She too swung both ways, and with her looks would quickly find a replacement for an oldie like CeCi. Still there would need to be phone calls to work things out, although Josyanne would sure as shit jump at the chance of house-sitting CeCi's Fifth Avenue apartment. So it was, with all these considerations in mind, that CeCi née Bodine and now using that name bedded down in London town.

Of all these projects, however, there was one uppermost in her mind, namely to become part of The Fubars' management team. She just loved those guys, and not only because they were friends with Dwayne, but because they were great young people who wrote great songs and played great music to go with them. In many ways, they reminded CeCi of the lifestyle her own parents told her of back in the halcyon hippy days of sixties San Francisco. Flowers in their hair. Making love not war. Preaching peace and civil rights and most of all protesting their right to be free because times were changing and parents shouldn't criticize what they couldn't understand. Good old Bobby Dylan, who now owned one of her paintings, and poor John Lennon who'd also preached peace and been shot to death on a New York sidewalk for his trouble. What the hell had happened to America since then, she wondered nearly every waking hour and often in her dreams. Crooked Tricky Dicky Nixon had been bad enough, but by comparison with the xenophobic, misogynistic, cheating, lying, conman psychopath currently in the White House, the guy had been an angel. And here were these kids, including her own son, writing the kinds of songs her ma and pa had played to her throughout her childhood, and not only on the record player either, also in person. Mom on piano, Pops on his beat-up old Gibson guitar. How *they* never made it into the music scene she would never know; they were surely good enough. But they were also grade school teachers, and those jobs took priority.

"Gotta keep the little guys in the groove," her mom Plume would say whenever the subject arose. "Music's fun, that's for sure, but it's the kids who're the future."

"Right on, hon," Pops Billy "Ocean" Bodine would agree. "Always those down home battles to fight."

And here CeCi was, half a lifetime later, *still* confronted with the same old battles, made even worse she reckoned by the me-me-mine and greed-is-good messages of the nineteen eighties and nineties. Plus the evils of the social media. Heaven only knew where Plume's and Ocean's "little guys" were now. You'd have thought the barking collapse of 2008 would have taught some lessons, but no siree. Instead, some years down the line we got Dougal Klank claiming on the campaign trail to be the saviour of the poor and disaffected, but once elected being the very opposite, the proclaimer of (him) self above all else. Thank whatever god did or didn't exist for this Fubar group of kids from all over the place singing new songs but with the same old protest messages from way back. CeCi Bodine wanted sooo much to be a part of that. She did what she could in her paintings, but it was the songs old and new that reverberated through her head as lasting tributes to a lost past and, she hoped, a better future.

It was with those thoughts in mind she called Dwayne one Friday evening and asked if she might come over to the Hackney house the following day.

"Sure thing, Mom, you'd be very welcome. Any special reason?"

"A little idea I have. But also I'd just like to be around you and the guys some. *If* that's okay?"

"I'm sure they'd all love to see you."

"Okay, then that's a date. Around what time?"

"Afternoon. You sleep late, right?"

CeCi laughed. "I sure as hell try. See you tomorrow."

~ * ~

As the UK's departure from the European Union continued to be obfuscated and delayed by extensions to the scheduled divorce date, Penelope Pringle went on, and on, and *on* proclaiming she would deliver the "will of the people" come what may. By "will of the people" she meant the four percent margin pro-Brexit decision produced by the serial cheating, lying, and sloganeering from the alt-right eurosceptic branch of the Tories, and dogged "constructive ambiguity" from Labour in the 2016 referendum. In furtherance of this ignoble objective, despite increasingly clear evidence it would spell economic ruin for the UK, she went on blithely tap dancing between bickering members of her own and other parties, as well as trying to sell the re-re-re-revised forty-fifth version of plan omega to Brussels officials who made no secret of their view the woman was either insane or full of shit, or both. It was all very frustrating for Penelope, especially when she smiled her most gormless smile, wore her prettiest most tit-enhancing outfits and applied more make-up than the average Soho harlot, that nobody, and *still* nobody would recognise her superior acumen and agree with her clever plans. Hence, the continued private sessions of headbanging a now badly dented wall at number ten.

The final straw in these troublesome times came on the day Dougal Klank, to stress his America First nationalism as a means of diverting attention from all his crimes and overseas diplomatic failures, announced his policy of selling American goods at inflated prices to all overseas countries except Russia, and imposing huge tariffs on goods imported from them. Which included Yurpeans of course, *and* Great Britain, the very nation with whom he was supposed to have a "special relationship." Penelope was flabbergasted. Had she not gone to Washington to hold hands with the creep immediately he was elected? Of course she had. But was he being nice to her in her hour of greatest need just when she wanted a trade deal with America most? The hell he was, the bastard.

"Aaaaagghhh," she said, as Wall sighed and prepared for further indentation.

Had she known Klank's announcement corresponded so closely to the ways Zobinski Snr, Hank Laplanque, and Anatoly Munchkov had intended to exploit Brexit, and that investigators in London and New York were already sniffing around that trail, she might have extracted some smidgeon of schadenfreude from the situation. But she didn't know. And even if she had, she'd have denied all knowledge and gone on pretending Klank was her best friend. In pursuance of which false hope she got straight on the super-triple-encrypted hotline to the White House and demanded to speak to Klank in person.

"And you are, ma'am?" said a voice sounding a lot like the droid R2-D2 in *Star Wars*. Which cheered Penelope. At least she was talking to one of her own kind.

"The prime minister of the United Kingdom, my man. Put me through to the president *if* you please."

"President is busy," said R2-D2, aka Gregor Klotz, Klank's latest appointee to the chief of staff role.

"Too busy to speak to another head of state?"

"Whut state, ma'am? Ohio? Nebraska? California? Oregon? We got a whole lotta states over here."

"The United Kingdom."

"That ain't one of *our* states, ma'am."

"Of course it bally well isn't. It's another *country*, The United *King*dom."

"Wow, you got a *king* over there?"

"Well a queen actually, but we're *called* a kingdom."

"Jeez, pretty weird, huh?" said Klotz, who'd never had top marks for anything at school, and no marks at all for history or geography.

"*Any*way," said an increasingly irritated Penelope, "what exactly is the president so busy doing he can't speak to me?"

"Signin' presidential decrees, ma'am."

Which wasn't true. What Klank was doing was fiddling with his smartphone to see how many photos of him were being telecast or posted that day, how his new toupée looked in them, whether the gruesome grin face looked better than the asinine grin one, if his latest denunciations of media, political, and legal enemies were gaining 2020 re-electable traction for him...and...so...on. Plus, of course, simultaneously firing off what he thought of as "vitriolicalistic" [sic] tweets further to enhance his tough guy, street-fighter image. So in that sense, Klank *was* busy.

Nonetheless, having heard the phone squawk its special Bald Eagle squawk, he left off the self-adulation—which irritatingly hadn't been forthcoming anyway—and wanted to know who was on the line.

"Some dame saying she's top minister of a kingdom, boss," said Klotz.

"*King*dom. Whut kingdom? They have dames in charge of *king*doms?"

"Yeah, weird huh, boss," said R2-D2 before checking back with Penelope, who was hitting the gin bottle hard. "Whut kingdom d'you say you was from, ma'am?"

"The *United* Kingdom. I am prime minister of it. My name is Penelope Pringle."

R2-D2 passed this news on to Klank, who said, "Aw, Christ, not *that* broad again. Man, she ain't even beddable. Tell her to go take a flying fuck at a rollin' donut, wouldya?"

Which R2-D2 did, while Klank went back to scrutinizing his appearances on as many media outlets as he could find.

Understandably, Penelope was infuriated. But she didn't let it show when she marched out onto the doorstep to face more press questions on the imminence of an as yet indeterminate Brexit with the normal set of fatuous replies, none of which included the hoped-for sop of an indulgent America to smooth her path.

~ * ~

When delivered back to Piddlington Hall by PCs Bartlett and Tomlinson, Lord Xavier Barr astonished Lady Hermione in two ways, firstly by being able to speak and secondly by being meek. Noticing the rhyming capacity of these gratifying developments, she even marked the occasion by composing the fragment of an ode to them. It went: "Hubby home and he can speak. Hubby home and he is meek." Not the sort of poetry ever to enter the canon of English verse, of course, particularly as Lady Hermione was yet able to compose any further lines and make a whole stanza. It did, however, serve as a peculiar mnemonic for the sudden and signal difference between the old blighter's past persona and what appeared to be his new one. How or why this metamorphosis had occurred she had no idea until Lord Xavier, who now wished to be known as Xavvy, sheepishly explained his bestial epiphany with Samantha and the lambs after falling off his bike into their ditch.

"Not the sort of thing one is used to," he told Hermione syntactically over tea and crumpets in the gazebo overlooking the estate's lake once PCs Bartlett and Tomlinson had taken their leave. "But, how can I put it…one's attitude to life has changed."

"Gosh. Top up your tea?"

Xavvy passed over his cup him*self*, which was per se an indicator of the new meekness. Never in their whole married life so far had Hermione witnessed such eagerness to accommodate, having become accustomed to finger clicking at any available flunkey (including her) to perform such menial tasks.

"More sugar?" she asked.

"Just pass me the spoon, darling, if you would be so kind," said Xavvy. "I'm sure I can manage the task myself."

Lady Hermione almost fell off her wicker chair at the "darling," this being the first time in the better part of twenty-five years she'd heard the term applied to her. Except by Sir George "Ginger" Wigglesworth, of course. But the only reason he'd employed it was to take her clothes off and bed her.

Xavvy managed the tea-stirring well. Held the spoon by the handle rather than the cupped end and twiddled it about like a person to the manner born.

"Mmm, tasty," he said, sipping at the Earl Grey when the stirring was over. "Thank you *so* much."

"My pleasure…darling," said Lady Hermione, herself not having used the word since being swept off her feet by the once handsome young peer at her debutante party. The even odder thing about his post-epiphanic self was Lord Xavvy was in some arcane way looking handsome again. Hair still grey, of course, but steelier somehow. And that old glint in the eyes was back. Lady Hermione almost felt her*self* transmuted back to some earlier time. It was all very bizarre; bizarre but nice.

"Should we perhaps make our way back to the hice?" she said when the teapot was empty.

"With the greatest pleasure, my dear," said Xavvy, taking her hand and heading off across the lawns. "Pratchetts still about are they?"

"No, I fired them for not keeping a proper eye on you as instructed and allowing you to escape believing yourself to be a fairy."

"Ah," said Xavvy in a tone he hoped would signal simple acceptance as opposed to the relief he felt at not having to face reminders of Milly's unusual sex acts in the way the woman had threatened should she and Max ever run short of money. "Gone far, have they?"

"I haven't the faintest idea. As far as possible out of my sight I told them, if memory serves. Unemployable as 'Help' anywhere, I said I would render them."

"Mmm, not around Little Piddlington In The Marsh any longer then?"

"Not so far as I know."

"Excellent. Good riddance to bad rubbish," said Xavvy with fingers crossed as they approached the portico.

"After you, milady," he added with a thespian bow and a jaunty sweep of his left arm.

Hermione giggled.

"Possibly time for a couple of brandy snifters, eh? What say, *ma chère*?" he said when they reached the immense lounge with its immense widows overlooking the immense estate. "I shall be Jeeves. Decanters in the same old place?"

Hermione nodded.

"Do make yourself comfortable then while I dispense."

And so it was that Lord and Lady Barr, for the first time in recent memory, spent the next hour and a half talking over older and better times and getting very sozzled indeed, *so* sozzled that instead of watching telly as Hermione proposed, Xavvy first tickled his wife's right kneecap and then her left breast before suggesting they both stripped and "had a bash at the old how's your father."

Hermione's eyes widened in yet further astonishment but what with being sozzled and everything, she complied with the eagerness of an eighteen year-old.

"Boobies not'z good'z they used to be," she slurred in mid strip.

"No problemo. No spring chicken meself, old thing," said Xavvy, struggling with his ditch-besmirched trousers.

And true enough, when they finally managed to become naked and fall back on the red-leather Chesterfield, these were not the sorts of bodies likely to feature in porno flics and both required careful manipulation before becoming fit for purpose. But once adequately titillated, all hints of middle age flew out of the window, and they went at it like youngsters.

"Wow!" commented Xavvy when it was over.

"Nnnnnnn, nice," sighed Hermione.

"Just between you and me, old thing, I'd pretty much forgotten how to use poor old Percy apart from peeing. So glad you reminded him."

"My pleasure, dearest. Fancy anozzer bash?"

Lord Xavvy sighed. "Body says no, but brain says…"

"Yes?"

"You betcha."

So they had another bash. Not quite as earthmoving as the first one but fun.

"Aaaaaah," they chorused, finally flopping back sated.

"What if Fergus Ulysses were to see us now," said Lord Xavvy. "What *happened* to him by the way? The memory's gone a tad fuzzy on the son issue. Bit fuzzy on *everything* since banging the old bean."

"Fetch me another shot of cognac, darling, and when you come back, I'll tell you," said Hermione, snuggling down beneath a Harrods blue silk throw, lying back in a sort of trance and drifting into a moment of poetic inspiration in which she added two more lines to her earlier ode.

"Gosh I'm a poet, and I didn't even know it," she murmured as a naked Lord Xavvy hove back into view bearing a tray with brand new snifters.

The two new lines were:

"Hubby's home, he's full of vim,

Hubby's home, and I love him (again)."

Again, not the sort of thing a Lord Byron or even a younger Paul McCartney would have been proud of, but at least they came from the heart. And, as Lady Hermione mused while Hubby fussed with the drinks, every poet had to start *some*where.

Twenty-three

Prior to her visit to the Hackney house, CeCi made another call to Dwayne but still made no mention of her "little idea." Said she was only calling to ask if all his housemates would be around when she came.

"Any special reason, Mom?"

"Like I told you last time you asked, I'd just like to spend a little quality time with you *and* the guys."

"Sure, okay, I figure I can arrange that."

Which Dwayne did. When CeCi climbed out of her cab and hit the doorknocker, the whole crew, including Andrea and Janine, were there to greet her.

"So great seeing y'all," she said, running into the lounge with open arms to administer hugs and kisses all around. When the hugfest was over, it was Desdemona who took her coat and asked if she'd like a cup of tea or, with a wink at Dwayne, maybe something a little stronger.

CeCi laughed. "My, now that *is* a dilemma. Tea would be great, but the 'stronger' is...?"

"Wine. Red or white."

CeCi shrugged and faux-winced. "Man, decisions, *decisions*," she mused stroking her chin actressly.

Dwayne smiled. "Last I heard, Mom, you were a WWW."

"A *WWW*?"

"A white wine woman?"

"Boy, some memory you have. Ookay, issue solved. I'm going with the white wine, Dezi."

So were the rest of the group as evinced by the trolley load of bottles Desdemona returned from the kitchen with. "Good choice, CeCi," she said. "Everybody just help yourselves. There're crackers, too, if anybody wants them."

Mutt pricked up his ears. He liked crackers and was pleased to see the others more interested in the vino. Only a question of politely biding his time, therefore, and the crackers would be all his. Which calculation was spot on and led to a bit of a mess on the carpet, but nobody worried about that. Mutt was Mutt.

Once glasses had been filled, quaffed, re-filled and re-quaffed, and everybody was sitting around in the little lounge, some on chairs but most on beanbags, CeCi approached her "little idea." Not normally tentative types, New Yorkers, and especially not CeCi, but even she didn't reckon an, "Okay, listen up, guys, I wanna be your manager" would fit the situation. The Fubars were already successful, and Tosh was the de facto manager, so who was she to butt in?

It was Dwayne who helped her out. "Mom, you told me on the phone you had this little idea you wanted to discuss with us?"

"Right."

"So go for it."

CeCi looked around at the upturned faces she loved so much. Would they understand she wasn't in it for the money? Did she have to *tell* them that? All manner of questions she had on her mind. Dwayne had never seen her so conflicted. What the hell *was* this little idea, anyhow?

"Mom, you okay?" he said.

CeCi took a deep breath and bit into her lower lip. "I'm okay."

"So?"

Which was when CeCi wondered out loud if The Fubars would mind if she had some small input into their management. Okay, she was mainly an artist, but she knew a little about PR and sales development stateside, and if that could help at all, then…?

Tosh was the first to respond. "You know we all love you, CeCi," he said. "And let's be clear, I don't know zilch about sales. I just got lucky with the band because they were so great, that's all."

"'Great' is the word, Tosh," said CeCi, before outlining her reasons for their greatness.

"Thank you. Thank you *so* much," said Tosh when she'd finished. "We do what we can. But any help from a friend like you would be welcome. Ain't that right, folks?"

Too-rights, bring-it-ons, and wowees from the folks, all of whom took to clapping and stomping rhythmically. They were a rock band after all.

"Gonna take that for a yes," said Tosh. "That right, guys?"

"*Raaf, raaf,*" said Mutt from amidst the heap of half-swallowed crackers.

"I guess that's the clincher, Mom," said Dwayne. "Hit us with your plan."

So CeCi proposed that, in junction with New Stars' Johnny Jimson, she and Tosh might put their heads together to organize a nationwide anti-Brexit tour, hitting all the biggest venues they could book. To judge by the second Hackney Empire gig, which had been a sell-out, she reckoned there had to be more audiences around the country ready to hear both The Fubars' music and their message.

"I ain't no expert," she said, "but it seems to me it's been far too long since we heard songs with any meaning, and I figure now would be the best of times to hear some more."

Nods all around the room.

"At the very time this country's goin' to hell in a hand basket. And, correct me if I'm wrong, but I ain't heard of *no*body else in that market."

"You're not wrong," said Fergie, huddled up on a love-seat beanbag with Aika.

"You're dead right," said Desdemona, who was still enjoying the image of her father cleaning toilets. Not for his political views sadly, but even so.

"We do a coupla silly love songs," said Tosh. "But, hey, with so much shit hitting so many fans in this country, so many lies being told, we'd have to be braindead not to say something about that, too. Get a few folks thinking a bit."

CeCi smiled. So humble these kids, but so wise.

"And if Brexit *were* further delayed, and there *were* another referendum?" said Maja. "Maybe we would have influenced a vote or two."

"Right, especially with the young ones. Think how many kids will have turned eighteen since the last one," said Andrea, picking up the baton. "Plus, how many of the old fogey Brexiteers have died. Not a nice way to look at it, but it's true. All the research shows the electorate profile next time would be quite different."

"And you can bet your bottom dollar, if we could just get them to turn out at the ballot box this time, the vast majority of the young ones would be Remainers," said Janine. "And what better way to fire them up than with good old rock 'n roll?"

Dwayne took his mother's hand and squeezed. "I guess you could call that a vote of confidence, Mom."

CeCi shrugged modestly, but inside her heart was beating double-time. "Sorry the idea had to come from some dumb Yankee broad, but it's just I've seen so much crap stateside since twenty-sixteen and done nothing, I figured now could be my time. And more importantly *your* time. Let's face it, we in America have the chance to dump Klank in another election or maybe earlier if the Special Counsel guy ever hits gold-dust, but if Brexit goes through, you guys are outta Europe for*ever*."

A brooding silence in the room, interrupted only by Mutt munching at cracker fragments then saying, "*Raaf, raaf.*"

It was Tosh climbing to his feet and going over to give CeCi the hug of her life that broke the human silence. "Okay then, so let's get out there and *do* something about it," he said.

This brought the other Fubars, Andrea, and Janine to their feet in a chorus of "For she's a jolly good fellow, and so say all of us," at which CeCi dropped her head onto Dwayne's shoulder and wept.

"Mom? Mom?" he said.

"It's okay, babe, I'm only weeping. Don't let anybody see."

"More wine everybody?" said Desdemona Britishly. An offer to which assent was assured.

And so it was, once CeCi, Johnny Jimson and Tosh had shared their considerable if diverse talents and uncovered *very* willing anti-Brexit mainland venues in Cardiff, Birmingham, Liverpool, Manchester, Glasgow, Edinburgh, Leeds and Norwich before heading back to London, that The Fubars hit the road. And not in some clapped out dormobile either. In a Mercedes Benz, super deluxe, customized, personnel carrier ironically paid for by CeCi from what was left of Dwayne Zobinski Snr's ill-gotten assets.

~ * ~

Anatoly Munchkov had been aware of being a wanted man when he was in the UK, hence his many disguises and furtive movements in that country, but reckoned he'd be free of the need for such subterfuges in New York City where to the best of his knowledge nobody knew or cared who the hell he was or what crimes he had or hadn't committed. Plus, he had the support of respected Wall Street banker Hank Laplanque, who was even reputed to have covert connections to the White House. Then there were his pals in the Russian Consulate General at East 91st Street from whom he could always be sure of a warm welcome. What could be cosier?

So it was that he strolled the sidewalks of the city that never slept without a care in the world. Sure, he wondered from time to time why he hadn't heard from Laplanque for so long but figured the guy might have taken a vacation or something. There was no way he could have known Hank was under house arrest, with a tracking monitor around his left ankle, or that he had already grassed up Munchkov to the cops with the accusation it had been *him* who'd masterminded and committed the Zobinski murder. How could he have? No way, that was how. Any more than he could have known his name had also reached the ears of Special Counsel Richard Michaels, who was interested in not only the murder case, but also the possible new link between Klank and Igor Ripurpantzov's meddling in American politics. Mind you, as any spook worth his or her salt will tell you, it is *never* safe to let one's guard down entirely because, even in apparently the most comfortable of comfort zones, lurk hidden dangers—meaning paranoia is always the recommended modus operandi in *all* circumstances.

Munchkov should have known that when he picked up streetwalker Suzie Labelle one midnight in Times Square and allowed her to take him in a yellow cab back to her apartment over the bridge in Brooklyn, but he didn't. Or rather, he was too pissed to care. A whole bottle of vodka can have that effect on a person, even a Russian. All Anatoly wanted was somewhere to poke his dick and Suzie in her mini skirt and thigh-high red leather boots looked just the ticket. A shame from his perspective that Labelle—real name Marcia Duval—was NYPD's most successful officer at working with girls in schools all across town to keep them from selling their bodies to feed their drug habits. How was *he* to know it was Marcia's practice once having enticed a client back to her apartment instead of providing sex, to lecture him about his complicity in the degradation of women, show him her badge, and after taking his details require him never again to indulge his obscene fantasies or face arrest? Legally speaking, this was a lie, of course, but sufficient to put the frighteners on nine clients out of ten, especially the pot-bellied, middle-aged ones with jobs, wives, children, and elderly relatives.

"Uh?" said Anatoly when she'd finished her spiel and also smacked him around a bit.

So Marcia repeated the message, this time requiring for her records evidence of Munchkov's parentage, place of birth, passport status, US residence details etc, etc.

"Uh?" Anatoly repeated.

"Just tell me your name, bozo," said Marcia, sitting herself down in front of her desktop computer. "I've got files for all kindsa names."

But you know how it is when you're legless. How hard it is to remember which alias you are currently using just off the cuff like that. And such was Anatoly's case. He tried and tried, but they just wouldn't come.

"Munchkov," he finally mumbled.

"First name?"

"Natalie."

"You're a *girl*?"

"Nuh-no. *Boy*."

"Ookay, *boy*, you wanna try that one again?"

"Nnnn...Anatoly," Munchkov finally managed.

Which...was...a...*very* big mistake.

"Ooo*kay*, Anatoly Munchkov," said Marcia tapping at her computer keys and, when her NYPD search was over and she'd seen the "Arrest On Sight" in red capital letters next to the name, taking a 9mm Glock 17 from her desk drawer.

"Hands on your head and walk this way," she told him.

"Bitch," said Munchkov, but that just earned him a spot of pistol-whipping so Anatoly walked this way while Marcia cuffed him and read him the few rights he had.

Then she shoved him back through the door to her apartment and down the stairs to the waiting black and white she'd urgently requested.

Back at downtown HQ, Carlos Benitez was gobsmacked, but pleased, when he heard the news. "Gonna be up for commendation, Officer Duval," he told Marcia when he picked up her call. "Maybe a very big *time* commendation."

"Thanks, Chief," said Marcia. "On our way."

Twenty-four

Andrea and Janine were warmly invited to join The Fubars' nationwide tour, but much though they would have liked to, they felt they must turn the offer down.

"You're sure, sure, *sure*, Mum," Desdemona pressed. "It'd be so good to have the both of you on board, even if just for moral support."

"And you'd have a ball, I'm sure of it," said Dwayne. "You could join us on stage anytime."

"Sweet of you." Andrea laid a fond arm around Janine's shoulders. "Only we're not the kids you are, and nowhere near as musical. You don't want two old fogeys tagging along."

Janine laughed. "I'm not ex*actly* an old fogey, but Andy's right... I'm not in your age bracket either. Plus you guys know all the routines and the songs are all yours, so..."

Tosh shrugged. "Maybe some other time for the odd gig?"

"With the greatest of pleasure," said Andrea. "But right now, I should really get back home, anyway, tour or no tour. My neighbour Alun Jones would look after the animals for as long as I asked him I'm sure, but *I* need to see *them*. They'll be missing me, I know they will. Call me a soppy old fool, but there it is."

"Don't worry, Mum. I understand," said Desdemona. "I'm pretty fond of those piggies myself. And of the dogs. What're they called again?"

"John, Sylvia, Herbert and Harriette are the piggies. And Barry and Hyacinth are the retrievers."

"I know what you mean too," said Fergie, remembering only too well his only pals William and Lucy during the bad old days back at Piddlington Hall. "A human's best friend, right? Always pleased to see you. Never shout at you."

"Raaf, raaf," said Mutt between chomps at his turkey-flavoured doggie bone.

Andrea smiled and mussed Mutt's wiry ruff. "You can say that again, Fergus. The only trouble I've ever known came from people."

"Ain't *that* the truth?" said Dwayne, reflecting on both his own father and the fates of those who might have killed him. Someday soon, he would need to get back to Matheson at Scotland Yard to see if there were any progress with the investigation.

"But those are not the *only* reasons," said Andrea, squeezing Janine's shoulder. "I did promise Janny a visit to Anglesey if she ever felt like it, and after Vincent's attack we're both a little shaky still, so..."

"Now would be a pretty good time," said Janine, rubbing the hand squeezing her shoulder. "There is a little more to that story though. D'you mind if I tell the guys and gals, Andy?"

"Go right ahead, darling."

"You see, Andy and are in love."

"Took us a while to find out for sure," said Andrea with a nervous glance at Desdemona, who just nodded and smiled.

"Some years ago it would have been a love that couldn't speak its name, but these days..." said Janine with a shrug.

"Who knows, *any*thing goes," said Tosh who was as much *au fait* with Cole Porter as he was with John Lennon and Bob Marley. "So great to hear the news! I sorta suspected it but didn't like to say anything. Shouldn't we drink to that, guys and gals?"

And the guys and gals, including Desdemona, loudly agreed they should.

"It's not that we're man haters like the sad old feminists," said Andrea while her daughter was away stocking and fetching the white wine trolley. "Please don't think that."

"I don't for one," said Dwayne. "CeCi's been batting for both sides as long as I can remember. Made no secret of it."

Andrea nodded. "And why not?"

"Why not indeed?" chorused Aika and Maja, which caused faux worried glances from Fergie and Tosh.

"*Any*way, rest assured we wish the both of you all the very best," said Fergie as Desdemona reappeared with the drinks.

It was she who proposed the toast once everyone had glasses in their hands. "Every happiness to my dear mum, Andrea, and her beautiful partner, Janine," she said, at which all The Fubars stood, raised their glasses, and repeated Desdemona's words. Minus the 'my dear mum' part, of course.

~ * ~

As per usual when out of the public eye (see above), Dougal Klank was furious. In public, he was all gimmicks and gestures and posturing and snide comments about his enemies, and how he was going to defeat them all. But in private, well away from the cameras and the microphones, he fumed and raged. Mainly at the Democrat women of the House of Representatives, especially its current Speaker, whose whole goddam purpose in life appeared to be to oppose every brilliant idea he had and make him look stupid. Manna from heaven for them had been news of how he cheated at golf, and *now*, the bitches also had the full version of Special Counsel Michael's investigation to play with.

What was currently obsessing and infuriating him, however, was the news that some Russian asshole called Minchykook had been arrested by the NYPD, and both he and another asshole called Leplink, an American, were under investigation in connection with the murder of the Zobinski creep in London. Not that he gave a shit about the dead guy or who'd offed him. Let them all rot in hell. What he *did* give a big time shit about, however, was *his* name, yet again, being dragged through the mud by the shit-eating "enemies of the people"—

aka the free press of the First Amendment—who were once again baying for his blood with their normal fake news. Over and over the "WHAT DID THE PRESIDENT KNOW?" and "IS THIS ANOTHER RUSSIA CONNECTION? headlines kept screaming as the story swept America. There were the same levels of interest in the social media and on TV. Except for Fox News, of course, who retained a guarded but telling silence.

"Holy Christ on a fuckin' scooter, Klutz, you gotta *do* sumptn about this," he shrieked at his new chief of staff.

"Like whut, Mister President? And it's Kl*o*tz," said Gregor who'd spent a lifetime the butt of 'klutz' jokes, and here it was all over again. "No use giving out denial statements this time. We done that with all your other crimes, and it makes no difference."

"I...done...never...committed...no...*crimes*," howled Klank, jabbing a forefinger into Klotz's chest. "How many *times* I gotta *tell* you this? One *more* time and you're *fired*," he added with such fury his toupée came loose, and he was obliged to reposition it. "Just make this story go away, O-freakin'-K?"

"Like how?"

"By sayin' I ain't never heard of these assholes. Never talked with 'em, never texted 'em. Never nudn with 'em. How dumb are you, Klutz?"

"Only thing is, Mister President, it ain't as simple as that. Seems like the cops, and the feebs, and the CIA got themselves evidence you *have*. Plus, we have the Brits breathing down our necks to extradite Munchkov to London for trial. Other guys he snuffed out there, they're saying. Russians pissed with Igor Ripurpantzov and giving out Kremlin secrets."

"Extra...?"

"Dite. Like we send him back to them?" said Klotz.

"Fan*tast*ic. So let's do it. Git the asshole outta my hair, wunnerful," said Klank, further re-adjusting his toupée.

"Like I said, it ain't so simple," said Klotz who despite his crappy high school grades had become a lawyer, nonetheless.

"Whaddaya talking about, *simple*? Simple *zimple*."

"First off, Zobinski was an American citizen. Okay, so he got iced in London, but I don't see Congress or the courts handing Munchkov over to the Brits just 'cos they want the glory. Plus, the Russians gonna have a say in this. They ain't gonna admit Munchkov did *any* of the crimes, in fact, for all we know, he is a national hero over there working outta the FSS or the FIS and gonna get a medal."

"Fuss 'n' fizz, what the fuck're *they*?"

"The old KGB, now the Federal Security Service and the Federal Intelligence Service."

"Kinda like the FBI and the CIA?"

"Kinda like that."

"Poor old Igor, huh? Man, gimme time. I am gonna close down the feebs and the Langley assholes. They're on my tail, too, ya know that, Klutz? I already fired some of 'em."

"Indeed, Mister President. But to return to the point, the Russians are sure as hell *not* gonna bring Munchkov to justice. Like I said, the exact opposite, so they're out of the picture same way the Brits are."

Klank frowned, trying his best to keep up with this logic and failing.

"Which leaves *us* to handle the case, which will take time," Klotz continued. "There's a procedure in law with foreign citizens, the federal government will have to get involved, etcetera, etcetera..."

"Federal government my ass. *I* am the government around here, in case you've forgotten, Klutz. I just write one of my presidential decrees, and zippity doo dah bingo the guy's outta here. Gimme the decree book an' a pen. Call in the cameras to see me doin' it. Soon as I fix my hair."

Klotz sighed. "Mister President, your decrees ain't been doing too good recently. You know how they keep getting overturned. And you know why that is? Because of the separation of powers into the legislative, executive, and judicial, that's why. You, Mister President, are only the executive. There's also the Congress and the courts, like I said."

"'Only' my ass. I am the top executive guy in all my companies and what I say *goes*. Gimme another term, and I'm gonna abolish the freakin' Congress and fire all the judges that won't do my will."

Klotz shrugged. "Well, good luck with that little endeavour, Mister President. Hasn't been tried before but…"

"America hasn't had a president like *me* before, either."

"*Any*way, to return, yet again, to the Munchkov question," said Klotz, eager not to get involved in what kind of a president Klank was. "Even if you *do* get him sent away somewhere, there's still Laplanque. The cops have *him* under house arrest in New York, and like I said, there's a trail that leads to this office. And it ain't too hard to find either. From him *and* from Zobinski."

"Details, details, details. Problems, problems, problems. Why I hire you, Klutz, is to make them go away. To make my life easier so's I got time to concentrate on my brilliant ideas."

"Exactly what I'm *trying* to do, Mister President. Acting on your behalf to keep you from any more…misunderstandings."

"Well, you're fucking failing. And people around here who fail me get YOU KNOW WHAT," said Klank, Klotz having inadvertently pressed too many bad mood buttons.

"Nice Christmas presents?" he said, going for humour in yet another costly misread. He should have known psychos like Klank didn't do humour unless at someone else's expense when the schadenfreude cup would spill over, but if the tables were turned, fearful furies were to be expected. Only Klotz didn't know. Which was why, when Klank took to struggling for breath, grunting bestially and turning an ominous shade of puce, he misinterpreted the symptoms as the onset of the heart attack he and others had long been hoping for. But like so many other things in his life—women in particular— Klotz had gotten it wrong all over again, as he discovered the moment Klank climbed from his chair, lumbered in his direction, pounced on him and pinned him to the carpet with all his flabby weight.

"*ASSHOLE, CREEP, GARBAGE BAG, SEWER RAT, MOTHERFUKKA,*" screamed the president swinging right and left hooks, which all missed as Klotz struggled for breath. "*YOU'RE FIRED. GET THE FUCK OUTTA MY SIGHT.*"

"With pleasure, Mister President," Klotz managed to gurgle. "And may you rot in hell," which was the remark that earned him the broken nose that caused the shriek that led to the minions entering the Round Room to see what all the fuss was about.

"Poor guy had some kinda fit an' fell over on his face," Klank explained. "I was just trying to give him....whatchamacallit?"

"The kiss of life?" asked minion numero uno, and next-in-line chief of staff hopeful, Darren Blink, only to receive the career-ending response, "Git outta my *SIGHT*, dumbo, I ain't no *FAG*."

"CPR?" tried minion numero due, and also chief of staff hopeful, Chuck O'Leary.

"Sounds good, what the fuck is it?"

"It means cardiopulmonary resuscitation, Mister President."

"Even better. Tell that to the enemies of the people, okay? Say how I saved the poor bastard from sudden death with that CTR. And your name is?"

"Chuck O'Leary, Mister President. And it's *CPR*."

"Nice name, CPR. You got a military background? I had it up to here with freakin' *law*yers," said Klank, raising his hand to his hairline only to discover he had lost his toupée in the ruckus with Klotz. It wasn't a good look.

"Matter of fact I do, Mister President. Served in Iraq and Afghanistan with the rank of major."

A lie, but Chuck figured Klank was too dumb ever to check.

"Where we won big victories, am I right?" said Klank, climbing off the writhing Klotz and allowing the newly arrived medics to carry him away.

"Yes sir, you surely are," said O'Leary, handing over the displaced toupée, which had finished up under Klotz's left trouser leg.

"Great, wunnerful, 'cos what I need right now is a big-victory-type guy. You wanna be my new chief of staff, CPR?"

"It's Chuck, Mister President. Chuck O'Leary, but hey what's a little slip of the tongue between friends? And I have to say I just *lurve* your style. Plus, you have nice hair."

"You're hired," said Klank, missing the irony of the hair comment. "That's the kinda talk I like around here. Not damn well en*ough* of it."

"To me you're a superstar," said Chuck, who'd done his homework on Klank and knew only too well how flattery got a person everywhere with a psycho narcissist.

"Walk with me this way, friend," said Klank, lumbering back to his desk. "I got me a small problem with some Russian killer dude I need wiped off all records. Plus some other American guy he was friends with. You figure you could help me out with that?"

"No problemo, Mister President. Just gimme the details. With record-wiping, I am shit hot if I say so myself. Lotta stuff happened in Iraq and Afghanistan nobody ever needed to know about," said Chuck, who had never set foot out of Mascot, Tennessee until, as deputy sheriff, he'd been accused of malpractices with underage girls and needed to hotfoot it away smartish. And where better to try his luck than in the Washington DC swamp?

Klank hoisted a happy eyebrow. "Guy after my own heart."

Twenty-five

Justices of the Peace Chalmers, Cuthbert and Galsworthy had been unanimous in their decision that Professor Vincent Vinicombe's punishment was entirely appropriate to his crime, although whether their sentence was delivered in expectation of reflection on his behaviour leading to remorse and possible redemption remained a moot point. Maybe as experienced JPs, that *had* been their objective, although another possibility was they'd had simply wanted him to suffer humiliation of the kind he had inflicted. Who knows? Crime and punishment can be such a tricky issue, can't it? Cure on the one hand, the potential for recidivism on the other. Over the centuries, whole tomes have been written on the subject—notably by Fyodor Dostoevsky—but *still* there's no conclusive answer, otherwise jails worldwide wouldn't be as jam packed as they still are.

*Any*way, in Vincent's case there was no question of the reflection/remorse/cure theory because he barely ever reflected on what he'd done and, if he did, was glad he'd done it. The only regret he had was that he'd been caught and then subjected to ignominy the likes of which no top-notch scholar of Renaissance Drama could *ever* have deserved, so the chances of rehabilitation were zero. Nor in these circumstances did he undergo the type of epiphany experienced by

Lord Xavier Barr. Okay, he didn't meet any helpful sheep during his lavatorial duties at King's College, but that was neither here nor there. Vincent Vinicombe was simply not the epiphanic type because, unlike some of the playwrights whose texts he taught, he lacked imagination in any form. Never dreamed, never reflected on the what-ifs and frequent non sequiturs of the human condition, nothing of the sort. Like Dougal Klank, the only thing that had ever fascinated Vincent Vinicombe was his solipsistic image of him*self*, the self that had been brought so low by the bitches on the bench at Woolwich Magistrates Court. And the only thing on his mind day and night was revenge for the cards dealt him by outrageous fortune.

To this end, instead of cleaning them, he further besmirched the lavatories under his supervision by leaving used tampons and condoms where they had come to rest *and* by adding extra items—dog turds and the like—he collected on his way to work. Activities such as toilet roll replacement and the wiping of floors, wash basins and lavatory bowls he spurned entirely, such that after only a few days, the facilities became stinky and unusable, which led to under- and postgraduates reviving the ancient art of student protest and marching around the campus chanting and waving banners proclaiming their dissatisfaction and disgust. "FIRE THE PROF OF POO" read one. "STICK HIS BOG BRUSH UP HIS ARSE," "COMETH THE HOUR, COMETH THE WANKER," and, somewhat inappropriately from a student destined for a third-class honours degree, "GET THEE TO A NUNNERY," read some others.

But was Vincent humbled? The hell he was. Instead, he picked up what he saw as the gauntlet thrown down to him and took to chasing after the demonstrators with balloons full of urine taken from his lavatories which he threw at their heads while yelling "gadzooks, foul demons, damn you all to Hades." Inevitably, there followed stand-offs, slanging matches, and occasional scuffles some of which spilled out onto The Strand and blocked traffic.

None of this could, of course, be tolerated by the university's Vice Chancellor, Professor Jocelyn Fothergill who back in the day had himself been an ardent demonstrator, sympathized fully with the students' complaints, and reckoned the Vinicombe creep had a bollocking coming to him in accordance with the supervision role assigned to him by the Woolwich magistrates. As a gay man and proud of it, Jocelyn found any form of sexual abuse abhorrent and was prepared under no circumstances to tolerate a convicted spouse abuser causing mayhem on his premises. It was at ten o'clock sharp on the Friday morning of only Vincent's second week of community service, therefore, that he was summoned to Fothergill's office, the same office Vincent had for so long cherished as his own at some future date but had been turned down without interview on every one of his VC applications.

"Sit," Jocelyn told him. "Over there," he added, pointing at a chair in the furthest part of the grandiose office beneath a shelf laden with the works of Laurence Sterne which he cherished as a former eighteenth-century lit expert, although he also dabbled happily in the twentieth-century French poststructuralist works of such writers as Michel Foucault.

"Fuck you, Jocy," said Vincent. Which wasn't a great start to the conversation. "I'll sit where I bloody well wish." It was Vincent's view that homosexuals should be either imprisoned or shot or both. Not because it was God's will, just because he loathed them.

"As you please, ex-Professor Vinicombe, now to business. The small matter of filthy lavatories and the entirely justified student protests to which they led."

"*Ex*?" spluttered Vincent. "Once I've served my time, I shall be back at my lectern telling students the *truth* about literature, not the piffle *you* used to peddle."

Keeping his cool, Jocelyn shrugged. "No you won't, old chap, not as long as you carry on this way. *Clean* the lavatories and *stop* fighting with students and pouring urine on their heads and there is an outside chance of you retaining your post. Continue in your current activities and there is none."

"We shall see about that. I shall inform the governors. I shall inform the press where I have influence. I shall…"

"Inform anyone you like, Professor Vinicombe, but first I would suggest you consult a psychiatrist. I doubt anybody would consider the daubing of toilets with poo and the bursting of piss-filled balloons on complainants' heads the result of a sane mind."

Well, as you can image, such comments didn't go down at *all* well with soon-to-be-ex-Professor of Renaissance Drama Vincent Vinicombe. Which was why he took to branding Jocelyn a pea-brained poofter as evinced by his pathetic choice of the eighteenth century, let alone Frenchie philosophy, as respectable areas for academic study.

"Laurence sodding Sterne, my arse," he commented, for example, while swiping off their shelf several books including *The Life and Opinions of Tristram Shandy, Gentleman*. "Muddle-headed Irish bog trotter with the brains of an average moke," he added jumping up and down on the tome, which he claimed could be read backwards or forwards and still make no sense.

But despite the violence perpetrated on his favourite text, Jocelyn continued to keep his cool, refusing to be drawn into yet another of the pusillanimous donnish spats that had so often brought university senior common rooms into mocking disrepute.

"There, there. *Du calme*, old fellow. All you've got to do is prove your worth as a reformed toilet cleaner and..." he said which, for reasons temporarily unknown, but time would soon tell, proved the tipping point for Vincent.

"*Don't* speak to me in...*that*...language," he yowled, advancing on Jocelyn with flaming red eyes and whirling above his head a lavatory brush.

"French?" asked the unflappable Jocelyn.

"*Any* fucking European language. You will have read my Brexit pieces in the national press. My views are well known. How those lying, robbing froggie *bastards* stole our sovereignty from us along with their allies, the krauts, the wops, the spics, all of them taking the *gggreat* out of Grrreat Britain."

Traitor *and* pervert is what you are," thought Jocelyn, who had not calculated on quite this degree of mania.

But by then, Vinicombe was marching towards him whirling his lavatory brush through the air with intent.

As a rugby scrum half, who still played regularly for his local seniors' XV every Saturday, however, Jocelyn was fast on his feet, suffered no damage at all from the smelly weapon aimed at his head, and tackled Vincent to the ground in seconds flat. But he took none of the revenge that might have been expected, not even an admonitory tap on the head, merely took his phone from his pocket and called the cops.

Which was how it came to pass that ex-Professor of Renaissance Drama Vincent Vinicombe was, yet again, arrested on an assault charge and appeared for a second time at Woolwich Magistrates Court before JPs Chalmers, Cuthbert and Galsworthy, who this time were much sterner in their judgement. Counsel for the prosecution Mack McGinity smiled as the ladies this time handed down six months in pokey without the option of remission plus mandatory attendance at an anger management course.

And, needless to say, that was the end of Vincent's career at King's College University of London although whilst in prison he was permitted by the governor Basil Harbottle, himself an ardent Brexiteer, to continue writing his inflammatory articles for red tops like *The Daily Snitch*.

You have to wonder, don't you?

~ * ~

Newly ensconced with Janine in the Llanddeusant cottage on the Isle of Anglesey, Andrea was unsurprised at her ex-husband's new sentence but, unlike a delighted Desdemona when she phoned with the news, expressed a degree of sympathy.

"Poor old sod, it was his upbringing that did it. You can take the boy out of poverty, but you can't take poverty out of the boy, never mind how posh he gets. The whole professor thing went to his head, I reckon."

"No need for him to become 'a' in the process though," Desdemona replied. "Anti-, anti-Muslim, anti-gay, anti-black, anti-women anti-European, anti bloody everything that we hoped to have changed since nineteen forty-five."

"Point taken, love. Trouble was there were Oswald Mosley-type brown shirts in his family background. He'll have heard those stories back in the East End. Cable Street riots, all of that. Must have stayed in his head somewhere."

Desdemona sighed. "And you fell for it?"

"I fell for the man I hoped he would become."

"But he didn't. Instead, he became an ambassador for the new populism. Just like Klank in the US."

"Quite. I'm so sorry, darling. We all make mistakes."

Desdemona relented. "True enough. And don't think for a second I'm blaming you."

"I don't, sweetheart. I'm just sooo glad you have Dwayne. Never do I see *him* going that way."

"Not with CeCi for a mother."

"Such a woman."

"Indeed. Anyhow, that's the latest news from the big city. Apart from the Brexit mayhem, that is. Someday soon, we'll come for a visit if that's okay. Just the small matter of The Fubars' nationwide tour, then…"

"You're welcome any time, love. Be safe and go well."

Andrea sighed when she put down the phone. "Messy business, life, eh?" she said to Janine who was sitting next to her on the couch.

"I got the gist of this particular episode," said Janine, leaning in with a shoulder rub. "The past, eh? If only we could put it behind us."

"We can, my love, together we *can*. And not just by 'drawing a line under it.' That's too facile. We have to make the conscious effort to erase what no longer serves and yet fight to keep in mind what *was* of value, and continue to cherish it in the present."

Janine nodded. "What's done can't be *un*done, though."

"No, it can't. But at least we can stand outside ourselves to see what can be salvaged and, as I said, *fight* to retain it. If we live blindly in the past, we're lost in it. You overheard what Dezi said about post-nineteen forty five?"

"I did. And she was right to name all the antis I also thought had been overcome or, at the very least, challenged. *I*, for one, grew up surrounded by very few of them."

"Indeed, she *was* right. Yet so many of those liberties are suddenly being trampled on by the new populism she mentioned. Human rights under threat again everywhere, and in only a few short years." Andrea clicked a thumb against a second finger. "Here in the UK, in Klank's America obviously, in Europe, and Latin America. All over the shop, progress wiped out like it never existed while liberals had their eyes off the ball thinking the battles were won. So much for learning from history! Its main lesson ought to be that it's cockups, not peace, we can only ever expect. My terrible fear is we're back to the nineteen thirties, and there are far too many Vincent Vinicombes roaming the earth just now taking great pleasure from their new kick-ass power."

Janine frowned. "That's some statement. I love you for so many things, Andy, but I didn't have you down as some kind of a bloody philosopher."

Andrea shrugged. "Out here in the outback, I've had plenty of time to think and I'm grateful for it. Not many humans to talk to, but plenty of nature and wise animals. I have a smartphone but no wish for false friends on Facebook. I only use it to make occasional calls. Let's just say I've grown up a little since the bad old days with Vincent. Also, I have a brilliant daughter who's working with a group of people who might just make a tiny difference to the shit that's hitting so many fans. I'll cheer them on all the way. Funny they should've called themselves The Fubars, eh?" Andrea chuckled.

Janine snuggled close and laughed. "But best of all we have each other to share ideas with now. Because of *very* peculiar circumstances, some might say, but let's not look gift horses in their mouths, shall we?"

"In case they've got rotten old teeth?"

"Exactly," Janine was saying as Hyacinth and Barry ambled into the tiny cottage lounge with meaningful looks on their faces, which translated as "garden pee time."

"You or me?" said Andrea.

"Me," said Janine. "I think they're starting to like me."

"Raaf, raaf," chorused Hyacinth and Barry nuzzling close and treating Janine to the full-face-lick routine.

"I think they are," said Andrea. "A glass of Pinot Grigio on your return?"

"With great pleasure. After Brexit, we might not see another bottle of that for some time, one that costs less than thirty pounds, anyway."

Twenty-six

Dougal Klank was over the moon when informed by Chuck O'Leary the little problem with Hank Laplanque and Anatoly Munchkov had been made to go away.

"Boy, I just knew we was gonna make a great team," he said, jabbing Chuck in the chest joshingly. "How'd you *do* that?"

"Kinda easy, boss. A two birds with one stone job."

"Wanna fill me in with the details? And don't...*do not*...tell me my name's written *any*place in connection with what you done."

"No way, Chief. Way I fixed it, nobody's ever gonna figure out what happened, or who was involved. Not *no*body"

"Okay, oo*kay*, great, wunnerful. So tell me. And keep it short and simple. I ain't good with long stories."

"No problemo, Chief," said Chuck, explaining how he'd used his influence with Klank's Russian contact at East 91st Street to warn of the potentially humiliating dangers of the court case being planned against Munchkov and suggest it might be to everybody's benefit if he were a) to be freed and b) to kill Laplanque for grassing him out

Even Klank was gobsmacked. "And they *bought* it?"

"Like kids given candy."

"Holy shit. And nobody knows you did this?"

"Nobody but me and the contact, and we sure as shit ain't gonna tell nobody except our higher-ups. You and…"

"Don't tell me the guy's name. I don't wanna *know* it."

"Good. How it should be."

"Great. And this Minchikev dude was *gotten* freed?"

"Yup. Also no details about how. Some insider dealings with a bent cop at the NYC jail is all I know."

"And he goes and kills Le Plank?"

"Who is still under house arrest, but yeah, he kills him. My sources say poison. It's his MO."

Klank's eyes widened in delight, then he frowned. "And Munchikiv?"

"Last I heard he was on a Russian military jet headed for Moscow."

"Holy cow, Chuck. Wanna pay hike? Wanna house in Florida? Wanna private plane to take you anywhere you wanna go?"

O'Leary shrugged again. "Only doin' my job, Chief."

"Wanna be campaign manager next time I run for president? I could use a guy with your talents."

"Sure, why not?"

"*Man*," said Klank, picking up the hotline phone to Igor Ripurpantzov. "I gotta tell my best buddy about this."

"No sir, you don't," said O'Leary, taking the phone from Klank's sweaty grasp. "Not a clever plan. Right now Rippo don't need to know zip. Like *you* said, the less anybody knows the better. All we're talking here is a crime that will always remain unsolved. That's the thing about it. *You* know, *I* know, but that's the size of it."

And for once, Klank took advice from another human being. "And the cops, and the feebs, and the CIA, and the freakin' Special Counsel?" he said. "Whadda *they* know?"

"Nudn, nada, zilch. Still starin' up their assholes wonderin' would be my guess. Whole thing happened in under twenty-four hours. Kinda fast in-and-out gig me'n the guys would do in Iraq and Afghanistan," said Chuck, although the actual reference was to bank robberies, and other heists he and his gang had pulled all across the US and Mexico, and never been caught.

"Where you were a major."

Chuck shrugged yet again. "Yup."

"In the wunnerful US forces I'm Commander in Chief of."

"The same, boss."

And so on and on and *on* the self-congratulation went. You know how it is with narcissism. How blind it can be. That Klank should have swallowed O'Leary's account whole would have beggared belief in a normal president, but Klank wasn't normal. He believed what he wanted to believe, namely that he was omnipotent, invulnerable and blessed with good fortune. Okay, so the part of O'Leary's narrative about Munchkov killing Laplanque and then being flown off to Moscow *was* true, but the claim that the cops, the FBI, the CIA, and Special Counsel Richard Michaels would be staring up their assholes dumbfounded was clearly no more than speculation. Yet Klank believed it because he *wanted* to, because it fit his worldview of himself as perpetual winner and his enemies as dumb dorks. But, as we saw in Vincent Vinicombe's case, behind each act of hubris lurks the spectre of nemesis. So it was that Klank's celebrations at being freed from yet another "fake" slur on his character lasted only a few days, after which he was forced to return to his default position of fury and manic tweeting.

And the cause of this sudden reversal? Leaks from the White House, and Carlos Benitez, Richard Michaels, and Marvin Matheson letting it be known they were not the clowns and imbeciles Klank took them to be. They had been aware of the Zobinski/Munchkov/Laplanque linkage to Klank for some time and were not fooled by the latest twist in the tale, as evinced in the top secret, hyper encrypted conference call they shared when news of Laplanque's killing by Munchkov was leaked by Washington DC deep throat Gregor Klotz who, nursing his humiliation and broken nose, had made revenge the mainstay of his life. Banned from the White House *he* might be, but he still had pals inside it, specifically Yolande Rattin whose job it was to monitor recordings of all Round Room conversations in case of any boo-boos that might need eliminating from the record. The one with Chuck O'Leary had been particularly interesting.

"Strange that O'Leary should have quit his job so soon after such a successful meeting," she told Klotz. "Nobody around here's seen him since."

Such was the deep throat info Gregor passed on to Richard Michaels.

It was Carlos who kicked off the three-way discussion. "My view this whole thing has Klank's paw prints all over it," he said. "Okay, I gotta carry the can for leaving Laplanque unprotected the way I did, and I am sorry, but..."

"No worries, Carlos," said Michaels. "You couldn't have known. And I agree on the Klank angle. Are we really supposed to believe the O'Leary creep alone could have swung the deal with the Ruskies to get Munchkov set free? I don't think so. It has Klank's deals with Ripurpantzov written in big letters."

Marvin Matheson, all those thousands of miles away in London, agreed. "Any help I can give just shout."

And so it was that the first seeds of doubt were planted and news of a thorough investigation of the whole story disseminated. But the factor that superseded even this initiative and drove Dougal Klank to the point of apoplexy was the story Chuck O'Leary sold for an undisclosed figure ($2.5m) to a social media giant—you might have read it—in which Klank becomes the architect of not only *this* crime but many other Russia-related ones. That was the flame that lit the media conflagration to come with headlines such as, "IS KLANK NOW AN ACCOMPLICE TO MURDER?" and "RUSSIA PLOT THICKENS," and, "TIME RUNNING OUT FOR KLANK." Even Fox News continued its deafening silence when it came to defending their champion. Not a bad day's work for an ex-bank robber turned double agent now safely in hiding in St Petersburg, eh? A pity from his perspective Klank never saw it coming, but that's psychopathy for you. Needless to report, he spent the following twenty-four-seven hammering out febrile tweets protesting his innocence and lambasting all and sundry for even *suggesting* he might be guilty, but Americans had become so accustomed to such outbursts, mainly they just shrugged. Apart from his staunchest supporters, the southern hillbillies and rednecks, that was. Sure, they took to grinding their teeth and blatting their brows but, nonetheless, a flash poll still suggested the majority of them believed their hero's version of events that he was the undeserving victim of a political witch hunt.

Meanwhile, Klank made two decisions. The first was never again to appoint a chief of staff and the second was, true to form, to change the subject, claiming he had insider knowledge of Muslims eating their own babies and threatening to start a nuclear "holy war" against Islam which he was sure all patriotic Americans would support. Which, alarmingly, many did. Amongst them were not the famous women in the House of Representatives, however. They just lapped up such last ditch hysteria from the White House.

"A bridge too far this time. Looks like we got the asshole where we want him," said speaker Norma Paolozzi to her best friend, Judy Daniels.

"In a jacket heading for the psycho ward?" said Judy.

"At the very least. I was thinking prison for a very long time with no chance of parole but, hey, a psycho ward would also suit me fine."

Amongst finally revitalized American liberals, visions of a saner future were therefore gaining traction, but on planet Klank everything was painted as still rosy. That weekend he played golf with three White House juniors he paid to beat and made sure there were photographers there to record his victory smiles.

~ * ~

Maybe it had been naïve of CeCi Bodine, Johnny Jimson, and The Fubars to think their eleventh hour, whistle stop, anti-Brexit tour around the country would pass off without incident when the nation was more divided than it had been since the civil war of 1642 to 1651. Okay, we weren't talking open hostilities between royalists and parliamentarians, more like futile mind-numbing verbal hostilities between politicians themselves. But, nonetheless, beneath the surface of apparently normal British day-to-day life, between the pro- and anti-Brexiters, there seethed the tinder-dry undergrowth of a forest fire awaiting only a spark to light it. On the one side, there was the unprecedented populist pro-Brexit alliance of the hard left and the hard right, and on the other, the defeated middle-ground, anti-Brexit liberals who no longer had a party to represent them but weren't going down without a struggle either.

And what was the spark that provided the initial kindling? The Fubars' trip, that was what. The first three gigs in Cardiff, Birmingham, and Liverpool passed off with only minor scuffles and a few arrests, but even they made it clear there was trouble in the offing. Eggs and tomatoes were thrown, there was some British National Party-type chanting when the finale, "Bye Bye Britain" was played, but no more than that, the sort of thing that might have been expected of teddy boys and beatniks, or mods and rockers way back in the twentieth century. Nonetheless, CeCi began to wonder about the wisdom of continuing the tour.

"Wouldn't wanna cause a riot further down the road," she said back in the Let's Rock Liverpool's dressing room after the show. "I'm starting to feel some bad vibes here."

Tosh nodded. "Hard to tell though, isn't it? If it was our message or just the regular pissed people out for a fight on a Saturday night."

"I guess." CeCi shrugged. "You know the country better than I do. But I still have this worried feeling in my bones."

"Don't overthink it, Mom," said Dwayne. "All we're doin' is singin' songs."

"Yeah, sure. But songs can have a lotta power, especially to irritate the crazies. You weren't around in the sixties, but my folks were and they told me all about it. Think Siege of Chicago in sixty-eight. Anti-war protesters singing peace songs, but what do they get in reply? Rifles in their faces and a whole lot of trouble on the streets."

"But this is England and it's the twenty-first century," said Fergie.

"A century with a *whole* lotta problems already, plus possibly even worse crazies, as you well know," CeCi countered. "But, hey, you guys figure we should continue on, we shall continue on."

"And we shall overcome," said perpetual optimist Johnny Jimson.

And so it was the show moved on to the Manchester Arena where, tragically, given the terror attack of 2017, the evil kicked off all over again. There was no suicide bomber on this occasion, and the only gun-carrying ticket holder was fortuitously mown down by a drunk driver as he was crossing the road to the venue, but the violent outbursts orchestrated by a Dark Web alt-right populist group were at levels well beyond scuffles, tomatoes, and eggs. This time it was social-media organized, and The Fubars were booed and hissed from the off, while their jubilant fans were infiltrated by pro-Brexit thugs with knives who took pleasure in beating the shit out of them, kicking them where they fell, spitting on them, and stabbing them. Immediately such violence started, The Fubars, shaken but not hurt, were called off stage by Johnny Jimson and a weeping CeCi Bodine. Some of the bloodstained guerillas tried to follow, but Mutt put paid to them by baring his teeth and growling his fiercest growls such that they cowed and ran.

"*GRRRRRR, GRRRRRR, GRRRRRR,*" he continued to howl until he was sure there were none left with the cojones to take him on, his warnings mingling eerily with the wah-wah-wahs of the approaching ambulances and police cars.

"God, oh *God*, what have I *done*?" CeCi howled, peering out at the mayhem in the auditorium. "I knew this would come to a bad end, now *this*!"

Tosh threw an arm around her shoulders. "Don't beat yourself up, love. We were *all* involved."

"But it was all *muh-my* idea."

"And mine," said Johnny Jimson. "Misread the situation, didn't I?"

One by one the other Fubars surrounded CeCi, gave her hugs and said it wasn't her fault.

"I see what you meant about songs though," said Dwayne.

"And what you said about the twenty-first century so far," said Fergie. "I am so ashamed to be British," he added, peering out at the scene on the floor.

It wasn't a pleasant sight. Police with tasers and dogs dodging blows and knife thrusts from defiant pro-Brexiteers, before managing to shackle them and march them off to waiting paddy wagons. Paramedics working with the injured and stewards combing the lavatories in search of those who might have escaped the violence but were too scared to come out. Blood on the ground wherever he looked.

"Holy *shit*," said Tosh, holding his head in his hands.

It was an hour later when the Manchester Arena had been finally cleared of debris and the injured that PC Maggie Jackson climbed behind stage to tell The Fubars it was safe to leave.

"And look, don't blame yourselves," she said. "How could *you* have known this would happen?"

CeCi was about to say she *had*, but Dwayne squeezed her hand too hard. Instead, she managed to say, "Anybody seriously hurt?"

"Too soon to say, ma'am. Early days, like. But reports I'm getting say there's nobody with life-threatening injuries."

"Thank God for that."

"Indeed, ma'am. Now, how about we get you back to your hotel? Sorry about it, but you're going to need blankets over your heads as we get you into the cars. Never know who else might be out there waiting, do we? Wanna follow me?"

"Raaf, raaf," said Mutt.

"Yeah, you get a blanket too," said Maggie, patting his head. "Reports say you were a real hero."

"Raaf," said Mutt sotto voce. Humbly almost.

~ * ~

Mercifully, nobody died or was seriously injured as a result of what the media were to dub "The Battle of Manchester," about which the EU Remainers were much relieved. Pleased they also were to discover a new poll suggesting support for the already tainted Leave campaign had dropped to a record low. It was a disgrace it took such violence to swing public opinion in this way but, to the horror of the parliamentary Brexiteers watching this counter-productive outcome for their cause, *if* there were to be a second referendum on the Europe issue figures suggested they would lose hands down. The embattled Penelope Pringle, who confusingly was both a Remainer *and* a Brexiteer, was furious at her latest exit plan being torpedoed by such "bloodthirsty hoodlums."

"Just when things were looking so *pos*itive with the Brussels chappies," she declaimed to her hapless cabinet, many of them twitching nervously with, "Not me guv' I had nuffink to do wiv it," written all over their faces, while others smirked at their discomfiture.

Things *weren't* going positively with "the Brussels chappies," of course. That was just Pringle's publicity pitch. In fact, the Brussels chappies reckoned she, her cabinet, and the entire British parliament were morons with whom they were no longer prepared to do any business at all. Nonetheless, they, too, royally condemned the events in Manchester. Already there was evidence of similar sentiments brewing in *their* countries, and they wanted none of it.

*Any*way, such was the political fallout on both sides of the Channel from The Fubars' final concert of the whistle-stop, anti-Brexit tour whose other venues had obviously enough been cancelled on police advice, and with the ready acquiescence of the band, and particularly CeCi Bodine.

"Thank God it's over, and nobody else got hurt," she said to Tosh & company over several bottles of white wine back in the safety of the Hackney house.

"Here's to that," said Desdemona, raising her glass.

"On the other hand," said the ever-positive Tosh, "at least those bastards did some of our job for us. Showed themselves to be the arseholes we sometimes sing about."

"True enough." CeCi couldn't deny it. "But enough was enough."

"Also, on the upside," said Johnny Jimson, "Fubar recordings are outselling the whole market. And the TV and radio talk show gigs are doing no harm with getting the message across."

"Also true," CeCi admitted. "I'm proud of them for that."

And she had every justification. Since their hasty return to London under police escort, Tosh, Maja, Dwayne, Desdemona, Fergie, Aika and the famous Mutt had been more or less omnipresent on all media outlets, and interviewed by even the most eminent of presenters, recording higher audience interest than any rock band since The Beatles. And Johnny Jimson was right. They *did* get their message across, such that another poll suggested support for a no deal Brexit fading even faster than the last one. Many professionals and ordinary observers suggested it was The Fubars' frankness yet humility that achieved this result. According to the BBC's prime time "Politics on Sunday" presenter Adam Moore during an interview with *The Times*, "In a political world beset with fake news and downright lies, the sheer honesty of their responses to my questions was a breath of the freshest air I've breathed since doing this job. No dodging, no hedging, no answering questions I *didn't* ask, just plain speaking. I'm not surprised people believed them. *I* for one did. If there were more kids out there with even a smattering of their intelligence and willingness to take part in politics, we'd be looking at a better world."

High praise indeed from one who'd been doing the job for fifteen years and a quote that gained in significance with each re-telling across the social media until it became practically a mantra in the chaotic early months of 2019.

Epilogue

The Personal and the Political.

Delighted at the outcome of events in the family arena, CeCi threw another of her Ritz parties. Along with the famous Fubars, Mutt, and Johnny Jimson she invited all those most closely associated with the band—the reformed Lord Barr and his newly besotted wife Hermione, Andrea and Janine, *and* the parents of Aika and Maja, who flew in at CeCi's expense especially for the occasion. The only surprise guest was Tosh's long lost mother Kenise, who somehow got wind of the bash and turned up professing undying love for her child and wondering if he could "lend her a few quid." Which Tosh dutifully did before accompanying her to the door and suggesting they meet again at some other place and some other time because there was a lot to talk about and The Ritz party wasn't the right occasion to do it.

"Meanie," said Kenise. "I got dolled up special and everything."

Kenise, a big woman, was wearing black leather trousers beneath a voluminous purple satin tent dress and decorated to the hilt with flashy bling.

"Mum, *please*? You and your bloke threw me out of the house and never gave a toss what happened to me. Now, I'm…"

"Famous."

"Right. Now I'm famous, here you are saying you love me. Funny, eh? Just take the money and get lost," said Tosh. "Leave a phone number, if you've got one, and I'll give you a call sometime."

Which was when Kenise took to weeping.

"Oh for *fuck*, Mum."

"I never meant you no huh-harm. It was juh-just the way things wuh-were. Nuh-now they're buh-better. Take the money back, boy," she said, thrusting the two hundred pounds in used notes back into his hand. "Don't want to be an embarrassment, so I'm gone. See you around. Like you said, sometime."

Which was when Tosh sighed, looked over his shoulder at the other mums and dads, relented, and said, "Okay, okay, come with me. I'll introduce you."

"I'll be nice, I promise," said Kenise.

Tosh laughed. "You behave bad, I'm gonna kick your ass."

"Sound like your pa," said Kenise, taking her son's arm and entering the throng.

The only family member missing from the guest list was Vincent Vinicombe, but he was banged up at Her Majesty's pleasure, so that was okay. Not that he would have attended even if he hadn't been banged up because, from the news that filtered into his cell, he was "disgusted, ashamed, and appalled" to hear his daughter had so "demeaned herself" by singing anti-Brexit songs with a bunch of ruffians whom he would have preferred to see shot. In order to quell such fury, particularly after he'd poured a bucket of PortaLoo piss over a warder's head while making this point, he'd needed to be sedated with a triple shot of Xanax.

*Any*way, this absentee aside, the party went with a zing. The Liberace lookalike was allowed to tinkle on his Steinway grand to his heart's content even though his version of The Fubars' greatest hits left something to be desired, but nobody cared about that. Great it was also to be insulated from the media by Montmorency who was stationed at the door dressed in one of his ex-all-in wrestler outfits ready to dissuade any crafty paparazzo with gatecrashing intentions. There was tasty morsel nibbling, there was drinking to excess, there was dancing, there were embraces between folk who'd never met but now shared a common pride. All in all a very private but very happy event crowned around midnight by CeCi calling for silence so she could say a few words.

"Never would I have thought…" she began, tearing up until Dwayne threw an arm around her shoulders. "That things might turn out this way. Such a helluva *mess* of a situation it was when everything kicked off. Lost kids, a murder, and look where we are now. Okay, we haven't changed the world, Klank is still screwing up my country, and Brexit yours, but maybe we made a tiny difference and maybe, who knows, the tiniest difference may blossom into something bigger. What is it they say? From little acorns you can get mighty oaks, something like that. But never mind the big bad world outside, at least we now have each other and *know* there is trust between us, trust and, in all cases, I hope," she said smiling at Tosh and Kenise who were holding hands, "*love*. For that, I am soo grateful, and I hope you will join me and raise your glasses in a little toast…to *us*."

Everybody stood, linked arms in a ring, hoisted their glasses with their free hands, and practically yelled, "To *U…U…U…USSSSS*," to the accompaniment of Liberace tinkling his idea of "Auld Lang Syne." Okay, it wasn't New Year, but that didn't matter. And once the glasses were emptied, they all joined in. With one arm around Lady Hermione and the other around Fergus Ulysses, it was Lord Xavier Barr who led the singing because he was the only one who knew—and miracle of miracles re*mem*bered—the words. And once that was over, there was kissing, firstly between partners, then between them and their relatives, then between anybody else willy nilly, Johnny Jimson and Kenise for example. Montmorency joined in, too, taking a fleeting break from his bouncer duties to get a special hug and kiss from CeCi.

"Man, that was *some* kiss-in," she said when it was over. "I got lip ache already."

The climax of the party was The Fubars jamming a few numbers with Liberace who, for the first time anyone could remember, stood up from his stool, wiggled his bottom and took to thumping the ivories in the manner of Jerry Lee Lewis or Little Richard.

Let's just say it was a hell of a party and a fitting way to find a happy ending to one strand of this story, the private and personal fubars that got resolved. What happened to all these folks next would have to be the subject of a whole *new* story—act six of a normally five-act play—for which there is no room here. So bye-bye the Fubar "family."

~ * ~

Finding a happy ending to the political scene—Klank's America, Ripurpantzov's insidious meddling in Western affairs, Brexit, and all their hideous ramifications—is sadly a much less easily achievable task except to say that "fucked up beyond all repair" remains the most apposite description of this snapshot of the turbulence of early 2019. So many false starts, U-turns, dashed hopes, and so much provocative prevarication that *any* definitive conclusion, let alone a happy one, was still way out of sight. Indications in many countries suggested that worse was yet to come as alt-right populism continued to make inroads into long held beliefs in harmony and continuity. Even the pope in Rome was under attack on the Italian immigration question and, despite the murder plot in which this story embroils him and the ongoing efforts of Special Counsel Richard Michaels to prove his involvements with Russia, Dougal Klank remained president and, some said, had every chance of being re-elected. Meanwhile, the parliamentary Brexit chaos continued in the UK whose citizens truly were as divided as at any time in their history. And, watching on, what did Igor Ripurpantzov do? Smiled with deep contentment, that was what. No light at the end of the tunnel so far, and no happy conclusion to this part of the story, therefore.

~ * ~

A funny thing history, isn't it? But only funny ha-ha if we look at it through the eyes of Sellar and Yeatman in their book *1066 and All That: A Memorable History of England*. Otherwise it's more like funny peculiar, which is the way we get taught it in school via the neat package normally written in retrospect by those currently holding the reins of power in order to make them look good. History then becomes *their* story. A pertinent example of this process is the normal manner in which wars are documented. First, there is a *cause* for whatever war is on the table—the bizarre defenestration of Archduke Franz Ferdinand of Austria by a Serb called Gavrilo Princip causing WW1, for example. Then, there are the *events* of the thing—millions of dead in fearful battles. Then, there comes a result; in this case, The Treaty of Versailles whose terms for German retribution lead to WW2 when the whole grisly process starts all over again. The same cause/events/ outcome methodology can be used to describe practically everything historical, including Henry VIII's divorce from Catherine of Aragon. Cause: Catherine is a Roman Catholic who can't produce a male heir. Events: Henry divorces her, waves two fingers at the pope in Rome and sets up his own church called The Church of England. Result: England becomes Protestant, gains sovereignty, and is freed from the impositions of horrid foreigners...which is a *good* thing, as evinced in Vincent Vinicombe's hijacking of the story for his pro-Brexit views (see above). There's nothing like a bit of history to make the case for one thing or another, is there? Normally to persuade one group of humans to hate some other group of humans and want to kill them. This occurs especially when both groups are either functioning on radically opposing versions of whatever ideologies are under discussion—frequently religion—or, more likely, have no idea what happened in the first place and are thus ready to accept *any* distorted interpretation that catches their fancy.

It is precisely into this void that populism steps and flourishes by asserting that history is best ignored because it was never lived and cannot therefore be proven except by dubious written accounts thereby leaving open the possibility of entirely new and different interpretations suited to its purpose. The burning of "unGerman" books by students in Opera Square Berlin on May 10th 1933, springs to mind as such a willful destruction of literary and philosophical history leaving the way open for the fabricated sloganistic mysticism that opened the gates to the high school dropout Adolf Hitler. In his novel *To Kill the Truth,* the writer Sam Bourne fictionally updates this phenomenon in relation to holocaust and slavery deniers in modern day America where historically inconvenient "facts" are regarded as the weapons of the liberal elite and so are also burnt. Only a fiction maybe, but a telling one when it comes to explaining how it is that manipulated fantasies can unhinge previously rational societies and lead to fragmentation and then dictatorships.

Gloomy? Sure it is, but it's happening all around us. "Dougal Klank" and the British Brexiteers are just the recent close-to-home tips of a very nasty Titanic-type iceberg we ignore at our peril, the same one that blinds us to our very own extinction if climate change is allowed to continue unabated. Several billion years of our past down the toilet just because of human greed. Having toyed with different definitions of history, even Georg Wilhelm Friedrich Hegel eventually concluded, "We learn from history that we do not learn from history." Whether he meant by this that we learn *nothing* from history, or all we learn is to continue repeating its mistakes *ad infinitum* remains a moot point. It was perhaps Shakespeare who got it right in saying: "All our yesterdays have lighted fools the way to dusty death," and the whole business is no more than, "A tale told by an idiot, full of sound and fury signifying nothing" (*Macbeth*, Act 5, Scene 5, lines 17-28).

Which may, of course, also be your verdict on this book.

Meet Paddy Bostock

Paddy Bostock was born in Liverpool and holds a B.A. in Modern Languages and History, a PGDip TESL, and a PhD in English Literature. Down the years he has been a barman, a road worker, a songwriter, an educational researcher, a translator, a book reviewer, a university lecturer and Chair of Department, and a high school mentor. He lives in London with his wife, writer Dani Cavallaro, and likes animals and bicycles.

Other Works From The Pen
Of Paddy Bostock

Mole Smith and the Diamond Studded Pistol - Only one way for PI gofer Mole Smith to win the hand of his beloved: to solve the ancient mystery of the diamond-studded pistol...

La Joie de Vivre - "Cherchez la femme!" — words Ambler will come to wish he'd never heard...

The Basque Head Case - Of heads found...and lost!...

The Hanging - Nothing is set in stone.

Chosen - It's only rock 'n' roll but...

Foot Soldiers - When will we ever learn...?

Jake Flintlock Mystery Series:

Two Down - Worry about your cellphone! Others may have spooky designs on it...

For the Love of a Woman - Family — you can't live with them; you can't live without them...

Hand in Glove - Never judge a zebra by its stripes...

Peace on Earth – Peace on earth? Don't bet on it...

Magical Mystery Series:

Noddy in Wonderland - Will wonders never cease?

The Bore - Funny thing, boredom...

What Ifs – "We are such stuff as dreams are made on..."

The Basque Head Case - Of heads found...and lost!...

The Hanging - Nothing is set in stone.

Chosen - It's only rock 'n' roll but...

Letter to Our Readers

Enjoy this book?

You can make a difference

As an independent publisher, Wings ePress, Inc. does not have the financial clout of the large New York Publishers. We can't afford large magazine spreads or subway posters to tell people about our quality books.

But, we do have something much more effective and powerful than ads. We have a large base of loyal readers.

Honest Reviews help bring the attention of new readers to our books.

If you enjoyed this book, we would appreciate it if you would spend a few minutes posting a review on the site where you purchased this book or on the Wings ePress, Inc. webpages at: https://wingsepress. com/

Visit Our Website

For The Full Inventory
Of Quality Books:

Wings ePress.Inc
https://wingsepress.com/

Quality trade paperbacks and downloads
in multiple formats,
in genres ranging from light romantic comedy
to general fiction and horror.
Wings has something for every reader's taste.
Visit the website, then bookmark it.
We add new titles each month!

Wings ePress Inc.
3000 N. Rock Road
Newton, KS   67114